An eden plain novel

A BIGGER LIFE

ANNETTE SMITH

NAVPRESS®

BRINGING TRUTH TO LIFE

OUR GUARANTEE TO YOU

NavPress
P.O. Box 35001
Colorado Springs, Colorado 80935

ISBN 1-57683-995-8

Cover design by Kirk DouPonce, DogEaredDesign.com
Cover photo by Superstock and Steve Gardner, ShootPW.com
Author photo by Jenny Leigh
Creative Team: Terry Behimer, Jeff Gerke, Darla Hightower, Arvid Wallen, Kathy Guist

Published in association with the literary agency of Alive Communications, Inc., 7680 Goddard Street, Suite 200, Colorado Springs, CO 80920 (www.alivecommunications.com).

Smith, Annette Gail, 1959-
  A bigger life : an Eden Plain novel / Annette Smith.
     p. cm.
  ISBN 1-57683-995-8
  1. Divorced fathers--Fiction. 2. Terminal care--Fiction. 3. Domestic
fiction. I. Title.
PS3619.M55B54 2006
813'.6--dc22

                          2006026228

Printed in the United States of America

1 2 3 4 5 6 7 8 9 10 / 10 09 08 07 06

For Mason's Dad

acknowledgments

THANKS ARE DUE MY AGENT, Beth Jusino, for her enthusiastic support of this project and her behind-the-scenes work on my behalf.

I appreciate my editor, Jeff Gerke, for his quick and witty responses to my myriad of questions and concerns. Thanks to the rest of the crew at NavPress for all they've done to turn my words into this lovely book.

I'm blessed to have good friends. Writing pals and dear ones, Laura Walker, Suzie Duke, Judi Braddy, Jan Coleman, Fran Sandin, and Rebecca Jordan encourage, instruct, and inspire me to higher standards and greater productivity. Jeanna Lambert, Sheila Cook, and Sheri Harrison were especially faithful to me during a recent season of personal funk. I so appreciate them for calling when I couldn't, sending cards and e-mails when I didn't, remaining interested in me when I could muster little interest in them. I'm also thankful for Leisa Wheeler. New friends are rare at this age. What a treat to come across someone so full of fun and so ready to pray.

Brenda Waggoner was an important person in my life this year. I so appreciate her wisdom, insight, and gentle counsel.

Abraham Valverde is a busy man. He works long hours, then goes to school. At home he sticks stars to the ceiling so a dear one can dream by their light. I'm grateful to him for taking time to read this manuscript. His twenty-something-year-old guy viewpoint helped keep the story real.

Michael Walker is one of the most creative people I know. It was with high anxiety that I took him up on his generous offer to read and comment on this manuscript. What a gift he's been. He read every line as I birthed it, made insightful comments and helpful suggestions, then spurred me on with enthusiastic pleas for more. Not every writer has such an encourager. How blessed I am that, on this project, Michael was mine.

Family is everything. My parents, Louie and Marolyn Woodall, are wonderful cheerleaders. My brothers, Dayne and Bruce, and their wives, Martha and Dale, encourage me too. I'm so thankful for the support of my children, Russell and his wife, Sarah, and Rachel and her husband, James.

My kind and gentle husband, Randy, is the best. No matter what, he's the one person in my life who is always, always on my side. I can't think of much else a woman really needs.

To God be the glory.

Heart-shattered lives ready for love

don't for a moment escape God's notice.

Psalm 51:17, *The Message*

chapter one

FROM MY SPOT IN THE SHADE, I count four cats crouched on top of my cinderblock back fence. There's nothing like the July smell of fish frying in hot grease to scare up hungry neighborhood strays. They sit motionless except for the tips of their tails. There's a big striped tom, two gray and whites, and a real small calico. The kids, none of which can reach up there, stand on tiptoe in the dirt, trying to coax the cats down with doughnut holes and Cheese Nips.

Uh-uh. Not happening. The cats are way too smart to fall for that business. They're here for the fish.

When I was little like them it was a bird I wanted. I was six, at a picnic on a hot day. My Uncle Cleve told me if I would put salt on a bird's tail I could catch him. A bird of my own! I was pumped. I would fix him a little box and keep him in my room. Feed him worms. There were lots of birds in Uncle Cleve's yard. They'd land on the grass, peck at bugs and stuff, then swoop back up. I remember running round and round the yard with the salt shaker, trying to do what Uncle Cleve said. I never even got close to a bird, but I got so worn out and hot I threw up, and my Aunt Irene made me come inside and sit under the fan with a wet towel over my head.

"Colton, no," I yell.

The other kids have lost interest and gone on to play

1

something else, but my son has decided to drag up a little plastic chair so as to get to the cats. He shoots me one of his looks. Do I mind my dad? Or not. He's considering his options.

"Go get the ball. The red ball," I yell. The good thing about three-year-olds is that they're not all that smart. Colton forgets about the cats and goes after the ball.

Sunday afternoons, five of us single dads hang out with our kids at my house. We cook. The kids play. It gets crazy. Usually the kids run around outside while we kick back in lawn chairs, like today. But not always. If the weather's bad or there's an important game on TV, we bring it inside. Talk about loud. You haven't heard noise until you've been cooped up inside with our bunch on Super Bowl Sunday.

Between us we've got five boys and two little girls. There's me, Joel, and my son, Colton. He's got my lanky build, his mother Kari's blonde hair and blue eyes. Kari and I've shared joint custody since we got divorced. Colton doesn't talk as plain as other kids his age, but we're seeing some improvement. He used to get ear infections a lot. Now he's got tubes.

My best friend Abe's daughter is five-year-old Sh'dondra, who Colton has a bad crush on. Colton follows Sh'dondra around like she's a mother duck. That girl is something else. Sassy? Smart? You have no idea. I tell Abe he better go back to college right now if he plans on being able to keep up with her.

Colton wants to do everything just like Sh'dondra, which I guess explains me catching him trying to pee sitting down last Sunday after everybody left. Me and Colton had to have us a little man-to-man talk about that.

Abe and I met five years ago when I went to work at Lucy's, a hair salon in Eden Plain, Texas, population 33,000, which is where we all live. I know you're wondering. Two guys. Who do hair. The answer is no. Abe and I are neither one gay. The other answer is yes. Abe is black. You probably thought as much from his little girl's name, which used to sound weird to me, a white guy, but doesn't anymore. Sh'dondra's mother is Jill. She teaches school. Abe and her still get together from time to time. They used to be married.

Our friend Pete sells insurance, which is why I'm the most well-insured twenty-seven-year-old I know. Life. Health. Disability. I'm good to go. Pete's kids are Brandon and Chase. Twins. They're six. Identical, except Brandon's got a reddish birthmark behind his left ear. Brandon and Chase have ADD. Their mother, Erin, gives them medicine during the week, but on Saturdays and Sundays Pete's on his own. Brandon and Chase are good boys. They just like to tear stuff up.

Sean's a department manager at Sears. Recovering alcoholic. He's the only one of us who has his kid full-time. Last fall Sean's wife, Brooke, left with some guy from their church. He's still pretty mad about it. I guess so is his daughter, Allyssa, who's two years old. Allyssa's a cute kid but you have to watch her because she likes to bite. A couple of weeks ago she took a chunk out of Colton's arm. Broke the skin in two places.

One thing. When you get a bunch of kids together, there are going to be fights. Over toys. Food. Who gets to sit where. We dads try to let them work stuff out on their own. Which is easy unless it's your kid who's crying because he got bit.

Casey's thirty-three. He's the oldest one of us. But not the most mature acting. It's because of Casey I had to lay down the law. No booze in my house on Sunday nights. No. Not even after the kids have crashed. I'm not sure Casey has what you'd call a drinking problem but he gets loud when he drinks and you can't have that sort of thing around kids.

His boys are Nathan and Andy. Five and six. Casey's a high school coach. He plays ball with his boys every chance he can. Nathan's probably going to be average, but Andy looks like he may have some real athletic ability. He's already got a pretty good arm. Casey and his wife, Darla, are separated. The boys are with her most of the time. Casey likes to talk about all the high school girls who hang over the desk in his history class. He says they're hot for him. I don't know. Maybe they are.

One thing is for sure. Casey can cook. Today he's brought over his fish cooker. If you've ever fried fish inside your house you understand why we're set up out in the yard. The kids line up and we fill their plates. Catfish. Potatoes. Hush puppies. Everything fried. None of them want salad, but Abe, who brought it, makes them all take some anyway.

"What kind of dressing?" Andy asks.

"Ranch."

Abe thinks none of the kids eat enough vegetables. Which unless you count catsup, which Abe says you don't, on the weekends is probably true.

It's after ten before everybody leaves. Sh'dondra and Colton are conked out on the couch. Abe and I have Mondays off, so he's not in any hurry to leave. He helps me clean up. I carry a paper plate of fish scraps out to the fence and put it up there for the cats. Then he and I sit for a while on my back stoop while I have a smoke. It's hot but nice out there. We don't talk much. After the noise of all those kids it's good to sit in the quiet.

People ask what made me decide to become a hair stylist. I guess it's in my blood. My granddad used to have a barber shop in Eden

Plain. It's closed now and he's dead, but when I was in grade school I'd go there sometimes after school to hang out. I'd sweep up for him and listen to the men talk, and when he wasn't watching me too close I'd sneak looks at the *Playboy* magazines he kept under the seat of the red vinyl chair next to the Coke machine that took quarters.

When I was in ninth grade I bought a set of clippers at a yard sale and practiced cutting my own hair. Then I started giving my friends five-dollar haircuts in the backyard. I seemed to have a knack for it. Took me a year after graduating high school to get off my butt and do it, but finally I signed up at Texas' Best Barber College, went through the program and got my license.

Nobody told me that barber shops were on their way out, or if they did I didn't pay much attention. All I knew was I planned on cutting hair for a living. So I was pretty surprised when I graduated to find out how hard it was finding a job. Took me a good three months before I talked this guy Mike into giving me a chance at his barber shop, which was on the corner in a rundown part of town. Talk about depressing. Place was shabby. Not even all that clean. Old equipment. Old barbers. Old customers. Most of them worried about their colons.

A lot of days it was boring as heck. But I needed a job and to get some experience under my belt because there's stuff about cutting hair you don't get in school. On-the-job training is how you learn it. Which I did. Because even though they were what I considered old, Mike and the other three guys that worked at the shop were excellent barbers. I watched them close and they watched me close so I could learn.

Which I did.

Until the day I had to quit.

It was a Saturday morning after I'd been at Mike's about six months. This black guy, about thirty-five, from Chicago comes in and asks if there's somebody who can shave his head. He was in town visiting his grandma who was sick in the hospital. The man had tears in his eyes when he told me he needed cleaned up because she wasn't doing so good and it looked like probably he was going to be staying for her funeral if things didn't change. My chair was closest to where he came in and I wasn't busy so I said sure. He sat down and I shaved him. It took me maybe ten minutes. When I was done, he paid me in cash. I told him I hoped his grandma took a turn for the better and then he left.

Which was when it all hit the fan.

Mike waited 'til the guy was gone but then left his customer and stomped over to my chair where I was sweeping up. His face was as red as one of those crazy zoo gorilla's big old behinds. I thought he might be having a heart attack or something, but no. He asked me what the heck did I think I was doing? We didn't serve blacks. He ran a clean, whites-only shop and didn't I know that?

Well, no, I said, matter of fact I didn't. Wasn't like there was a sign or anything. *Whites only?* This was the year 1998.

I'm six feet, two inches tall. Mike was maybe five-three. I just stood there looking down at him dead in the face but feeling crazy mixed up inside. Stunned. Embarrassed. Mad. Like some little kid who has just gotten a spanking in the aisle of the grocery store for doing something he didn't know he wasn't supposed to do.

I honestly could not believe what the man was saying to me.

After Mike got through yelling at me, the shop went dead quiet except for this one squeaking ceiling fan that needed oil and old Rush Limbaugh ranting on the radio the geezers kept on in the back. Over Mike's head I could see none of the other barbers were looking up but they were sure listening. Hard. All three had customers but they'd stopped cutting. They'd every one laid down their clippers and their scissors and picked up their combs.

I guess I was supposed to apologize. Tell my boss I was sorry and that I'd never do such a terrible thing again.

But I couldn't.

So for the longest time we just stood there looking at each other like a couple of yard dogs ready to fight. Then Mike started in coughing. Then he started sounding like he was choking. Guy couldn't quit harking. I was about to get him a glass of water but then he pulled out his asthma inhaler, which fortunately helped. After he took a drag he sort of slapped me on the back and told me not to worry about what had just happened. No harm had been done. He realized that I didn't know any better, which was probably his fault but that now I did know better. We could rest assured nothing like that would happen again.

After all, blacks had their own places to go. They liked it like that and sure didn't need to be coming to us. Here's what I was to do from now on: Black guy comes in what doesn't know the policy, I just tell him I'm too busy to do anything for him and send him back out the door the way he come in.

Then he told me to finish sweeping up and clean my clippers real good. He went back to working on an old guy's comb-over. And everybody else in the shop started back to what they were doing just like normal.

Normal.

It's a wonder the next three customers I did that afternoon came out of my chair with both of their ears still attached. I nicked all three of their necks. You know how it is when you're so mad about something you can't even think? Your mind goes ninety miles an hour and your heart feels like it's slamming against the wall of your chest and your hands sweat like a thirteen-year-old kid moving in for his first kiss. You want to say something. You say ten things to yourself but you know you can't say any of those things out loud because it would be really bad if you did and so it builds up and builds up until you feel like maybe you're not going to be able to breathe if something doesn't give.

That is exactly the way I felt the whole rest of that day.

I hated prejudice then and I hate it now. Treating people bad because they're different or because you disagree with something about them is not right. Here's the deal. Growing up, I went through some stuff. Bad stuff that I'm over now but that has a lot to do with how I still am.

When you're a kid you just want to fit in and be like everybody else. If you or somebody in your close family is different than most everybody else, you get made fun of. Kids tease you. Teachers ask stupid questions about stuff that isn't any of their business. People say things behind your back but where you can hear them. You get your feelings hurt. You get mad. Sometimes you get into fights. I know because it happened to me and to other kids, too.

For my friend Josh it was his mother who caused him grief. She weighed over three hundred pounds and couldn't hardly walk because her butt was so big.

My buddy Mike got teased because his little sister was in a wheelchair. She drooled and she couldn't talk. People acted like she was a monster or something even though she was just a little girl.

Evan's dad was in prison for writing a bunch of hot checks. Other kids' parents didn't want them hanging around Evan because of what his dad did, which wasn't fair because as far as I know, Evan never stole anything in his life.

For me, it was my dad, because after I was born he decided to be gay.

Everybody knew because he didn't try to hide it. Where you

live maybe folks buttering their bread on both sides is not such a big deal. But in small-town Texas where if you don't own a hunting rifle people talk behind your back about how you must be queer, being gay is not something people can know about and think you're all right.

Truthfully, I hated my dad being like that. It was embarrassing. People called me gay because of him. I wanted him to be like a normal dad.

But he wasn't.

Ever.

But he was still my dad. And I loved him.

Which put me in a really bad place. A place no kid should ever have to be.

I learned early that there's a lot of hate in this world. Which explains why I could not work for somebody like Mike.

After that day I never went back.

Quitting put me in a bad place. No job. No money. I could not find work. I tried every barber shop in town, but there weren't all that many. Word about me had gotten around. Two months I went without work and things seemed like they were just going from bad to worse in my life. I was feeling real sorry for myself.

But then my luck changed. Through the grapevine Mrs. Chan who ran Lucy's heard about what had happened to me over at Mike's. She told somebody to tell me to call her up. When I did, she offered me a job. Over the phone. Sight unseen. Even though I was a barber and not a stylist, which meant there was a lot I didn't know how to do.

I believe in being loyal to people who help you out when you're down. Mrs. Chan's not the perfect boss by any means, but let me tell you, I will do anything that woman asks me to do. She's a good person and she was there for me in my hour of need.

Sometimes I get ribbed for working in a salon with, not counting Abe, all women. When we're having a slow day and the talk turns to PMS I can see their point. But I look at it this way. There are other ways of making a living but I am not a highly educated guy. Without a college degree I could be working out on somebody's ranch. I could be a foreman in a factory. I could work construction.

But why would I want to? I've got an inside job. When it's hot out, I'm cool. When it's cold and wet, I stay warm and dry. I'm surrounded all day by pretty women who smell good and have nice voices and clean teeth. You tell me: Who's the smart one — me or the guy with the sunburn and the grease under his fingernails?

I do both men and women's hair, but probably two-thirds of my clients are female. Naturally cuts are what I'm best at but we're a full-service salon so I've learned to do color and perms, too, even brow and lip waxing, except most women are embarrassed to have that done by a man. I picked up the skills by coming in on my days off and watching some of the more experienced stylists work. I also read stuff and watched training videos. It wasn't as hard as you might think. As a barber, legally I'm allowed to do everything a stylist can do except cut wigs, which is not a problem since there's not a lot of call for that around here.

What I make is not a great living but decent. Counting tips, I cleared $32,000 last year. Enough to pay the rent on my house, make my truck payment, and keep up on my child support, which I pay to Kari even though I've got Colton nearly half the time.

chapter two

COLTON'S MOM, KARI (YOU say it *CAR–ee*, like the kind you drive), and I went to high school together, but there were three hundred in our graduating class. We probably had some classes together but if we did neither of us remembers it.

The summer after graduation we both got jobs as lifeguards at the city swimming pool, which is where you could say we actually met. Kari wears her blonde hair in a shoulder-length bob now, but back then she had a long blunt cut. Every day she'd come to the pool, climb the ladder up to her stand and, without taking her eyes off the kids, she'd pull that great hair back and twist it into a braid that went nearly to her waist. She was something else. Not just great hair. Kari had great everything. With her on duty in the stand across from mine, in that pink bikini of hers, it was all I could do to keep my eyes on the kids in the pool.

Once a week they had a meeting all the lifeguards had to go to. Without making it too obvious, I did my best to sit next to Kari every time I could. When she didn't have a pen to fill out a form they made us do, I let her use mine. When I opened a pack of gum, I offered her a piece and she took it, but I still couldn't tell if she liked me or not. Kari was friendly but not one to flirt, if you know what I mean.

It was late August before I got up the nerve to ask her out.

Our first date, we got sandwiches from Subway and ate them on top of the roof of Leslie Johnson's two-story house. Leslie and I'd been good friends since back when we were fourteen. Before she left for college, I was over at her house three or four nights a week. My parents were divorced and I lived with my dad so he didn't care. Leslie and I'd eat supper with her folks, then watch a movie or something. After they'd go to sleep, me and her would climb out her bedroom window and sit on the roof of the garage talking and smoking 'til sometimes two or three in the morning.

Sounds cheesy now, but I'd heard Kari tell somebody at work how much she liked to look at the stars. I knew the roof was a good place to lay back and stare up at the sky. Leslie and her folks were on vacation, but I was bringing in the papers and the mail and feeding the animals so I had a key.

Even though it was hot and I was sweating like I don't know what and Leslie's dog was barking his head off at us the whole time we were up there, I guess the date went good because Kari agreed to go out with me the next night and again the night after that.

Before you knew it, Kari and I were seeing each other every day. I knew right off she was the one. I liked everything about her. The way she looked, the way she talked, the way she smelled. Kari said she liked everything about me except for how I smelled. And how I tasted. Which was why I cut way back on my smoking and finally quit.

So as not to upset her parents, who thought we were too young, we waited a year to get engaged. Another year before we tied the knot. Kari came from a well-off family and so our wedding was really big. Seven attendants. A horse-drawn carriage. Pink roses from here to Oklahoma. Her family paid for everything.

Kari made Cs in high school. I got mostly As and Bs. Don't ask me why, but college was not something either one of us considered. Guess we didn't see the need. None of our parents had gone. Besides, by the time we got married I'd finished barber college and had my job at Lucy's. Kari worked as a receptionist at her dad's mobile home company. We were doing okay. A couple kids playing house. We both had decent jobs. We went out with our friends on the weekends. Back then Casey and Darla were still together and they had a boat. Bunch of us went to the lake every Sunday during the summer. Things were rocking along pretty good.

But then Kari had a falling out with her dad, quit working for him, and got a job as a nurse's aide at the hospital. You should hear all the stuff she had to do. And for minimum wage. Why anybody would want that job is beyond me. But Kari loved it. There were a lot of old people on the floor where she worked. Some of them might stay for a week or more. Every day she'd take care of them. She'd get really attached. When one of them would pass away, if it was a person she'd gotten to know pretty well, it would get her real down.

Kari's got a real tender heart.

One time she was taking care of this sick old man who was blind. When she went into his room to tuck him in for the night he thought she was his wife. He patted her hand and called her his little darling. Since he was blind Kari didn't think it would hurt anything. So she patted his hand and told him he was her little darling, too. Which was fine until the old man puckered up for a kiss.

"What'd you do?" I asked her.

"Why, I kissed him," she told me.

"On the lips?"

"Of course. Where else would a man kiss his wife?"

I should have known better than to ask.

Kari's face is the kind people remember. Besides being pretty, she's got these blue, blue eyes that are hard to forget. After she went to work at the hospital, it got to where we couldn't go to Wal-Mart or Safeway without some old person stopping her in the aisle to hug her neck.

Which, even though it was a pain, made me really proud of her for people thinking she was so nice.

Kari had been working at the hospital for a year when she got the idea to become a nurse. She could go to community college to get her associate's degree. The hospital had a tuition plan. They'd pay for half her expenses if she'd keep working while she was in school and sign on to stay there for two years after she graduated.

I was pretty surprised she wanted to do it.

"RNs make good money," she said. "Twenty dollars an hour starting out."

"Yeah?" That was a lot more than minimum wage. We could probably get us a boat. "How long will it take?"

"Three years. Maybe more. They said I'd need to take some basic courses before I apply to the nursing part. It's pretty hard to get in. This year a hundred and forty applied. They only took twenty-three."

Not just a boat. Maybe a jet ski.

"They'd be nuts not to take you." I gave her a kiss.

"So you think I should try?"

"Sure. Why not?" Three years was a long time but it wasn't like we were going anywhere.

That was in May. In June Kari started taking her prerequisites. Chemistry and speech. Speech made her really nervous and a couple of times she cried because chemistry was so hard. I thought maybe she should quit. When her grades came in the mail, she was so scared she made me open the envelope. Two As.

She was so excited she started jumping on the bed.

In the fall Kari signed up for four classes, including anatomy and physiology. Two days a week they had lab. She'd come home with a bad headache and a real funny smell in her hair. Formaldehyde. They had to cut up a cat. Can you believe it? The same one for sixteen weeks.

A year after she started taking classes, Kari got accepted into nursing school. We went to Red Lobster to celebrate.

She came home after her first day of nursing school with a bunch of stuff she spread out all over our bed. Five hundred dollars' worth of books. Two uniforms. White with blue trim. White shoes. Shoe polish. One of those things you listen to people's hearts with—a stethoscope—and a pair of funny-looking scissors with rounded, crooked ends.

"What are these for?" I asked.

"I dunno. I guess to cut stuff with."

I tried them out. "Not very sharp." No way you could cut hair with those.

"Come here," she took the stethoscope out of its wrapper and put it into her ears. "Let me see if I can hear your heart."

She unbuttoned my shirt and put the thing against my chest. "What do you hear?" I asked.

She put her finger to her lips. "Shhh."

"What's it sound like?"

She concentrated real hard. "Bomp bomp. Bomp bomp."

"Cool. Let me listen to yours now," I said, happy for any excuse to lift up her shirt.

"Hear anything?" she asked. She stood very straight and very still.

"Not yet," I said, moving the stethoscope and pretending to listen really hard. "Wait. I think I found it. No. Not there. Uh. Let me try over this way a little."

"You!" Kari laughed when she caught on.

Later that night, we lay spooned together in our bed. "They gave us a big talk today," Kari said.

I was nearly asleep.

"The director of the program said these next two years are going to be really stressful."

"Probably," I said.

She rolled over to face me. We lay on our sides, knees touching knees.

"You'll get through it." I yawned.

"She said nursing school is really hard on a marriage. Even people who start out with strong marriages get divorced before it's over because of the strain."

"That's hard to believe," I said.

"She said it happens every year and that she thought we should know it going in."

I grabbed her hand and pulled it to my lips. Why did they have to say stuff like that? Stupid if you asked me. "Nothing like that's going to happen to us. No way. You're wasting time even thinking about it. Come on. Let's get some sleep."

And so we did.

Back then Kari was easily convinced.

chapter three

ABE'S LANDLORD IS HAVING the house he rents sprayed for bugs. The guy does it every year even though Abe says he doesn't see why. He's got allergies and the chemicals they use make him sneeze. For the next three days or so, 'til the fumes wear off, he's staying with me.

Fridays and Saturdays, instead of closing up at six the salon stays open 'til nine. Mostly walk-ins. We rotate. Half of us work Friday nights. Half Saturdays. Tonight is my Friday. Abe is off. When I get home I can hear out in the driveway he's got the CD player turned up real loud.

I come in the back door.

Whoa.

There's Abe's backside.

Two hundred and forty-something pounds of sweaty black man, wearing nothing but his tighty whities. He's mopping my kitchen floor. His dreadlocks are flying and he's singing along with the CD.

Opera.

There's one thing about Abe. Well, actually there's a lot of things about Abe, but this is one. He's got a thing about people doing him favors. He does not like it. So, no matter what it is you do for him, you can bet Abe's gonna try to pay you back.

When he sees me, he goes and turns off the CD but comes right back and starts mopping again. "Hey, man."

"Hey," I say. I guess he got hot. My floor has never looked so good. I take off my shoes so as not to track dirt.

"I used the last of the Mr. Clean."

"Okay."

"You eat?"

"No."

"T-bone's in the oven. Salad in the refrigerator."

I head to the bathroom. By the time I come out, Abe's finished the floor and put on some clothes. He's in the living room reading a book, highlighting parts as he goes. I sort through the mail. When the kitchen floor looks dry I make myself a plate. Abe has scrubbed the inside of the fridge and put one of those orange boxes of Arm and Hammer on the top shelf next to the milk and eggs I guess he went and bought.

The steak is tender. The salad's good. He's made deviled eggs, too. "Thanks," I say, holding up a bone.

"No problem."

I eat. Abe reads his book.

I get up to take my plate to the sink.

"You been to church much?" Abe asks.

"When I was little my Aunt Irene took me some," I say. "Why?"

"Jill's been going. Taking Sh'dondra. After me to come with them."

Abe and Jill get along better than any divorced couple I know. She's a good person. We don't talk about it, but I think he'd like to get back together with her. "Maybe you should go," I say.

"Been thinking I might. Sunday. You want to go with me?"

Sunday is the only day I can sleep in. "Not really."

"They got Sunday school. Jill says Sh'dondra likes it."

I guess Sunday school is something good for kids.

"Don't start 'til ten," Abe says.

"I'll think about it."

But on Sunday, Abe goes by himself. Me and Colton share a Grand Slam breakfast at Denny's and go to the park to feed the ducks our leftover pancakes. Later, after all the guys and their kids have come over to the house, I ask Abe how it was.

"Okay," says Abe. "It was okay."

Maybe Colton and me'll go next week.

Kari bought one of those assemble-it-yourself desks at Target. She needed a place to study away from the TV and everything so we cleared the junk out of the spare bedroom. Once we got it put together, I moved the computer in there for her and got it all hooked up. She put stuff in the drawers and set one of our wedding pictures up next to the monitor. We didn't have cases for all those books so I stacked two-by-fours on bricks to make her some shelves. When we were about done, I sat down in her computer chair and looked around. Her new office looked pretty good. "Look at you. My wife the college student," I said.

She put the last group of books on the shelf then came and plopped herself in my lap.

"Taking classes. Eating lunch in the student center." I patted her rear. "What if some university boy catches your eye? Think you might decide to trade me in?"

"No way," she said. "You're the only man for me."

"Because I'm so good-looking?"

"Well, that," she said, grinning, "but mostly 'cause you do such a great job on my bangs."

Her first semester in nursing school, Kari learned to take vital signs and give bed baths and do head-to-toe assessments, which is like a physical exam but the kind they let nurses, not doctors, do. At the college they had a fake person in a real hospital bed that they did all that stuff to. For some things, that worked good. For other things, they were supposed to practice at home on somebody real.

I thought my arm would fall off before Kari got the hang of taking blood pressure. Before she even asked, I told her I was drawing the line when it came to shots. She sat at the kitchen table and practiced on an orange. Pumped that sucker so full of water it's a wonder it didn't bust.

She made it through that first year of nursing school okay. I won't say it wasn't tough on both of us, because it was. We had to keep reminding each other that it would all be worth it when she got through. To get in her hours at the hospital Kari worked twelve-hour shifts at the hospital on Saturdays and Sundays. During the week she went to school Monday through Thursday. Fridays were her one day off.

We didn't see each other much. When we did, she was tired.

I started smoking again. Just at work. Behind Kari's back. I knew she would get mad if she found out, and with everything else, that was one place I did not want to go.

I didn't intend to start back, but one afternoon a couple of us were in the break room shooting the breeze. It was a slow day. Sharon and Kim, two of the stylists, were going out back to smoke. "Wanna come, Joel?" Kim asked. She was new. "Sure," I said. I intended to just sit out there with them, but for some reason when Kim offered me a cigarette I took it. One was all it took for me to start back. I bought a pack when I stopped for gas on the way home.

I kept a toothbrush and some Scope at work. Since I did the laundry and changed as soon as I got home, Kari never smelled my clothes. Fridays when I'd get off she'd be studying. I'd head straight to the shower. My truck had a problem with the exhaust system so to make extra sure, I rode home from work with the windows down. If I smelled like anything it was exhaust.

Only once did I nearly get caught. Kari's afternoon classes got canceled and she surprised me by dropping by the shop to see if I'd had lunch yet. I was out back smoking. It was Abe who came to get me.

"Kari's here," he said.

I put my cigarette out, took a swig on Abe's Diet Coke, swished, spit, then went back into the shop and grabbed a broom.

"Sorry, babe," I said, sweeping up, not getting too close. "Got a one o'clock cut and highlights. See you tonight?"

"What are you doing?" Abe asked when Kari was gone. "Sneaking around. Lying. You ain't got one thing on your book for this afternoon. This ain't middle school. She's your wife for crying out loud."

I told Abe to stay out of it. I had enough people in my business without him on me, too.

Kari was an only child. Her parents were something else. Her mother liked to keep stuff stirred up. I can't tell you how many times she would call and have Kari crying by the time they hung up. Her dad could be just as bad. Kari wanted more than anything to not make her parents mad. I wanted more than anything for them to leave us alone. It was one of those lose-lose situations for me. Kari wanted me to take her side, but if I ever said anything about either of them, she'd get mad.

They got killed on a Friday night.

It was in October of Kari's last year of nursing school. A night I was off. Kari'd had an argument with her mother over us not coming over there as often as her mother thought we should. Soon as she'd gotten off the phone we'd gone out to eat Mexican. On our way home, we stopped at Wal-Mart to get toilet paper and some bread. We came in the back door just in time to catch the phone. It was somebody Kari knew from the hospital. They told us there'd been an accident and we needed to come.

Took us only ten minutes to get back in the car and drive over there, but it was too late. Nobody ever said but I still believe Kari's mom and dad were already dead when the hospital called. The Malibu they drove got hit broadside by a train at a crossing two blocks from their house.

That is not the kind of news you give to a person over the phone.

Maybe somebody can tell me: How does a person handle something like that? What are you supposed to do? How do you help your wife when she cries for four days straight and her hair starts falling out and she won't eat or talk to you or even get dressed? I am twenty-seven now and I don't know. I was twenty-three then and except for changing shampoos, which sometimes helps people experiencing hair loss, I did not have a clue what to do to help her.

Not only did we have Kari's parents' deaths to deal with. Turns out their finances were in a real mess. Their business was in the toilet. They'd borrowed against their house, and they'd cashed in their life insurance policies. What that meant was that there wasn't even money for their funeral. Kari and I had to take out a loan to give them decent burials.

The teachers at Kari's school were understanding. But only up to a point. A couple of them came to her parents' funeral and they gave her a week and a half off. After that she had to keep up or they would kick her out. Which I thought was cold-blooded because couldn't they see how bad off she was?

The night before her time off was up, Kari was standing at the sink rinsing out a casserole dish somebody had brought over. People who knew her folks had loaded us down with funeral food. King Ranch Chicken. Green bean casserole. Chicken and dressing. All of it good but you cannot believe how those dishes stacked up. I came up behind her and wrapped my arms around her waist. She leaned back against me. We stood there, not saying anything. Finally I turned her around, picked up a dish towel, and dried off her hands. Then I walked us into the living room. I sat down on our old green couch and pulled Kari into my lap. She curled up against me, her chin on my chest.

"I love you, you know," I said to the top of her head.

She nodded.

"I don't know what to do to help you."

She didn't say anything.

"You sure you want to go back to school?"

"I have to," she said.

I didn't think she had to do anything. "You could take a break. Start back in January."

It didn't work like that. Kari told me if she stopped now, she'd have to wait 'til next fall to start back. She'd lose a whole year. Worse, if she dropped out, the school didn't have to let her back in at all if they didn't want to, which to me seemed like a total rip.

"You going to be okay?"

I wanted so bad for her to say yes.

"I don't know," she said, real low. "It doesn't feel real. I pick up the phone to call my mom and then I remember I can never do that again. I miss my dad. It's so weird. I didn't realize what it meant to me to know that they were there. I thought they always would be. Nothing feels safe anymore."

I held her tight. I wanted to tell my wife she was safe with me but the words did not come. I hated not knowing what to do to make her feel better. I figured whatever I said would probably make it all worse. So instead of trying to tell her how I felt, I kissed her and touched her and coaxed her into bed.

It had been more than a week.

Afterwards, Kari cried in my arms and I wondered what it was I had done wrong. That was the night our son was conceived.

chapter four

COLTON IS ALWAYS CRANKY when he first wakes up from a nap. It took me awhile, but I've got it figured out. If you leave him alone, let him go on and pout and be mad at the world for no good reason without trying to do anything about it, he'll get over it by himself soon enough. This is not a problem unless he sleeps until right before you've got to have him up and going somewhere. Trying to get Colton fed, dressed, and into the car when he's just woken up is not a good thing.

For a little guy he can pitch one mother of a fit.

My house has three bedrooms. One bath. Twelve hundred square feet. On the outside it's white frame with blue trim. There's no garage. Not much landscaping; just a few shrubs. I'm not much of a decorator and I'm not the cleanest person in the world but I keep stuff pretty much picked up. Colton sleeps in his room in a little youth bed with dinosaur sheets I bought for him when he outgrew his crib. He'd rather sleep with me, but Kari read somewhere that kids should learn to sleep in their own beds. I figure she knows more about all that than me so when she tells me something that has to do with raising kids, I pretty much go along.

Colton's crazy about my friend Pete. Calls him Pee Pee, which Pete's twin boys think is the funniest thing they've ever heard — especially when we run into the three of them in some public place.

"Pee Pee! Daddy, there's Pee Pee!" he'll yell out at Wal-Mart or Burger King. Brandon and Chase crack up. The boys are playing summer league T-ball and tonight they've got a game. I've got Colton for the weekend. Me and him are going to go watch them play. But first we head out to get us something to eat. I ask him. Taco Bell or McDonald's?

Like I didn't already know.

After one chicken nugget and two fries, Colton's full. He wants to play on the playground too bad to worry about eating. I put his Happy Meal back in the sack to take with us to the game. He can eat it later. Right now he's got his eye on the slide. I stand below and watch him climb up. He has no fear until he gets to the top. Then all of a sudden he is not so sure. There's bigger kids behind him telling him to go. Colton's in position but he won't let go of the sides.

"Come on, buddy," I call. "You can do it. I'm right here. I'll catch you."

"Go on," says one girl.

Colton sits tight.

"Hurry up," says a boy.

My hands start to sweat.

"Baby," says somebody else.

He can't do it.

So I climb up the little ladder, bump my head on the bar at the top, scoop my son up, and bring him down. He's sweaty. Crying. Getting snot all over my T-shirt.

"S'okay, Colt. S'okay, buddy," I tell him. I rub his back. His arms have a death grip around my neck and he tucks his face into that space below my left ear. "Next time," I tell him. "No big deal. We'll try again next time."

Dumb kids. I shoot them a look.

Colton gets over it.

Quicker than me.

Casey's house is on our way home from the game. We decide to stop and see what he's doing. When Colton and me pull up, I see Casey in the driveway of his next-door neighbor's house, working under the hood of an old blue station wagon. The neighbor's Mexican. Really dark. Five feet tall. Maybe a hundred pounds. Muscles and teeth. He's under the hood, too. Nice guy. Been living next to Casey for about a year. Doesn't speak much English.

Casey doesn't know Spanish, but he's all time doing stuff for the man. Guy's got a wife and some kids, a daughter in a wheelchair. He must have just gotten the car because I know Casey's been taking the little girl to the doctor and giving the man rides to the store.

Me and Colton get out. From the sound of the car and the smoke coming out the back end, I don't think Casey's done with giving the guy rides.

"Hey," I say to the neighbor.

He nods. Wipes his hand on a rag and shakes my hand.

Casey raises up. "Colton. Gimme five, man."

Colton's hands are sticky and stained red from the snow cone he had at the ballpark, but Casey doesn't care.

"What's the problem?" I ask.

"Leaking oil."

"Where?" I know a thing or two about cars.

"Everywhere," Casey says.

"How much he pay for it?"

"Eight hundred bucks. Worth fifty cents."

But Casey's got it running, which is better than before. His neighbor's happy. He shakes Casey's hand. Tells him thanks, then goes inside. It's hot out. We head back over to Casey's air-conditioned house. Colton wants to play with the dog. Casey wants a cold beer.

The dog's name is Steve. Medium sized. Brown. Hairy. No telling what breed. Casey tells everybody Steve's a Curb Setter. His mama was settin' on the curb when his daddy walked by. Colton loves to play with Steve. Tonight it's tug-of-war with an old sock. The two of them are having a big time. They're pretty evenly matched. But then Steve gets hold of the sock, runs under a chair, and before any of us can stop him he swallows the thing.

"Did he just eat that sock?" Casey asks.

I've never in my life seen a dog do that.

Swallowing a sock can't be good for Steve so Casey calls up the vet, who says there's not much to do except keep an eye on him and bring him in if he starts to act sick.

Which he does real quick. Steve starts gagging and coughing, his whole body goes stiff and he makes this awful urping sound. He does this for what seems like forever. Then up it comes. First the sock. Then some dog food. It's gross, but we're all glad because now we know Steve's going to be all right. Casey pets him and tells him he's a good dog but he can't be eating any more socks.

Steve isn't finished. He starts gagging again.

Something else is on its way up. We wait and watch.

But not for long.

I look at Casey. He looks at me.

Panties. Little ones. Red with black lace.

"Somebody 'round here lose something?" I ask, playing dumb.

"Shut up," says Casey. He's grinning even starting to clean up the mess.

Not long after, somebody knocks on the front door. It's the neighbor's wife. Twice her husband's size. Callused hands. She doesn't come inside but passes Casey something wrapped in foil on a flowered plate. Tamales. Two dozen. I didn't know she was

Casey's neighbor, but I recognize her. She sells her tamales door-to-door to businesses around town. Only for her does Mrs. Chan, the manager at Lucy's, make an exception to the "no soliciting" rule.

Casey gets out some paper plates and a roll of paper towels. Even though we've all three already eaten, it doesn't take us long to polish off half of what she's brought over. Man. You've never had tamales so good. Even after cleaning up dog puke, they hit the spot.

Just so I'm clear.

I can't even think what it would be like if we didn't have Colton. I won't deny he was an accident, but even after everything that's happened, nobody's going to say me and Kari having our son was a mistake. Colton's the best thing we ever did. Which makes me feel really guilty about how upset we were when we found out he was coming.

Two weeks before her parents died, Kari caught a wicked cold. She coughed so much it sounded like she was going to break something loose. A girl in her class gave her some antibiotics she had left over from when she was sick. I was glad when they worked because then we could finally get some sleep.

A month later Kari's period didn't come. She was never late. The test she did at home came back positive. A little pink plus sign. Kari and I stood in the bathroom, both of us chewing on our nails. We looked at the thing sitting on the edge of the sink, then at each other. Impossible. She must have done it wrong because no way we could be pregnant. Besides. How good could a test you buy at the Dollar General be?

Kari threw the little tray with the plus sign into the trash. "I'm not worried," she said. "Stress messes your hormones up. I'll probably start in a couple of days."

She was lying but I went along.

When two more weeks went by and she still didn't get her period, we got nervous. I went with her to the doctor. Kari was pregnant, all right. Two months along. Due in June. He asked her if she'd missed any of her pills. She hadn't. But then he asked her about other medicine. When she told him about the bootlegged antibiotics he nodded his head.

Yep. That explained it.

Antibiotics can sometimes cancel out birth control pills.

You think they'd tell you something like that.

Then, like it was no big deal, the doctor patted Kari on the knee and shook my hand. Told us congratulations and asked us which we wanted, a boy or a girl. He gave Kari some vitamins and some pamphlets to read and made us watch this video about what all she was supposed to do and not do while she was pregnant. After that we made another appointment and walked back out to the car way different than when we came in.

Us.

Parents.

It did not seem real.

For a good week I'd say we were in shock. "How did this happen? We can't have a kid now," I remember saying.

Kari was mad at me for getting her pregnant. Like us having sex was all my fault. Except for when her parents died I had never seen her so upset. She didn't speak to me or touch me for three days. She did her best not to even be in the same room with me, which in a house as little as ours was no small thing.

Those three days felt like a month.

Here's the deal: It wasn't that me and Kari didn't want kids. We never talked about it and I always figured someday — like maybe in five years — we'd have a couple. But her pregnant now? The timing stunk. We were barely holding on as it was. Between both of us working and her going to nursing school we never saw each other. Kari's classes were hard. If she made less than a B they could kick her out, so she studied all the time.

I'll admit one thing right off: I should have been more understanding instead of acting like a jerk. My wife had just lost her mom and her dad. She didn't feel good. But there are two sides to everything and it was like Kari changed all of a sudden.

Before starting nursing school and finding out she was pregnant, Kari was always laid back, easygoing. That was one of the things I liked most about her. But after everything happened, she became obsessed with stuff being done exactly her way. Life at our house stopped being fun. Besides sleep, pretty much all Kari did was go to work and school, come home, study, and gripe at me. She was always tired and always in a bad mood. Nothing I did was right. When I bought paper towels with designs instead of plain ones she got so mad I thought she was going to make me take them back.

Paper towels.

I may not be the brightest bulb in the strand but I am no idiot either. Which is exactly what Kari treated me like.

Our house was a wreck and the walls were so thin I couldn't watch TV without her complaining about not being able to concentrate and asking me to turn it down. Which meant I spent lots of nights watching *Seinfeld* reruns sitting about a foot away from the screen with the sound turned almost all the way down.

As Kari got further along, she got bigger and bigger but instead of buying maternity clothes she started wearing sweatpants and baggy T-shirts of mine. She stopped wearing makeup and she had me cut her hair really short, which did not look all that great with her face, which was puffy and broken out. You hear about women letting themselves go after they have kids. Best I could tell at the time, Kari was getting a head start down that road.

Just to get along, what I did mostly was try to keep my mouth shut at home and stay gone as much as I could. Anybody wanted off at the salon, I took their shift. A couple weeks I pulled sixty hours. I hung out at Casey and Darla's so much Darla started setting a place for me at the table. I joined a gym and started working out every other day.

It got so bad with me and Kari that I started to wonder what exactly was the point. What was such a big deal about her getting to be a nurse? Had things been so terrible back when we were both just working at regular jobs? I didn't think so but I knew better than to say anything to her.

Kari told me I needed to look at the big picture. To remember what she was working for. A better life for us. More money. All that sounded good until about six months into all this, when it hit me. Forget us saving up for a boat once Kari got to be a nurse.

You can't take a baby out on the lake.

She was taking psychology that fall. I saw this form she'd left out on her desk. You were supposed to fill it out to find out what level of stress you were under. The way it worked was you got stress points for different stuff you were going through in your life, then you totaled it up to see how bad off you were. It had things on it like changing jobs, buying a house, losing a loved one. I wasn't surprised when her score at the bottom of the page was up there way high.

Stress was the word of the day at our house.

Every day.

chapter five

SAY ANYTHING YOU WANT TO me about pretty much anything and I'll take it. Except when it comes to how I'm raising
my son. I don't claim to be the perfect dad, but most days I can
look at myself in the mirror and know that I'm giving him the
best I've got.

I see people who don't have kids and I think that unless you have
one there's no way you can understand how it changes everything.
One day you're just going along. The next day you're a dad and you
have this little person who can't do anything for himself. Your life is
not the same anymore. He needs you for every little thing.

I used to drink some. And I'll admit to smoking a joint once
in a while. Now? I might have one or two beers but I go easy and I
pass on the weed. Once Colton came I knew I didn't ever want to
be so messed up that if he needed me I wouldn't be able to be there
for him one hundred percent.

Not everybody agrees with me. Casey's like, unless its his
weekend with the boys, he's off the clock. He's entitled to his
opinion, but that's not how I see it. Even if Colton's with Kari,
what if she got sick and she had to call me to come pick him up
or they were in a car wreck or something? I can't get stuff like that
out of my mind. You've got to keep a clear head all the time once
you are a dad.

Your kid has got to come first because if you mess up—it's gonna mess things up for him. That's something I know for a fact.

Because when Kari was five months pregnant I messed up big.

"Day gots a potty?"

"Yep," I tell Colton. "You need to go?"

"Poo," he says.

Not good. Colton doesn't give you much lead time when it comes to number two. "Okay, buddy. Hold on. We're almost there." I pull into a parking spot at the dentist's office and hope to God their restroom is empty and easy to find. It's Colton's first visit, his first checkup with this dentist who's supposed to specialize in kids.

"Is coming, Daddy! Is coming!" Colton's eyes are big and his face is red, which anyone who's got a kid knows is not a good sign.

"No, Colton. Wait." I slam the truck into park and turn off the key. "You can't go now. We're here. See? You got to wait. Okay?" I reach across the seat, unfasten the latch, and lift my son up out of his booster seat, ready to sprint him inside.

"Daddy?" His face and the stink when I stand him up say it all.

Man. You can't cuss around kids. And I don't. But one very appropriate curse word comes pretty close to crossing my lips.

Yep.

That would be the word.

Colton's been out of Pull-Ups and into big boy pants for a few months now. It's been going pretty good. So good that I didn't think to bring him any extra clothes. I reach for the box of wipes

I keep behind the seat. It's empty. We are already running late for his appointment, which took six months to get and Kari will kill me if I miss.

It's a hundred degrees outside. Ten seconds after killing the engine it feels like ninety-nine inside my truck. I wipe Colton up as best I can with a bunch of leftover fast food napkins and a plastic Wal-Mart sack, getting you know what on my shirt, his shoes, and the seat of the truck. He's crying. I'm mad. Mad at him for messing in his pants. Mad at myself for not being prepared. Colton's shorts only have a little bit of poop on the leg so I put them back on him, pick him up, and toss his underwear into the dumpster in the parking lot.

Once we get inside, I take him to the restroom and wash both of us up.

"I'm sorry I yelled at you," I tell him. I'm rinsing the leg of his shorts off in the sink. "It wasn't your fault. I know you couldn't wait."

Colton stands there in his shirt and his shoes. He's shivering in the air conditioning, sucking his thumb. He doesn't answer me.

"You be a big boy while the tooth doctor looks in your mouth and we'll go to Sonic on the way home."

That brightens him up. He likes Sonic Tator Tots with cheese.

When I get to work, late, Alice Dunn, one of my long-term customers, is sitting waiting on me. She's reading *People* magazine and slurping on one of those frozen drinks from Starbucks.

"Right with you, Alice," I tell her.

In the break room, I drop my backpack on the floor, stash my lunch in the fridge, and swish a swig out of the bottle of Listerine

I keep on a shelf in the employee restroom. When I come out, Mrs. Chan's doing a cut. She catches my eye, looks up at the clock, and gives me one of her looks. I know. I know. I'm already twenty minutes behind and my book is full.

I'm not going into it but I can't help thinking, if only she knew.

I nod to Alice that I'm ready for her.

"Morning, Joel," she says and sits down. "How've you been? How's Colton?"

"He's fine," I tell her. "Growing. Talking. Took him to the dentist this morning before I dropped him off at day care." I tuck the collar of her blouse inside then put the cape around her.

"That does not sound like fun," Alice says.

"You have no idea." Alice is short so I raise up the chair. "Let's just say the experience of taking a three-year-old to the dentist has got to be the best form of birth control I know."

"No future slipups, then," says Alice. She's laughing.

"Not a chance." I hold up three fingers. "Scout's honor. What are we doing today?"

"Just a trim. Unless you've got other ideas."

A month ago I talked Alice into an all-over medium brown, which was not easy. I promised her we could go back to her blonde highlights if she didn't like it, but her hair turned out really pretty. Going brown took a good five years off her face.

You've heard the jokes about Texas women and big hair. You really don't see so much of that anymore. I do a lot of natural looks where I use nothing more than a round brush and a blow dryer to get the style. Hair should move. And even though we sell the stuff, I try to talk my customers away from using lots of styling products and hair spray, which can dry out the hair real bad and take away the shine. But there is one thing about Texas women and their hair that's true. I'd say eighty percent of my customers who color go for blonde highlights. I've done foils on girls young as eleven. Sometimes an older lady thinks keeping highlights makes her look younger. But that's not always the case.

I comb through Alice's hair. "Roots still look good. Little snip to the ends, you'll be set." She's a nice Baptist lady. Midforties. A few pounds overweight. Teaches third grade at a little Christian school across town. Alice and her husband, who she's been married to for twenty-five years, have got two grown kids. I cut his hair, too.

"What'd Rich think about your new color?" I ask.

"He liked it. But old Pancho barked at me when I first came in the door. Guess I scared him. He's used to it now."

I've been doing Alice's hair since the first week I went to work at Lucy's, which would be going on five years now. She is a very kind person. Conservative but not judgmental like you might expect. We talk. She always asks me how it's going with me and Kari and Colton. Alice was real understanding back when Kari and I got divorced. Said she was praying for me, which I told her I appreciated very much. When I was going through all that, I told Alice a lot of stuff, probably more than I should. But she never acted shocked or told me I was a bad person or anything like that. Last Christmas she bought Colton a present.

Only thing about Alice. She is all the time telling me stuff that's in the Bible and inviting me to come to her church.

"You'd like it, Joel," Alice says to me while I rinse her out. "You should come. Just one time. See what you think."

I don't want to hurt Alice's feelings because she's a good person and I don't believe in putting anybody's personal beliefs down, but I'm not sure the Baptists would know what to do with somebody like me.

"One of these days, Alice," I say. "One these days maybe I will."

After Alice is gone, I start to sweep up.

"You ever going to Alice's church?" asks Abe.

"Nope."

Abe shakes his head.

It's not that I've got anything against church. I believe in God. I think the Ten Commandments are important and I don't understand why there's all this fuss about trying to take them out of courthouses and all that. But that's about as far as me and religion stuff go.

Alice asked me one time if I prayed. I told her the truth. Not much. When I was in seventh grade we had this basketball coach. Made us kneel in a circle before every home game and say The Lord's Prayer. I remember it, and I guess it's a good thing, but I still don't understand most the words.

When *The Passion of the Christ* came out, everybody who came into the shop was talking about it, so of course I went. Man. It blew me away. No way you could see something like that and not be affected. So of course it gave me a lot of respect for Jesus. No ordinary man could have gone through all that stuff that he did.

I've got customers who don't know my background. Christians, I mean. I'll tell you this right now: The way they talk about gays and religion—well, that's something somebody like me has a hard time dealing with. My dad had a lot of problems and he let me down some, but he was still my dad. Everybody is entitled to their own beliefs. They might be right but I don't need somebody telling me my dad's going to burn in hell.

But I don't like getting into arguments. When talk like that comes up I keep my mouth shut. Problem is, some people don't get the message even when you all of a sudden get quiet. They keep running their mouths. One guy even handed me a bunch of pamphlets with Bible verses about how homosexuals were all condemned by God, thinking I'd help him out by giving them to my customers.

"Sorry, man. No can do," I told him.

He never came back after that.

Bradley Lopez is my next customer after Alice. "How's it going, man?" He steps over and hops up into my chair.

"Sorry you had to wait," I tell him. According to my book, I'm running a half hour behind.

"No prob. Saw you weren't ready. Went and paid my light bill," says Bradley.

Now about this church business, Bradley might have the right idea. The guy's one of a kind. Tips me five dollars for a twenty-dollar haircut every time he comes in. Claims he's a pastor. Runs a limousine service on the side. Weddings, proms, whatever you want. Bradley wears all these gold chains. Big gold nugget cross. Pinky rings on both hands. Fake-alligator skin ankle boots with zippers on the sides. Looks like he could be a pimp in some movie except he's white. I don't know where the Lopez comes from.

"Joel, starting me up a new church," Bradley tells me. The man's always got either a matchstick or a toothpick between his teeth. "Gonna meet over at the Lone Star Diner. Know where that is? Back behind that old closed-down skating rink off Fourth. They got a private room in the back. Haven't gone non-smoking like every other place in town."

Cigarettes are not good for diabetics and Bradley is one. If I was as bad off as him, I don't think I'd be smoking. He takes three shots a day.

"Church is gonna start at two o'clock every Sunday afternoon."

"How come so late?" I ask him.

"So's all the winos and the hookers and dopers'll have time to sober up and get over their hangovers and still be on time." He starts laughing. "Figure they's the ones need saving. May as well make it where they won't have to worry about being late."

You never know when Bradley's being serious or when he's trying to put one over on you. "Sounds like a plan, man," I say. "Sounds like a plan."

"Let you know when we get it set up. Case you and that boy o' yours want to come."

"You do that," I say. I'm thinking: Yeah, right. Some out-of-the-way diner with hookers and drunks is exactly the kind of place I want me and Colton to be spending our Sunday afternoons. I put the cape on Bradley and take up my comb. "How about we try something different? Take some of this off your neck." Every four to six weeks, Bradley comes in for me to clean up his mullet, which I have not yet been able to talk him out of and would rather not lay claim to because it looks so bad on him.

"Nah. That's okay. Regular cut'll be fine."

It's his hair.

So I'm cutting. Bradley's talking. Telling me some wild tale about this girl he met at his Wednesday night Narcotics Anonymous meeting. Speculating on whether her boobs are real or fake. He claims he can usually but not always tell just by look-ing. But then Bradley's voice sort of trails off and I realize he is all of a sudden sweating like a pig. Water is pouring off his head and neck. He's still with me but he has gone real pale and sunk down in my chair.

I know right off something is bad wrong.

"Mrs. Chan!"

She comes over. So does Abe.

"What happened?"

"Get him some water."

"No. Get him a Coke."

"He can't have a Coke. He's diabetic and we're out of diets."

"Bring him a real one. He needs the sugar."

"Bradley. You okay, man?"

Nobody even thinks about calling 911.

Where's Alice when you need her? Times like this, knowing how to pray would come in handy.

Bradley is trying to say something but he can't get his mouth to work. It's like he's doing everything in slow motion. He's fumbling when he reaches into his pocket and pulls out his keys and some change, which he drops on the floor.

"Whoa, buddy. You're not going anywhere," I tell him. I take his keys from him, which makes him look like he would hit me if he had enough in him to raise his hands. "You're sick, man," I tell him. "Something's wrong."

Then Bradley reaches back into his pocket and pulls out one of those little tubes of cake icing. Pink. His hands are shaking but he tries to get the cap off it.

Abe grabs it out of his hands, breaks the top right off, and squeezes the stuff into Bradley's mouth. Abe's sister is diabetic, which is how he knows what to do.

I have never seen anything like what happens next.

Bradley gets okay. I mean like in less than a minute he's back to himself. Or close anyway. He's still real pale and all but he's talking normal and sitting up straight in my chair. "Joel. Can you give me a towel?" I see his hands are shaking when he tries to wipe up sweat from his head.

"You need go to hospital?" asks Mrs. Chan.

Bradley shakes his head. "Nah. I'm all right now. Or I will be."

"What happened, man?" I ask him.

"Sugar dropped," he says. "I was going to get some lunch soon as you got done with me. Should have waited to take my insulin."

This is my fault. I was running late.

"I think maybe I'll take a rain check on the haircut," Bradley says, "I got to get something to eat."

Of course he does. One of us should have thought of that.

Then Bradley starts to get out of my chair, but you can tell the man is not a hundred percent. So I make him sit down, and I go to the back and grab my lunch. Two ham sandwiches and a banana that's on the edge of being too ripe. He eats it while I cut his hair. After I'm done, he tries to pay me but I tell him no.

"This one's on me."

But when he leaves Bradley slips me a five-dollar tip anyway.

Even though she got big by the end, Kari did not gain that much weight when she was pregnant. It was only at one of her appointments that her doctor told her she needed not to eat so much. She was supposed to gain about a pound a week. At her five-month checkup, we found out she'd put on seven pounds in only four weeks.

"Mrs. Carpenter, it's true," her doctor said after she stepped off the scale, "you're eating for two. But one of you is very, very tiny. Only about this big." The guy was Asian. Real short. Dark black hair. He held his hands about six inches apart, like he was showing off the size of a fish he'd caught, one not big enough to keep. "He does not eat very much. Be careful this next month. Try to cut back. Just a little. Especially on fried food and sweets."

On our way home, Kari and I went through the drive-through at Dairy Queen to get stuffed jalapeño bites and Butterfinger Blizzards. She was craving them bad. We laughed about what the doctor had told her. "Good thing he can't see you now," I said.

I don't want you to get the wrong idea. We could joke about it because Kari had been real careful about her diet starting the day we found out she was pregnant. She ate lots of fruit, drank milk with every meal, even gave up Cokes.

"Don't you know the rule?" Kari said. She had a red bandana on her head and she was wearing white Keds. Sitting in the sunshine her eyes were as blue as the sky. I remember she smelled like peaches. Lotion, I guess.

"What rule?" I asked. We were eating, sitting thigh to thigh on the back stoop of our house. Even though it was February, the late afternoon weather was sunny and nice, sixty-something degrees, which if you live in Texas you know is not all that unusual. I looked over at Kari. She had a Blizzard mustache, which made her look like a cute little kid. I reached up and wiped her mouth with my thumb.

"The day you go to the doctor is a free day. You get to eat anything you want." She scraped the bottom of her cup with her spoon.

"That so?" I teased her. "You read that in one of those pamphlets?"

"Page twenty-one," she said. "You gonna want all of your peppers?"

I gave her my last two. "Now remember, Mrs. Carpenter," I held up my hands, slid my sunglasses way down on the end of my nose, and tried to sound like a doctor, "one of you is very, very tiny. He doesn't eat all that much."

Which made Kari laugh and have to go in to pee.

That was a nice day. A really nice one. Everything felt good. And right. But there weren't very many of those kind of days that fall and winter. I loved Kari and she loved me. I don't believe that was ever the issue. But the truth is, I don't remember much laughing during those months she was pregnant. What I remember is her being tired and me having lots of stuff I was supposed to do.

When Kari and I first got married, we never worried about how clean our house was. Before her mother died, she used to come over and fuss because the kitchen floor needed to be swept and our bed wasn't made. Kari blew her off. Stuff on the floor didn't bother us. What was the point of making up the bed if you were just going to get back in it in a few hours? Being newlyweds, we'd have spent a big part of every day making that bed up if we'd tried to fix it back every time we crawled out from between the sheets.

We didn't have a washer and dryer so we'd let our dirty clothes stack up pretty high. When we ran out of anything to wear we'd load everything up and spend an afternoon at the Laundromat. Sometimes we waited a day or two too long. Like the time I caught Kari wearing a pair of my white Hanes because she didn't have any clean panties. Girl had them on backwards. Because they fit better that way.

Our yard was mostly weeds and I didn't always mow it as often as I should. Kari's mom generally had something to say about that, but honestly none of that bothered either of us. It's not like we were slobs or the health department was going to come after us or anything. Compared to some of our friends' places you could have called us Mr. and Mrs. Clean.

We were just a couple of kids hanging out, basically playing house, having a good time.

I guess there must be some chemical that kicks in when a

woman gets pregnant, because almost from the minute we found out Colton was coming, things changed. My laid-back wife got majorly obsessed with things being clean.

Which would have been fine if she'd left me out of it, but she didn't.

I hated coming home from the salon and finding a list of stuff she'd left for me to do. It wasn't that I minded helping out. Okay, maybe I did. But at the end of the day I wanted to kick back, shoot some baskets in the driveway, or watch some TV. Cleaning the ceiling fans, folding clothes, scrubbing the shower, or weed eating around the trees was not how I wanted to spend my time. What guy would? But there it would be. My list of things to do. Kari made sure there was no way I could say I forgot. It was all there in black ink stuck with a magnet on the refrigerator door. Either I did what she said or I didn't.

Most times I didn't.

Kari got really big into all kinds of lists. Not just chore lists, but running grocery lists, which we'd never used before, lists of things she had to do for school, lists of which bills needed to be paid when. There was this one long list of all the things we needed to buy for the baby. Not just a bed and diapers like you'd think, but stuff I'd never even heard of. Out beside each item she had what it was going to cost. It added up. But Kari had it figured out what we were supposed to buy every month so that we'd have everything we needed by June, when he or she was supposed to be born.

What was the point of all this organization? I didn't see the need.

Once after a big fight over me not pulling my weight, I told Kari she needed to lighten up. To chill. Everything would work out. She was still beautiful, but where was that fun girl I'd married?

Which was when she told me to get over myself. To stop being such a selfish jerk because it was time for me to grow up.

It was the same week as that good day, the one when Kari and I ate our Blizzards on our back stoop, that I met up with an old friend. I was at work, between customers. It was a slow morning. Neither me or Abe had a customer and we were both nearly asleep slumped down in our chairs when somebody came up behind me and covered my eyes with their hands.

"Guess who?"

Even though I hadn't seen her in three or four years, I knew who it was right off. Leslie. My friend from high school. The one I spent so much time with up on the roof of her house.

"Girl!" I spun my chair around, jumped up, grabbed her and swung her around in a bear hug. "How are you? What are you doing in town?" I put her down. Leslie looked exactly the same. Beautiful. Five foot one. Big boobs. Gorgeous brown eyes. Sweet, sexy smile.

"I came to get my hair trimmed." She grinned up at me. "Anybody around here any good?"

Abe cut in. He shot me a grin. I knew what he was thinking. "I've got time."

"Sure. Now he's awake," I said. Then I introduced the two of them. "Back in the day Leslie and I were best friends. She knows all my deep dark secrets."

"Yep. The tales I could tell." She laughed.

"What you doing in town?"

"My mom and dad are moving to Florida. I came down to help them sort stuff out and get packed."

"They're not selling their house, are they?"

"Yep. Getting rid of lots of stuff. We're having a big garage sale next week."

"So you're here for how long?" I asked.

"Couple of months. Drove in day before yesterday."

"That's great," I said. "And so you really came in here to get a haircut?"

"I came in to see you, you idiot," she frogged me in the arm. "But since I'm here, yeah." She climbed up into my chair. "Show me your stuff, Joel. Make me beautiful."

Abe's eyebrow shot up.

Beautiful? She already was.

chapter six

INSTEAD OF COOKING, WE decide on pizza for our Sunday single dad get-together. I order. Pete, Casey, and Abe chip in. Sean brings sodas and water to drink. After ten minutes of discussion about what kind everybody wants we end up ordering sausage; pepperoni; three meat combo; and a mushroom, pepper, and onion for Abe, who avoids processed meats and looks to me like any day could cross over to vegetarian. When the pizza comes I tip the guy four bucks and everybody dives in.

The bigger kids are excited because tomorrow's the first day of school.

"Spent fifty bucks on school supplies," Abe says.

"For kindergarten?" I'm surprised.

"Your day's coming. You should see all the junk they've got to have," says Casey. "Not just scissors and glue and notebooks and stuff. I'm talking Kleenex, wet wipes, paper towels."

"Sh'dondra had to have a disposable camera," Abe says. "What's with that?"

"I go school," Colton says. He's picking the pepperonis off his pizza and eating them first.

"You do not," says Pete's son Brandon.

"You're too little," says his other son Chase.

"Am not." Colton can't decide whether to hit Brandon or

49

Chase first.

"Colton goes to day care," I say. "He calls it his school. You guys want cookies?" I head them off. "Tell your dad to get you some. On top of the fridge."

We have a good time, but since the kids need to get to bed at a decent hour everybody leaves pretty early.

Except for Sean. Allyssa's too young for school and so is Colton. We don't have to worry about getting our kids in bed any certain time. I mean it's not like you have to worry if they fall asleep at day care because what's it going to hurt?

Sean and I've known each other couple a years. He looks like what you'd expect somebody named Sean McDonald to look like. Short red hair, light skin. Freckles. Average height. Five ten or so. Not built big but lately getting a piece of gut on him. Allyssa's asleep in his lap. She's the cutest thing. All girl. Long, light brown hair, curly eyelashes, fair skin like Sean but with round cheeks that are always pink. She's the kind of little girl who'll grow up to be the kind a woman who'll end up breaking a bunch a guy's hearts.

Colton's on the floor, sitting Indian style watching The Food Channel. He loves Emeril. Go figure. Weird, I think, for a three-year-old to get into something like that, but I'm not too worried. I figure it might be good for both of us if someday he learns how to cook.

"You hear anything from Brooke?" I ask.

Sean's arm's gone to sleep. He shifts Allyssa's position on his chest, then shakes his hand, trying to get it to wake up. "Talked to her yesterday. She calls couple times a week."

"Where's she at?"

"Don't know. Won't say. I figure out of state. She won't ever stay on the line long. She wants to see if Allyssa's okay."

I think its pretty obvious that a two-year-old girl without her mother is not okay. "Still with what's his name—that guy from your church?"

He nods. "Ross. Youth pastor. She was always helping him out. Nice guy." He shakes his head and starts in.

I've heard all this before. Actually I've heard it several times but he needs to talk so I let him run on.

"The man was real friendly. Kind of person makes you feel like you've known him for a long time when you only first meet him. I felt sorry for him not being married. Figured he was lonely. Can you believe it? I ran into him at Ryan's the week they took off. We were both by ourselves so we sat at the same table. I even paid for his lunch." His face flushes red just talking about it. "I was pretty stupid not to know something was going on."

Six months Brooke has been gone. You don't have to be a shrink to see Sean's hurting bad. She didn't leave a note or anything. Just one day, out of the blue, Brooke calls Sean up and asks him if he can pick Allyssa up from day care on his way home from his job at Sears because she has something she has to do.

Some*body*, more like.

When he got home with Allyssa that afternoon, Brooke was gone. So were all her clothes, her jewelry, her shoes, her makeup, and stuff. She called Sean that night. Told him she loved that Ross guy and couldn't take being his wife anymore. When he asked her what about being a mother anymore, Brooke hadn't had an answer, just said that she didn't expect him to understand.

"Figure you'll get divorced?" I ask.

"I'm not filing," he said. "If Brooke wants a divorce she's the one who'll have to get it." Sean reaches for his root beer, takes a sip, then sets it down and rubs Allyssa's back while she sleeps.

It can't be easy having Allyssa full-time. I'm no way proud of this but it's the truth. Sometimes I count the hours 'til time to drop

Colton off at day care or take him back to Kari's place. And I've only got him half time. Sean's responsible for Allyssa twenty-four seven. He never gets a break. No matter how much you love your kid they can get on your last nerve. I'd never hit Colton. Kari and I don't believe in spanking. But there've been times I've had to go outside away from him so as not lose it.

Last Saturday was one of those times I'd about had it. It had been me and Colton all day in the house together because it was nonstop rain and, three days before payday, I was too broke for us to go anywhere. I'd played with him, read to him, fixed him exactly what he wanted to eat for three meals straight. That night when he started whining and carrying on about something stupid, I lost it. My head was killing me. It looked like the rain outside was never going to stop. When Colton started that whining, I caught myself feeling sorry for myself and yelling at him about how he didn't appreciate all the stuff I did for him.

Now that was real smart. Me, a grown man, yelling at a three-year-old about appreciation. What kind a fool goes there?

When I got done cutting and styling Leslie's hair, it was time for my lunch break so she and I decided to go eat together even though I had a sandwich waiting on me in the break room. We'd talked while she was in my chair, but it was kind of hard with everybody around and me using the blow dryer and all. Having lunch would give us a chance to really catch up.

Mrs. Chan looked at her watch when we headed out the door. I got her drift. "I'll be back for my 1:30," I told her. "On the dot."

She rolled her eyes.

"My car?" Leslie said.

"Sure. Where you parked?"

She pointed to a baby blue Mustang in the second row.

"No. That's yours?" The 1970 model. Loaded. Mint condition. "Sweet." I ran my hand over the hood. "Girl, you've come up in the world since your minivan days. Business must be good." Back when we were in high school, Leslie had to drive her family's old Aerostar or walk. She hated that thing.

"Fair," Leslie grinned. "Wanna drive?" She tossed me the keys.

"Sure. Rosa's okay?"

At the restaurant—a rowdy dive where you can get four different kinds of Mexican beer, tamales to go, and the best fajitas in town—the two of us hunkered down in a back booth with chips and salsa while we waited for our enchilada specials.

"Cool place," Leslie said.

"Yep." I reached for a chip. "Enchiladas are $3.99 on Thursdays. For that you get your meal, a drink, Tejano music, and the occasional friendly roach."

"What a deal."

"Glad you approve."

"You look great, Joel," Leslie said. She wiped off a spot of something that was on her spoon, then stirred two packets of Sweet'N Low into her iced tea. "Kari must be taking good care of you. Everything's going okay?"

"Things are all right," I said. "Kari's parents died in October. Car crash."

"That's terrible. I'm so sorry."

"She's going to nursing school."

"That's great."

"And she's pregnant," I said.

"Get out of here!"

"Five months."

"Congratulations! That's wonderful."

"Yes." I coughed on a chip stuck sideways in my throat. "It is wonderful. Timing's off a little, is all." I drank some tea, then filled her in on how we'd not planned on having a baby for a while.

"May be hard now, but it'll work out," Leslie said. "I'm happy for you. My old buddy." She touched my arm. "Next time I see you, you'll be a dad. Pretty cool. Is it a boy or a girl?"

"Don't know. Doctor did a sonogram. Baby wasn't turned right." Leslie being excited about the baby made me feel good.

Then the waitress brought our meals.

"So, you and Robert," I said. "How's it going? Figure you'll stay in Nebraska? Y'all plan on having kids soon?"

"We're doing fine. As for kids, that's another story. We've been trying the past two years. No luck."

Did I ever feel bad when I heard that. Here I'd been griping about having a kid too soon while Leslie was wanting one. Me and my mouth.

"At first, trying to have a baby was fun. Robert and I were up for the challenge." She smiled, but in a sad way. "But when we tried for months and nothing happened, we started in on all the tests, following a schedule, all that." She looked down and stirred at her rice, quiet for a minute.

"That's tough," was all I could come up with to say.

"You don't want to know. It's put a strain on our marriage." She pushed her hair behind her ears. "Robert's sick of all the baby talk. Even though I know that, sometimes I can't make myself think or talk about anything else. I blame him. He blames me. They can't find anything wrong with either one of us, which sounds crazy but makes it somehow even worse. The whole thing is depressing."

"I feel bad for you, Les."

The waitress brought us more tea.

"Thanks," Leslie said. "Now I wish I hadn't told you all that when you've just given me good news. I don't know why I did that. I'm happy for you. I am. And I don't want you to feel like you can't talk about the baby around me. I want to hear all about it. Everything. Is Kari feeling okay? Must be hard for her going to school. Working, too."

"We hardly see each other."

"That's not good."

I shrugged. "It's mostly okay. When it's not, what are you going to do?"

That night when Kari got home from work, I told her I'd seen Leslie. They'd barely known each other in high school, but I'd talked about her enough over the years that Kari knew who she was.

"How's she doing?" She took off her name badge and kicked off her shoes, then peeled off her scrubs and tossed them in the hamper.

"Okay."

"How long's she here for?"

"Couple of months. Helping her folks pack up so they can move. We had lunch at Rosa's." I told her about Leslie and Robert not being able to get pregnant.

"That's so sad for them," Kari said. She was wearing one of my T-shirts, standing at the bathroom sink with her toothbrush in her hand.

When she was finished, I brushed my teeth, too, thinking she might be in the mood.

"Did you iron those clothes I asked you to?" Kari asked.

"No." I was already in bed.

"I need a uniform for tomorrow. That's the one thing I asked you to do."

"Sorry. I forgot." I pushed back the covers and got up to go do it because I didn't want to argue.

Which was just too bad.

Because Kari was in the mood all right.

To argue with me.

chapter seven

THE DAY AFTER OUR LATE-NIGHT fight, Kari was off work. I came home to a warm kitchen and the sight of my wife wearing an apron that said, "I kiss better than I cook."

She'd made dinner. My favorite meal. Chicken fried steak. Baked potatoes. Salad. Even a cake. Kari's a good kisser and a good cook. After we finished eating, she apologized for blowing up at me. Glad it was over and not seeing any need to go there again, I told her to forget it, it was okay, and that she should go sit down because since she cooked, I would clean up.

"Uh, the kitchen can wait," she said. "Let's go to the living room. We need to talk."

Man. I hate those words.

I knew what was coming. We went and sat on the couch, her straight up with one foot curled under her butt, me leaned all the way back, my legs stretched out in front of me, my arms across my chest. Kari smiled at me. She put her hand on my leg. She told me how much she loved me. She said our marriage was good but that there were things we needed to work on.

We.

Yeah, right.

Then, like I knew from past experiences to expect, my wife spent the next hour nailing me on the hundred and ten ways I was messing up and letting her down.

🖘

Leslie called me at work to see if I was interested in anything of her mom and dad's. "Garage sale's this weekend," she said. "They're selling some pretty good stuff. Couple leather couches. A TV. Thought you and Kari might want a preview."

I told her I'd stop by on my way home from work.

Leslie was sitting on the front porch with a mug of tea when I pulled up in my truck. "Where's Kari?" she asked.

"Working. She gets off at eleven."

"Those are some long hours."

"Yep." *Enough about Kari* was what I wanted to say. I was still hacked off at her from last night. Leslie and I went around to the side door. I ran my hand over the peeling paint on the fence that ran beside it and looked up at the mature oak trees shading the house. "Can't believe your folks are actually selling. I always thought this was the greatest place."

"Good memories," Leslie said. "Hard for me to comprehend I won't be coming back here to visit. I realized yesterday when I leave Eden Plain this time, it'll probably be for the last time."

"What? You won't come back for our class reunions?" I pretended to be shocked.

"Get real."

Neither of us was the class reunion type.

Leslie pushed open the back door and, like almost every time I'd ever been over to her parents' house, you could smell something good cooking soon as you stepped inside. The two of us went through the laundry room and into the kitchen where her mom, Mona, was unloading cabinets, packing and sorting dishes and glasses and stuff. Mona was short like Leslie. I gave her a hug and a kiss on the top of her head.

"You're just in time," she said after we got past all the how-are-you-how've-you-beens and she fixed me a glass of iced tea. "I can't reach these top shelves. Mind handing me down the stuff that's up there?"

While I did that, Leslie stirred something her mom had going in the crock pot. "Stew?"

"Beef. Should be about done. Turn it down to low, honey." Mona washed her hands at the sink, then turned to me. "Joel. Stay over and eat supper with us. There's plenty. Allen'll be back any minute. He'd love to see you. It's been too long." She got a little teary, which Leslie had told me she'd been doing pretty regularly during all the getting ready for the move.

I glanced over Mona's head and caught Leslie's eye. She nodded I should stay. "Thanks. That'd be great." I gave Mona another hug. She blew her nose and started pulling stuff out of the refrigerator to make a salad.

Leslie's folks were two of the kindest people I've known. They had money but you wouldn't know it. Both had hearts as big as Dallas. Took anybody in. Leslie said things were different now that they'd gotten a little older and especially now that they were planning on moving, but back in the day she never knew who — besides me three or four times a week — she'd be eating supper with.

Her parents had this big oak table and even though there were only three in their family, lots of times you had to work your way in to get a spot around it. There'd be high chairs and wheelchairs crowded in, along with the regular wooden ones that went with the table. Always plenty of food, even if sometimes it was sandwiches or chili out of a can. Way it looked to me, if you were poor, sick, had just gotten out of jail, if you were eight years old and didn't know who your daddy was, if you and your wife's combined weight was six hundred pounds, if you were a little bit mentally off, down on your luck, or just plain didn't have anywhere else to go, you were welcome at Allen and Mona's table.

They were that good.

I'm ashamed of myself now, but sometimes back then Leslie and I would make fun of all the misfit people her parents fed. Behind their backs of course. It was years later before I came to realize I was no different than any of the other folks they took in.

When Allen got home I saw he had aged more than Mona, but he still had the same brilliant blue eyes and wild hair—used to be blond, now gone white—he used to. At first he shook my hand but then he gave me a hug. He wanted to know all about how I was doing. He was thrilled when I told him about the baby. When the stew was ready, we sat down to eat. Allen said a blessing. Mona opened a bottle of wine. We ended up sitting around the table for a good two hours. Laughing. Talking. Remembering. Eating way too much. By the time we all moved to get up, my rear had gone numb.

Leslie and I told her folks we'd clean up, which they said was great. While we were doing that they'd take their evening walk even if it was a little later than they usually went. The two of them left out the back door, went around the side of the house, and headed toward the street. I stood at the window and watched them. It was eight o'clock by then. Dark in a half hour or so.

Mona and Allen went a few paces but Mona was kind of limping. She must have had something in her shoe because they stopped. Mona held on to Allen's elbow while she bent, took her shoe off, shook it, and then put it back on. Looked like they were

set then. But before they started out again, Allen bent and gave
Mona a little peck on the lips and patted her on the rear. She said
something and they both laughed. Then they started out again.

Leslie showed me the garage sale stuff. There wasn't much I
wanted. Just a couple of CDs and a rod and reel of her dad's. Our
house wasn't all that big and with the baby coming we didn't have
room for a bunch of extra stuff.

"This has been nice," I said when we got done looking. "I
better head home."

"Don't leave," Leslie said. "This's been such a good night. Didn't
you say Kari's not home 'til eleven? Why would you go home to an
empty house? I've got a better idea," she said. "Let's go out on the
roof. Bet you could use a cigarette."

She was right. "You still smoke?" I asked.

"Hardly ever. You remember I never got very good at it. But
tonight I'll have one for old times' sake."

I wanted to stay but didn't know if I should. "Won't your folks
wonder where we are when they get back and see my truck but
we're not in the house?"

"We'll holler at them when they come up the drive. They won't
care. They're in bed by nine-thirty. Both of them are early risers
these days."

So Leslie and I climbed the stairs. The hall felt more narrow
than I remembered and the light was burned out in her old bedroom. It was a sewing room now. We groped our way around
plastic crates and boxes her mother had out to start packing up
stuff in. It was hot and stuffy. I guessed they didn't have the air on
upstairs. Smelled musty.

"Shoot." Leslie had on flip-flops and she stubbed her toe on
the leg of a chair.

"You okay?"

"Yeah."

I raised the window and we climbed out.

The two of us sat on the edge of the roof, letting our legs hang over the side so we'd be sure to see her folks. Leslie rubbed her toe.

When Mona and Allen came up the drive they waved at us. "Good to see you, Joel," her Dad yelled up. You'd have thought seeing his grown-up daughter and her friend on the roof of his house was something he saw every day of the week.

"Thanks again for supper," I yelled back.

"See you in the morning, honey," Mona called.

"Good night, Mom."

The sky was nearly dark by then. No clouds. Because it was still early, there were only two stars out. Within a couple of minutes they'd be all over. Leslie picked up some acorns that had fallen on the roof. She arranged them in a little circle beside her. From all the leaves, it looked to me like it had been awhile since Allen had cleaned out the gutters. There were some loose shingles. A few missing. Which was no big deal since they were moving.

After a bit, Leslie and I scooted back so we could stretch our legs out and lean against the slope. "We spent a lot of hours up here back in the day," I said.

"Ever wish you could go back?" Leslie asked. "To when we were teenagers?"

Leslie has always been one to get into deep discussions. "Sometimes."

"We had so many choices back then," she said. "And we didn't even realize it. Tell me. If you knew then what you know now would you do anything different?"

"I don't know. Would have been fun to have taken a road trip. Some us guys talked about it. We were going to drive to California.

Planned it all out during history class, but we never got around to it. Once we graduated, everybody lost touch. One guy got a job. Somebody moved off." I slapped at a mosquito on my arm.

"I miss the way it was back then," Leslie said.

I knew what she meant. Everything was so easy. "What if you had a do-over," I asked. "Would you take it?"

"I don't know." Leslie looked down. She got busy rearranging her acorns. "Everybody makes choices. Maybe I'd make some of them different."

"You mean like where to go to school? Where you'd live?"

"More than that," Leslie said. She snagged a cigarette out of my pack. I handed her my lighter. She took a quick drag in, then exhaled slow. "Okay. You ready? Here's how I think it all works. We all get basically two choices. We choose to live a life that's safe, or one that's not. We decide to follow the rules and do the predict-able thing, or something else. Something with chances and risks and adventure. Know what I'm saying?"

I nodded. Now that guy who worked with the crocodiles. He lived what I'd call an adventurous life.

"Way I see it, everybody gets to pick one or the other," Leslie said. "If you pick the safe life, things will probably turn out like you expect. If you don't, they probably won't. Not saying either choice is wrong. Or right. There's a price to pay whichever way you go."

"Once you make a choice, you can't change your mind?" I asked. "You can't decide to take the other path?"

"Most people don't," she said.

"You went way off to school. Married a guy nobody'd ever met. Moved way off. I guess I know which one you chose," I said. "Me? I never thought about it but I guess I chose the safe life. I'm still here in Eden Plain. Married to a hometown girl. Big adventure for me is eating Chinese food instead of Mexican."

Leslie looked away. "It's not about place. Or even about a person. It's way deeper than that."

"Sounds like you're going through some stuff," I said.

"Maybe. Mostly I'm lonely. Really, really lonely. And you know who I'm lonely for? Myself. Isn't that dumb? But I feel . . ."

"Like you've lost who you are," I finished. "Or who you were."

"Exactly." She wiped her eyes. "I'm such a whiner, aren't I?"

I smiled at her. "You always were."

She smiled back. "I've got a good job. We have a nice house. Robert's a good husband."

"What would make it better then?" I asked. "A baby?"

"Maybe," she said. "Probably. Sounds crazy, but I don't know anymore. Some days I just want more. More of everything. A bigger life. I think about running away. Going someplace where nobody knows me. Starting all over."

"Which would mean leaving Robert?" I said.

"And which I'm not going to do. I love him. There's nothing wrong with him. Not one thing. He's a good man. He treats me well."

"What nerve," I said.

Leslie laughed. "I know. None of this makes sense, does it?" She blew her nose.

"It makes sense," I said.

"You ever feel trapped?" she asked. "Like you wish you could go somewhere else, have somebody else's life. For just a little while?"

"Only about twice a week," I answered.

Leslie scooted closer to me and leaned her head against my shoulder.

I took her hand. "My take? Everybody has to figure out for themselves what it is they want. Unfortunately, that's not the hard part. Once you figure out what you want you have to figure out how to get it. And if it's worth it."

"Joel, what do you want?" Leslie whispered after a time.

I rubbed her thumb. "You really want to know?"

"I do."

"I want what your mom and dad have."

She sat up. "A house like this?"

"No. Nothing to do with a house. I want a family. To be part of one of those old couples you see who've been together so long they look alike. I want to be sixty years old, gray, still with my gray-headed, chubby wife that I've been married to for forty years. I want to be a good person. To do the right thing, whatever that is. I want to be generous. Unselfish. Your parents are the most unselfish people I've ever met. I want at the end of it all to be able to look at Kari and at our kids and grandkids and both of us say we've had a good life. What's scary is that I don't know if I can pull it off, because mostly I'm a big failure when it comes to being a good husband. I sure as heck don't know how a person goes about being a dad."

"You'll be a great father," Leslie said.

"I'm going to try."

"You're a good person. One of the best I've ever known."

"You must not know many people," I said.

"Don't put yourself down."

"I only know one thing. I don't ever want to hurt Kari," I said.

"I don't want to hurt Robert, either. It's just that sometimes I feel like I'm going to die if I don't—I don't know how to say it—get some kind of relief."

We stood up. I gave Leslie a hug.

I knew just what she meant.

And so I went home and did everything on my list.

chapter eight

ABE HAS DECIDED TO JOIN Jill's church. Get baptized. Go the whole nine yards. He tells me this after work on Tuesday. We're in my truck on our way to the gym. His car's in the shop. Transmission.

"That's great, man," I say even though I'm surprised. He's been going awhile but I didn't realize he was ready to join up. "If that's what you want, you should go for it."

"I know what you're thinking," he says. "This doesn't have nothing to do with Jill."

He's right. That is what I'm thinking. But what would be wrong with that? Joining Jill's church is a good step to take for him to get back with her. She's gotten really into it over the past year or so. Be good if they hooked back up.

"I came to this on my own," Abe says. "Did a lot of reading. Not just about Christianity. Buddhism. Islam. Some other religions, too."

Abe most all time has his head stuck in some book.

"What made you decide?" I ask.

Abe doesn't answer me. I look over to see if he was even listening to what I said. He's chewing on his jaw, staring out the window. The guy's about impossible to read. He's got the kind of face that unless he's smiling has the look he's hacked off at you about something even when he's not. Before I got to know him, I thought he was mad about eighty percent of the time.

"Why now?"

"Can't say, except it feels right," he says. "Really, really right."

"That's good." I'm afraid Abe's about to cry. I didn't intend to get something started up so I change the subject. "Want to get something to eat after we work out? Jack's running two-for-one burgers."

Abe doesn't answer me about eating but at least he's not bawling. "Been holding back on this for a long time. Finally figured it out. Not about all that religious mess. You know, I never had any use for that. Still don't. Big buildings. Rich people. Fancy cars. Preachers always wanting your money. No place in that for me."

Me either is what I think.

"So what changed your mind?"

"The man."

"Must be some preacher," I say.

"No. No," Abe says. "I'm talking about Jesus. In the Bible. I started in reading this new Bible. Jill gave it to me. Every night I open it up and read some. Some of what's in there'll blow you away. Book's written like people talk now. None of those thee's and thou's."

Thee's? Thou's? I nod like I understand but I don't have a clue what he's talking about.

"Everything Jesus did and all the stuff he said—when I read it for myself, it tripped me up. Church people done sold us a line, Joel. You read about Jesus and you find out it wasn't them he hung out with. It was the sinners. The bad folk. The people nobody wanted around. Jesus understood where they came from. He knew all about what they done. But he didn't judge them. He loved them. When I read that, it changed everything because . . ."

He stopped to put some gum in his mouth. "You've known me a long time. I'm no church man. I'm just me. A messed-up guy who messed up his marriage. I got skeletons in my closet. Pushing like crazy to get out. No telling what's gonna hit the fan when they do."

Yep. I knew.

"I'm ready for something different. Ready to start over. Looking to be clean."

"Sounds like you're sure. That's good. I'm glad for you."

"More sure than I've been about much of anything in a long time. Sunday's when I get baptized. Big day. You want to come?"

"If you want me to."

"Mean a lot."

"Then sure," I say, even though as a person who does not know what you're supposed to do at a baptism, I'm not at all sure. "I'll be there. Let me know where and when."

A week or so after I'd been over to Leslie's house to look at the garage sale stuff, I got off work a little early, came home, and was surprised to see Kari's car in the drive. Then I remembered she'd switched shifts with somebody. She was off tonight. Maybe we'd go out to eat. See a movie. I'd let her pick what she wanted to see.

I got out of my truck and started around to the back door. If Kari hadn't had the windows open airing out the house because of the cabbage she cooked last night, I would have gone on in. She'd have known I was home and I'd have missed something that gets to me every time I hear it.

Music.

Kari was playing the piano, which is something she only does when she thinks nobody's around. She's never believed she's any good. But she is. When we first got married I asked her to play for me. I mean why else did me and four guys kill our backs hauling that thing, which weighed about as much as my truck, up our back steps but for her to play it? That was before I figured out how shy she was about it.

Before she died, her mom blamed Kari's not wanting anybody to hear her play on this music contest they put her in when she was fourteen. She was sick that day but didn't tell anybody and went on in to play for a bunch of judges. No big surprise. She bombed. Forgot her song, started crying, and ran off the stage. Later they checked her temperature. One hundred and four. Thinking about it still makes me mad. Somebody should have seen she was sick. A little girl should not have to go through something like that.

Couple of times right after our wedding I talked Kari into playing while I was home. She played classical stuff. Bach. Beethoven. I don't know who all else because that's not usually my kind of music. But I loved listening to it when she played it and I loved watching her. You could just see in her face how much she was into it.

But me watching and listening embarrassed her. For real. After a couple times she flat wouldn't play when I was around no matter how much I asked her and teased her about it. I've never figured that one out. The woman'd let me see her naked but she wouldn't let me listen to her play the piano.

Even though she was shy about it, I figured out pretty quick playing was something Kari had to do. Like scratching an itch that won't ever go away. So I got to where I'd tell her I was leaving to go somewhere but would hang out just outside the back door hoping once she thought I was gone she'd sit down and play.

Lots of times she did.

When that happened I'd open the back door a crack and prop it with a brick. Then I'd sit down on the back stoop and listen.

She never knew.

So that afternoon, when I stepped out of my truck and heard my wife on the piano I shut the door real easy so she wouldn't know I was home. With our crazy schedules it'd been a long time since I'd heard her play, probably a long time since she'd had the chance. When I got up to the back door, I sat down and listened for a good twenty minutes.

This probably sounds weird, but Kari's music is one of the things I miss most about us being married. On that afternoon, hearing her play was like putting some kind of medicated cream on a sore. It made me feel better. About her. About us. I was tired and I needed to go to the bathroom but I'd have stayed put even if she'd played for an hour. I remember sitting and listening and catching the smell of somebody in the neighborhood cooking steaks out on a grill. I remember the feel of the hard concrete under my butt. I remember too, looking up and seeing a flock of geese heading south, a sight that has always struck me as sad.

It'd been a long day. An even longer week. I'd driven home from work tired, and I'll admit it, I was feeling sorry for myself for how hard I had it.

I'm not proud of it, but I get like that sometimes.

But that afternoon, out there on those steps, all I could think about was how much I loved Kari. How bad I missed us getting along good. And how glad I would be when she was through with school and wasn't pregnant anymore because then everything would get back to normal.

A week later Leslie and I were sitting on bar stools in my kitchen having Dr Peppers and Oreos. "I should not be eating these," she said. "I need to lose weight."

"Where?" I asked.

"What do you mean where? My rear. My belly. Pretty much all over." She unscrewed her Oreo and began to lick off the filling.

"I don't know how you can think that. You don't need to lose weight," I told her. "You look good the way you are."

Leslie and I were listening to a couple of CDs I'd burned for her. Coldplay. She'd stopped by to pick them up, but I think both of us knew the CDs were one more drummed-up excuse for her to come over to my house.

She'd been in town for four weeks and so far we'd seen each other more than half a dozen times, always when Kari was at school or work since she didn't know Leslie all that well and wouldn't have cared about getting together with her anyway.

Three days before, Leslie had stopped by to bring me some old pictures she found when she was cleaning out her room. Two days before that it was to get me to listen to her car, which was making some kind of funny noise and since she was in the neighborhood she figured I might as well check it out.

Every time we were together it was like old times. Easy. We laughed. We talked. Since we were in the same place, Leslie and I understood each other. When she told me about the distance between her and Robert, I understood because I felt the same way with me and Kari. When I told her I felt sometimes Kari treated me like one more thing on her list of responsibilities, Leslie got it because lots of times Robert looked at her that same way.

Because we were such good friends, Leslie and I even joked about our nearly nonexistent married sex lives. We laughed about how new clients at the shop usually assumed I was gay but about how that was too funny because if only they knew. Leslie said she had a hard time believing people really thought that about me because to her it was way obvious I wasn't gay.

Talking to each other was good for us, we said. It was better to let off steam to each other than for me to take it out on Kari and for her to let Robert have it over the phone or when she got home. We counted ourselves lucky to have each other to talk to, even if we both knew it was only for about another month.

That afternoon in my kitchen, Leslie had kicked off her shoes and was swinging her feet back and forth, telling some story. Her toenails were painted bright pink. While she was talking, several times she reached up to brush her bangs to the side.

"You keep messing with your hair," I said. "Did I leave your bangs too long?" I reached up and touched her forehead. Looked like I might have not gotten them exactly straight.

"Little longer than what I'm used to."

"No problem. Sit tight. I'll get my scissors and trim them up for you."

"You sure? I could run by the shop tomorrow."

"Nah. Won't take a second."

I came back with my scissors. "Lift your chin up. Hold your head straight."

"Yes, sir," she said. "Since you're doing this at home, I hope you're not expecting a tip."

I stood in front of her stool and wet her bangs with a comb. "Shh. Don't talk. You're moving your head."

"Just take a little off." Leslie was holding a mirror I'd brought from the bathroom so she could see. "Half inch. Maybe not even that much."

"How's that look?" I was done after a couple of snips but I

didn't move from my spot between her knees.

She reached up and ran her fingers, slowly, really slowly, over where I'd cut—taking so long I thought I'd not pleased her, I hoped she didn't think I'd cut too much, because hair is shorter when it dries than it is when it's wet.

"Something wrong? I take too much off?"

The CD had ended and the house was quiet.

"No. You did a good job." Leslie was looking at herself in the mirror, not at me. She kept touching her hair. "They look nice. You got it right, Joel."

"What then?"

Leslie set the mirror down on the counter. She wouldn't look at me.

"Hey. Something's wrong. What's the matter?"

She still wouldn't look up.

"It's you, Joel. You always get it right. There's never been anybody in my life who's gotten me like you do. All these years. Nobody. Nobody like you."

I wish I could say I stepped back, shoved another cookie in my mouth or moved to get another soda out of the fridge. I wish I could tell you I cracked a joke. If only I could tell you I went and put a CD in the changer. It crossed my mind to do every one of those things, but I did none of them. Instead, I stayed rooted to the floor. Leslie let her right knee relax just enough that it came to rest against my hip. She turned her head to the side. I saw that her eyes were wet—and something in me got torn down. I put my hands on her shoulders and she put hers on my face and we kissed each other for the very first time.

Once you cross the line there's not much chance of going back. Maybe it wouldn't be as bad if I could claim I was caught up in the moment, that it was like a dream or like being wasted or something and that I wasn't actually aware of what we were doing. But I can't. It wouldn't be the truth and if there's anything I've learned it's that lying to yourself is like shooting your own head. The truth is that when we kissed, when we touched, when Leslie slid down off that stool, I was more aware of what I was doing, of the decision I was making, than I've ever been aware of anything in my life.

I knew I was moving over from one place to another, but I did not stop myself.

During that next month, I'm surprised I didn't have a heart attack. Seriously. There's no telling what my blood pressure would have read if Kari had taken it. My heart pounded from the moment I woke up until when I went to sleep, except that I couldn't sleep. I'd start thinking about the last time Leslie and I were together and I wouldn't be able to catch my breath. My hands were constantly sweaty. I lost eight pounds because my stomach was knotted up so bad I couldn't stay out of the bathroom.

Abe asked me what the heck was wrong with me and if I was doing coke.

Kari got worried about me, too. She bought me some vitamins, told me to stop putting in so many hours at the salon.

I blew both of them off. Made excuses to Abe. Told Kari not to worry so much. It wasn't good for the baby and besides I was fine.

But I wasn't.

All I could think about was Leslie and when we would be together again. I knew what we were doing was wrong and I was eaten up with guilt, but being with her was like a drug. I had a wife I loved and who'd loved me since we were eighteen years old. We had a child on the way. Life was basically good. But none of that was enough to keep me away from Leslie. I was greedy. I wanted more than what was rightfully mine.

Our affair went on for that whole last month she was in town. I don't remember how many times we were together, but it was more than a few. We took advantage of pretty much every opportunity we could to see each other without getting caught.

It would be easy to blame my affair on Kari, on her maybe not being the perfect wife during the time that it was all going on, but I need to make this clear. No. Things were not good at home but what happened wasn't her fault. She didn't deserve me cheating on her. No way, no how. I don't blame anyone for what happened except myself.

On the day Leslie left, we told each other good-bye in the driveway of my house. We hugged each other. But if you'd been a neighbor watching from your window you would have seen it as a brother-sister kind of hug. You wouldn't have thought one thing.

This may surprise you, but our good-bye was clean. No tears. Not even any talk of us staying in touch. Most people would at least pretend to love the person they were sleeping with to make it feel okay. But we were honest. Leslie and I never did pretend to love each other that way. All I'll say is that at one time we did love each other as friends. But that changed. You can't be friends with someone you've cheated on your spouse with.

It will not work.

Looking back, I actually believe we were both relieved the craziness was over. The whole thing had been too intense. Sneaking around and lying wears you out. And even though we never said it out loud it was way obvious there was no place for us to end up but bad. The embarrassing truth was that Leslie and I were both cowards, not strong enough to be faithful but not willing to give up our marriages. We didn't want Robert or Kari to find out because neither of us wanted to lose what we had going at home.

A person tells themselves all kinds of lies to cover up guilt. I convinced myself the day Leslie left that no harm had been done. Our affair was a one-time thing. I was closing that door. It would never happen again and Kari would never find out. I told myself that in a way, me and Leslie getting together had even been a good thing because it had taken some of the pressure off Kari and my relationship at a time when things could have easily cracked if there hadn't been some relief. I decided that as long as I was a good husband from here on out things would be fine.

And on the outside I was pretty much able to pull it off. It was inside my head where things weren't fine. What I found out was that my secret created this huge abyss between my wife and me. She believed I was this one person. I knew I was not that man anymore and wondered if I ever had been what she thought of me. I'm not judging anybody but myself, but what kind of person cheats on his pregnant wife? I don't claim to be the perfect husband, but I swear. Never in a million years would I have thought that person would be me.

Those first few weeks after Leslie left I went through all the motions of things being normal. But I didn't feel normal. I couldn't even remember what normal was. Sometimes I felt like I was an actor in a movie, or like I was watching myself from somewhere way off. I'd lie next to Kari in our bed, feel her arm around my waist and her breath against my back, and I'd be a thousand miles away.

I would have given anything to go back to being the person I was before my thing with Leslie. Now that it was over, I could not believe what I had done. Over and over I'd ask myself the same questions. *What* had I been thinking? How could I have *possibly* done such a thing?

Problem was, there was no way I could go back and undo my mistake, my betrayal, the lie I carried on my back like a two-ton weight.

So this is what I decided to do.

I would love my wife the best I knew how. And for the rest of my life, I would do everything in my power to make up for cheating on her. Whatever she asked of me, I'd try to do. Whatever she wanted, I'd do my best to get it for her. I determined I'd try my hardest to be a good husband to Kari for as long as she lived.

Maybe, just maybe, that would be enough.

chapter nine

LUCY'S IS LIKE MY SECOND home. And no wonder, since I spend nearly as much time at work as I do at my house. It's in a little strip mall, which is handy because there's always plenty of places for you to park. There's eight stations, two shampoo bowls, and a little place where customers can wait. Mrs. Chan has the place decorated pretty nice—green plants, some art on the walls. She's been talking lately about expanding. All I can say is I hope she doesn't bring somebody in to do nails. I'm sure it would be good for business, but all those chemicals they use would sure stink the place up.

I've got Alice in my chair. We're doing her roots today. She's past due. Her gray's showing, especially at her crown. "Don't wait so long next time," I tell her. "We need to touch you up every six weeks."

"I know, Joel," she says.

I drape a hot pink cape around her front, then snap it at the back of her neck.

"Trying to stretch my dollar. Don't take this wrong. You're worth every penny, but keeping this up is expensive. I'm not used to it. I could go three, sometimes four months between color appointments when we were doing highlights."

"Forget it," I say. "You're not going back blonde. Your hair looks great. Lots healthier. You look younger."

Alice smiles. She's sipping on a bottle of water. "I know. You're right. Problem is I've got too much Scottish blood in me," she said, "We're savers, not spenders."

"Which is a good thing up to a point," I say while I section her off. "Bargain groceries are fine. Nothing wrong with stocking up on peanut butter and toilet paper when it's on sale. But here's you some free advice. There are two things you should never, ever scrimp on. Two things, Alice, where you should go for the best money can buy."

"Since you're such the financial wizard," Alice is grinning, "I'm listening."

"First one's your hair. You wear it every day. Spend whatever it takes to keep it looking good."

"Okay. Makes sense. What's the other one?"

"This one's important, so listen up." It's hard for me to keep a straight face but I pull it off. "The good places are higher. I know. But you've gotta bite the bullet. Don't look at the difference in prices because remember, you get what you pay for, at least when it comes to this."

"And what would *this* be?"

I stop what I'm doing and turn her around so I can look her dead in the eye. I've got her this time. "Young lady, I do not want to see you going out and getting yourself any cheap tattoos."

Alice gets so tickled she chokes on her water and I have to stop, take off my gloves, and set her bottle on the counter so I can slap her on the back. Mrs. Chan looks over at me from the other side of the salon. I know she's wondering, after Bradley's diabetic reaction, what's going on in my chair now. I mouth to her that Alice is okay, but she keeps her eye on me anyway.

By the time Alice can talk, she's laughed and coughed so much she's got tears running down her face. "Oh, Joel." She's still laughing. "You've got my word. I will not get any cut-rate tattoos."

"Good girl. Just so you're sure." I've finished applying her color. "Need anything?" I pat her on the knee.

"I'm fine."

"Okay, then. While you process, I'm stepping out back for a minute. Fresh air break."

"Right," Alice says. Then she points to my lighter, which I've left at my station.

She is so on to me.

After she's done processing and I'm back to rinse her out Alice asks me where Abe is today.

"He's off," I tell her. "Had to go to some class this afternoon at the church. He's joining. The one where his ex, Jill, goes."

"Really," Alice says. "That's wonderful. I didn't know Abe went to church."

"Yep. He wants me to come on Sunday. Be there when he gets baptized."

"You going?"

"Can't let my man down," I say, wishing now I hadn't brought it up. Alice is probably going to start in on me about coming to her church. I've got my scissors in my hand. She needs a cut, too. "How 'bout we take a little more off the back this time?"

I guess Alice figures it out because she lets it go. We talk about Colton, about her dog Pancho being sick, about the new pizza place that's opened up across from the shop. Not 'til she's paying does Alice say anything and then it's only, "Tell Abe I'm real happy for him."

This is Kari's weekend to have Colton, which I'm glad about because I'm nervous enough going to Abe's church without having to worry about keeping my son quiet.

When I was a kid my Aunt Irene took me to her church a few times. She'd give me a box of animal crackers to eat and a coloring book and some crayons to keep me busy so I wouldn't make noise. Which worked pretty good except I ate the crackers way too fast and one time I got in big-time trouble for coloring in the song book that was in the rack on the bench in front of me. Other than that, what I remember about Aunt Irene's church is that it was long, the preacher yelled a lot, and a bunch of fat ladies always hugged me so hard I almost couldn't breath but some of them gave me gum.

Except for those times with my aunt, I've maybe been to a church a dozen times in my life. Living with my dad, and him being the way he was, church was not exactly some place me and him hung out.

When I was a teenager I went a couple times with this good-looking girl I liked. Her church had some funny beliefs. At our school's Valentine's Day banquet, where the girls asked the guys, she and I went to the first part where they had food and where they crowned the king and queen. But because her church said it was a sin and she was a good Christian girl, when the dance started we had to leave. Instead of dancing, we sat out in the parking lot in my car listening to music and making out until her midnight curfew when I took her home. Since I liked making out way better than dancing anyway, that was cool with me.

Kari and I had our wedding in a church, of course. We went a couple of times after we got married because her parents wanted us to. It was all right, but then we started going to the lake on the weekends. I've been to a few funerals that were in churches, but usually they have those in a funeral home.

Around here it's mostly rich people who go to church regular.
Sunday mornings you pass by some the big churches in town, all
you see in the parking lots are late-model SUVs and nice trucks,
Lexuses and BMWs. Two of the churches in Eden Plain have their
own schools. Everybody says it's because they don't want their kids
going to school with blacks and Mexicans, but I don't know if
that's really true.

Sunday morning I get up, shower, and wonder what I should
wear. I figure not jeans but khakis. I'm not one much for dressing
up, but since it's church I run over my shirt with the iron, but
there's something wrong with the steam thing and it spits rusty
water all over the sleeve. Just what I need. I go with a polo instead
of a button-up and hope I'm okay.

Abe's given me directions. I see the sign out near the street, and
so I turn in to the parking lot of an older strip mall near the edge
of town. "Hope Community Church" is painted on the window of
a space between an insurance office and a music store with a video
rental place on the other side. Abe says they play guitars so I guess
the music store's real handy in case somebody breaks a string. I see
people going in and there's a bunch of cars in the parking lot—no
high-dollar vehicles here, mostly old four-doors, a couple of beat-
up minivans—in the spaces in front. So I park and lock up since
this isn't exactly the best part of town.

I don't think I'm late, but there's already music playing when I
get inside. There's this little lobby area, kind of like in an old movie
theater. A black guy, maybe fifty, wearing a green suit greets me,
tells me he's glad to see me and to go on in.

So I do. Inside it still sort of looks like an old movie house.
Maybe they used to have plays or something here. No benches.
Instead, rows of folding theater seats, about half of them full.

There's a raised stage area up front. A wooden cross hanging on the back wall. A table over to the side with a blue cloth on it holding a big loaf of bread, one wine glass, a bottle of wine, and a lit candle on it. Sitting on steps leading up to the cross, there's a woman and a man playing acoustic guitars. Over to one side there's a keyboard but right now nobody's on it.

Standing at the back, it looks like this church is mostly all black people. They're dressed up. I hope it's all right I didn't wear a tie.

I guess Jill's been watching for me, because about the time I get ready to sit down in an empty seat near the back, she starts waving at me from about halfway down to the front. Abe and Sh'dondra are with her, too, which is good, because I was afraid maybe they weren't here yet or Abe had changed his mind.

I sit down next to Abe. Jill's on his other side. Sh'dondra in a seat beside her.

"Hey, man, glad you made it," Abe says real low.

"No prob." I lean forward and wave at Jill.

Sh'dondra squeezes past her mother and daddy to climb up into my lap. She puts her arms around my neck and gives me a kiss. "Where's Colton?" she says out loud.

"Shh," Abe tells her.

"He's with his mama today," I whisper in her ear. "You sure look pretty. I like your dress."

"My daddy bought it for me," she says.

I look over at Abe. He's holding Jill's hand.

Church lasts about an hour and a half. The preacher's okay. The music's good. Everybody sings. You'd have to be dead not to feel something when you hear "Amazing Grace."

When they say it's time for communion, people file out into the aisles to go up to the front like you see done at a funeral when people go up to view the dead. The preacher and a lady I guess is his wife are down there waiting with the loaf of bread and a full glass of wine. I don't know if it's such a good idea that everybody is supposed to drink out of the same glass. At least it isn't flu season. Except for me and this couple over on my right, everybody in the church goes down to get some. I can't hear the words, but as each person takes it, the pastor places his hand on their shoulder and says something in their ear.

Turns out Abe's church doesn't have a place to baptize people. They believe in dunking you all the way. So after the service the whole church loads up and drives to the state park, which is about ten miles out of town because that's where Abe's baptism is going to be. In the river. I'm thinking it's a good thing this is August because that water is going to be cold.

Abe says I can ride with him and Jill but I'll need to wait because he's got to change. They'll bring me back to my car but I tell them no thanks, since I'm not sure how long I can stay I'll drive myself.

It looks like a funeral procession. People dressed up. That long line of cars all pulling into the park. People get out and everybody goes down to the edge of the river. Since Abe's not here yet, we have to wait, but not for all that long. Everybody's pretty quiet. Finally, when Abe arrives, him and Jill get out of their car and come down to where we are. The pastor says something to him I can't hear. Then the two of them ease their way out into the water. They stop a few yards from the bank. The water's barely up to their waists. The pastor, who's got Abe's big hand in his, starts to talk.

"Dear ones, we've gathered to witness the death and resurrection of our brother. Abraham Marcus Tyler stands here before you on this day, ready to die to the old man and put on the new," the pastor says. He's a medium-built black man, wearing wire-rimmed glasses, black pants, a white shirt, and a black tie. His voice is gentle, not all that loud. By the gray at his temples I'd guess he's past sixty years old.

"Amen," say about three people scattered in the crowd.

"This is a good day," someone else says.

"Thanks be to God," I hear a man behind me say.

Abe, six-four counting his dreadlocks, is something to see. He's wearing white pants and a long white shirt, which makes his face look darker than it is. There's sweat on his forehead. His feet are bare. His lips are quivering. Every so often he reaches up with his one free hand to wipe at his eyes, to rub the back of his hand across his nose.

"When he goes down into this water, the old Abraham gets buried and a new person will be born. What was before will be no more. He'll be clean before God. No regrets. No worries. The past will be gone. Abraham will come out of this water to walk in the grace of our Lord."

I did not expect to feel anything, but seeing Abe and hearing the pastor's words make my throat tighten and my jaw ache.

"In the name of Jesus."

"Yes, Lord."

"Praise be to Him."

The pastor half turns to face the river. Trees line the water on the other side, but we're standing in a grassy clearing. The bank slopes easily. No rocks. No weeds. Beautiful blue sky. Bright Texas sun. The man stretches his hand toward the water and speaks to Abe. "Are you ready, son?"

"Yes, sir," says Abe. "I am." He looks over at Jill, who's standing next to me. She starts to cry, then hands Sh'dondra over to me.

Sh'dondra's hot in my arms. She lays her head on my shoulder and I can smell the lotion her mother has put in her hair.

"My mama cry," she says.

"Your mama's all right," I say in her ear. "She's okay."

Then Abe and the pastor wade out farther to where the water is up to their chests. All of us on the bank move closer. Somebody begins to sing about the blood of Jesus washing you clean. Then the pastor asks Abe if he believes that Jesus is the son of God and that he came to earth, died, and was raised.

Abe says that he does.

The pastor asks Abe if he's ready to live for God, ready to become his child.

Abe says that he is.

Then like he's holding a baby in his arms, the pastor gently lowers big old Abe farther and farther back until he is all the way under the water. Laying him back is one thing. I'm watching to make sure he can bring my friend back up, but he does. And when Abe comes up, wet as an old dog, he's crying and laughing and smiling so big about all you can see is his teeth. He comes up out of that water, raises his hands up to the sky, then like a kid playing in a swimming pool, jumps straight up, then sinks back down to dunk himself under again three or four more times.

People on the bank clap.

Some of them cheer.

Somebody starts in on a song about this being a happy day.

I guess Jill can't stand it anymore because all of a sudden she takes off her pink church shoes and even though she's got on a dress I'm pretty sure is dry-clean only, she tears out into that water to where Abe takes her up in his arms and holds her like he is not ever going to let her go, like there doesn't exist anybody else in the world.

And I am glad I've come.

chapter ten

COLTON'S GOT A 103.6 FEVER. Kari's out of town. Not answering her cell. I don't know what to do. I've given him Tylenol and Children's Advil, but his temperature won't come down. I figure it's his ears. But what if it's meningitis or something else real bad? Should I call the doctor? Take him to the emergency room where I know from past experience we'll have to wait for four hours? Is it okay to hold out 'til morning?

I should have known something was wrong. He didn't act right all day. Instead of running and playing with the other kids when he and I went to the park, Colton mostly hung around me. I bought him ice cream on the way home but he only ate a little bit of his cone. When we got in the house, he didn't want to do anything but sit in my lap, which, as active as he is, he normally doesn't do for a long stretch. Colton used to be real cuddly but lately he's gotten on this major independent streak. Acts like he's too big or doesn't have the time for all that baby stuff. So actually, I enjoyed him laying around on me. We watched some TV together. After a while he ended up falling asleep. I needed to get some stuff done, so I went and laid him down.

Then I lost track of time. At eight o'clock I realized he'd been asleep for three hours. I went to check on him. Colton had thrown up in his bed. It was in his hair. All over his clothes. He cried while

I cleaned him up. When I asked him where it hurt he couldn't tell me. I felt terrible for letting him sleep for so long without realizing something was wrong.

So it's now three in the morning. Since one, Colton's fever has just kept on going up and I can't get him to eat anything. I don't know what to do. He's had diarrhea twice but he hasn't thrown up anymore.

He should drink. I remember that. Carrying him, I go to the fridge. "Come on, Colt. Let's have some Coke." Kari and I don't let him have sodas very often. They're bad for his teeth. Which means he usually thinks he's getting away with something great when he gets to have one from a can.

But not tonight. He takes one sip, then lays his head back down on my chest.

"Drink some more," I say. "A little bit more."

He's limp against me. His skin is hot. His eyes don't look right. He doesn't want any more Coke.

I hate this.

Where is Kari?

And why isn't she answering?

I call the hospital. They won't tell me anything. Give me some freakin' one eight hundred Ask-A-Nurse number to call. I try it over and over again but all I get is a busy signal. When I finally do get through, one of those automated answering systems puts me on hold, where I stay until the machine hangs up on me. I slam down the phone.

Those people don't care. Nobody does. I'm sitting here alone in my house in the middle of the night, scared and stupid, holding my sick son, not knowing what I should do even though I'm the adult and I'm supposed to have it together. There's nobody to ask. Nobody I can turn to and say, "Hey, what do you think we should do here?" I am completely and totally alone.

Being a single parent stinks.

People I've talked to who go to college say that things usually wind down the last couple of weeks of a semester. Not so with nursing. The people at Kari's school kept everybody in her class scared they were going to fail or get kicked out right up until the week of graduation. I thought she was kidding about being so worried until she showed me her grades and told me what she had to make on her final to pass.

She was at the top of her class, but that didn't matter. It was going to be close.

Two people in her class actually did fail.

But not Kari.

Being big pregnant and all, she wasn't sure she wanted to go through the actual graduation ceremony. You didn't have to and a few of her classmates were so sick of school they said they weren't coming. The school would mail your diploma if you didn't show up, but I told Kari no way. She had worked hard for this. I wanted her to enjoy her big day. I was proud of her. If her parents had still been alive they would have been proud of her, too.

In her cap and gown, you really couldn't tell Kari was due in a month. She just looked fat, like everybody does when they graduate. Even though her ankles were swollen and she hadn't been able to reach her feet for over a month, when they called her name, my gorgeous, smart wife marched up those steps, shook some guy's hand, smiled for the photographer, and got her diploma.

When she did, I cheered.

Casey and Darla and their boys were there. Abe and Jill and

Sh'dondra, who was about two years old back then, came to watch her graduate, too. After the ceremony everybody came over to our house. Darla had made an Italian cream cake. We put steaks on the grill. While they were cooking, Kari showed Darla and Jill the baby's room. I'd painted it yellow one weekend and we'd put a white crib in there. Kari's nursing classmates gave her a baby shower the last week of school.

Diapers, blankets, clothes. We had it all.

Because it was her big day, when we got ready to eat I didn't let Kari do anything. I made her sit down and I fixed her plate.

After everybody left, she and I sat outside for a while longer. It wasn't all that late. "Thanks for the party," Kari said. "It was nice."

"You deserve it," I said. She had her feet up in my lap. "What's it feel like?" I asked her. "Knowing you're really done with school?"

"Weird," she said. "It hasn't sunk in. I keep thinking there's something I should be studying for."

"You'll probably feel like that for a while," I said.

"Yeah. I'm figuring until at least the end of the week." She grinned. "I could get used to being a bum, laying around, working part time, not going to school, letting you fix my plate and rub my feet. You have no idea how good that feels."

Kari leaned back in her chair and closed her eyes while I stroked her heels. I thought she might be going to sleep, but then I saw her smile.

"What?"

"Baby's kicking." She patted her basketball belly.

"He's glad to be out of school, too," I said.

"Probably."

"I don't know how you did it," I said. Kari knew what I meant. "I think maybe I would have quit."

"You don't know how many times I wanted to, how many times I started to."

"You never said."

"If I'd ever said it out loud, I was afraid I'd do it and I'd have regretted it for the rest of my life." She looked toward the moon, which was just coming up in the sky. "These past couple of years haven't been all that great for you, either."

"It was okay."

"Lots of times I wasn't myself. I stayed on your back about a lot of dumb stuff. I don't know why. I just did."

"Don't worry about it."

"I just want you to know I'm sorry about all that. And I'll make it up to you." She gave me one of her cute crooked smiles.

"Nothing to make up for," I said. I didn't like her talking like that. The way I looked at it, me and Leslie had way more than evened out the score. It was something I thought about every day. I figured whatever Kari did to me or said to me to hack me off for the next fifty years or so, I had it coming.

Kari yawned.

I set her feet down, stood up, and offered her my hand. "Bugs are starting to bite. Let's go in."

Kari stopped working June the first. The hospital would have let her work right up until the baby was born, but by me putting in extra hours I'd paid ahead on some of our bills, so she went ahead and took off. I was glad when she did because I knew she was tired and those late shifts weren't good for her. Her ankles swelled and we had to keep an eye on her blood pressure in case it got too high.

Our due date was June twentieth, but on July first Kari was still pregnant. I felt sorry for her but there was nothing I could do. You cannot believe how big she got. She had constant indigestion, her back hurt, and she wasn't just hot, but burning up twenty-four seven. We had to keep the house so cold the only time I got warm that whole month was when I went to work.

I worried that something might be wrong, but every week Kari and I went to the doctor and he said everything was okay. The baby would come when it was ready and that it could happen just any day.

It gets to you, waiting and waiting on something like that. Kari didn't sleep good. She tossed and turned and made funny sounds. About five times a night I'd wake up and ask her if she was sure she was all right. Most mornings, we'd both be so worn out with trying to sleep it was a relief to get out of bed.

Finally, on July third, Kari's water broke. We were at home when it happened. It wasn't like some big gush or anything. More like a little stream. Not as much as when you take a leak. I wanted to load up and go to the hospital right then, but Kari said we had time and there were a couple things she wanted to do.

Like what?

Water the plants.

Empty the dishwasher.

Fold and put away a load of clothes.

Since nothing I said convinced her we should head on out, I followed her around with a bath towel mopping up the trail of water she left on the floor.

Good thing we didn't have carpet is all I've got to say.

Kari had read all these books about childbirth. I'd looked through a few of them. We went to three classes. After the last one, which told you all the problems you can have with painkillers,

Kari decided she was going to have our baby natural. Without any drugs. Her doctor said epidurals aren't that bad, but Kari didn't want one of those, either.

I could see both sides, but since Kari didn't want to take anything, I agreed with her plan. If she got into labor and changed her mind, I was supposed to talk her out of taking anything. Help her breathe and focus and stuff. That was my job.

Which sounded really good until about five hours into it, when Kari told me she didn't think she could take it anymore. She hurt so bad.

"Joel, I can't do this." She was squeezing my hand so hard I thought I heard a bone crack. "I changed my mind. Make them give me something."

She did not have to ask twice. I was out of that room you cannot believe how fast. "Where's my wife's nurse?" I asked the lady mopping the floor outside our room.

"I guess down there." She pointed to the counter at the end of the hall.

"She wants something for pain. Now. Can you get it now?"

Epidurals are wonderful. It took about half an hour for them to get hold of the guy that does them, but once he came and got that thing in her back, within a couple minutes Kari went from crying and carrying on to sitting up playing cards.

If you ask me, that natural childbirth stuff is garbage.

Nothing can prepare you for what it's like to see your child for the first time. When Colton came out, they put him right up on Kari's chest. I was standing next to her head. When I looked into his big eyes and when I touched his face it was like somebody started my engine. I felt this power in my body, this surge like I've never felt before. I don't know if it was love or protectiveness or what, but it was something new.

Kari cried.

I cried.

Colton cried.

He still had blood on him and his skin was weird looking, spotted and sort of swollen bluish like a fish. He moved his arms and his legs like in slow motion, like he was finally here and he had all the time in the world. I know they say babies can't see good right at first but I don't believe it. For the longest time he stared at us both with these big, serious-looking, blinking eyes. It was like he'd been waiting to see us forever and he wanted to take us all in.

I know we couldn't take our eyes off of him.

"He's perfect," I said to Kari.

She couldn't say anything. Tears were running down the sides of her face.

I was one dumb jerk back then. Twenty-three years old. I didn't know much about anything at all. I had no idea what it took to raise a kid. But even so, there is one thing I knew for sure. As ignorant as I was, in that moment I've never loved anything ever in my life as much as I loved my wife and my son.

I would have done anything for them.

Anything.

And the truth?

I still would.

For Colton, yes.

But for Kari, too.

Some things won't ever change.

chapter eleven

COLTON'S FINE. BACK TO NORMAL.

I sweated it out with him all that night, took him to the doctor's office the next morning, still wearing his pajamas and running a fever. We were there before eight when they opened the doors of the clinic. Even though we didn't have an appointment, right away a nurse put us back in an exam room. Probably because we both looked pretty rough and they didn't want the patients in the waiting room to get whatever it was Colton had.

We waited an hour before the doctor got to us. Wouldn't you know, by then, Colton was fine. When she came in to see him, he was eating the banana I'd brought with us, sucking down Coke from a can, and climbing all over the place. The doctor said it was probably a viral infection, which is what I think they tell you when they don't really know what's wrong.

That's one thing about kids: They can be sick as dogs one minute and running around crazy the next, which is the reason Kari says she'll never work in pediatrics. She says sick kids can go bad on you too quick, and she'd never forgive herself if she missed something or did something wrong and the patient was a child.

There are nursing jobs all over. Anybody looking for a career, that's a thing they should sure look into it. Seriously. The Sunday paper is full of places looking for RNs. Kari says she looks at the ads every week but since getting out of nursing school she's worked at the same place, one of the regular medical units of the hospital. She takes care of diabetics, people with pneumonia, infections, heart trouble, stuff like that. No surgery patients. And no kids, since both those have their own unit.

You'd think that, working with sick people all the time, nurses would be sick a lot themselves, but Kari hardly ever is. Only once since our divorce has she not been able to take Colton when it was her time to have him, and that was last winter when she had a bad case of the flu. Kari says your immune system gets stronger when you work around sick people all the time. You build up some kind of a resistance to illness.

I'm glad for her. Wish I had a few of those immunities. Working at the salon, so close to people coughing and blowing their noses, I usually end up with about three bad colds every winter. You'd think people would cancel if they came down with something, but most of them don't.

Kari and I've been divorced almost two years now. For nearly the whole first year, she had Colton the majority of the time. According to the judge, I got him every other weekend and every Tuesday from eight in the morning until eight at night. My attorney said that was pretty standard visitation and that there shouldn't be any problems as long as I kept up on my child support.

Visitation.

I never could get used to that word. Actually, I hate it. There's something wrong with a father *visiting* his own son. But at the time we split up there was so much hurt between me and Kari that I didn't want to cause any more so I went along. I figured the thing I could do for Colton and Kari was lay low and be the best part-time dad I could.

I don't mean to take anything away from how hard single

mothers have it, but being a part-time dad, having your child for only a few hours a week, puts a lot of pressure on you.

It's not hard to spot a weekend dad. You see them on Saturday afternoons all the time. At the park. The mall. McDonald's. The movie rental stores. You know, that tired-looking guy you see with no wedding ring who's buying stuff for cranky kids dressed in mismatched clothes with their shoes untied and their hair not combed?

Ten to one he's a divorced dad.

Trying to make up for lost time.

It's like this. Because you've only got a few hours with your kid, you try to make it good enough that they'll want to come back and so that next time maybe they won't cry when you pick them up. Because when they do cry it makes you feel terrible and makes your ex suspect you aren't treating them right when you have them, which would explain why they act like they don't want to go with you.

Never mind the fact that those same kids' tears dry up about the time you've backed out of their mother's driveway.

I'm not speaking for all divorced dads, but my friends who are single live for the weekends when they get their kids. They love them. They want to be good fathers. They know they've messed up their marriages—I'm the first to admit it's almost always mostly the guy's fault when a marriage busts up—but they don't want to mess up their kids.

At the same time, dads who don't have custody have lives apart from their children. We have to or we'd go nuts. What we've done we've already done. No matter what regrets we've got, life goes on. Jobs. Friends. Our day-to-day routines. It can be hard fitting your kids in when you do have them, which makes you feel guilty. So you try that much harder, which puts pressure on them. They get cranky. And who wouldn't, being shuffled back and forth like they are? I'd be cranky too if I woke up and half the time couldn't remember which bed it was I fell asleep in last night.

It takes awhile to figure things out.

Right after the divorce, on my weekends with Colton I'd try to take him all kinds of places. What was I thinking? He was only a little over a year old. But there me and him would be. Saturday mornings. Him in his stroller, lots of times crying. Sometimes asleep. At the park. The zoo. The children's museum. Neither one of us having much fun, but me trying to do the right thing.

Thankfully, after the first year that changed. Our original custody arrangement is still on the books. We didn't ever go back to court and I still pay child support, but one day, Kari and I sat down and had a long talk. She knew I loved Colton. She knew I was a good dad. If we agreed on anything it was that we wanted what was best for him whether or not it was the best for either of us. We agreed. Starting that day, forever and ever, our son would come first.

It's worked out pretty good. These days we divide up the week so he's with both of us about half the time. Kari and I try to figure it out where we work mostly opposite days. Her schedule at the hospital can get changed at the last minute, which makes it hard, and sometimes I've got appointments on my book a week ahead, but we try our best to fix it so Colton has to go to day care only a couple days a week. Having him with me three or four nights every week isn't the same as living together as a family, but it is way better than being an every-other-weekend dad.

For a divorced couple, me and Kari have worked it out as good as anybody could.

Nothing can prepare you for that first week home with a new baby. When he was born, Colton weighed seven pounds and six ounces. How somebody that little can totally change your house is beyond me, but that's what happened. Total chaos. We were up all hours of the day and night trying to keep him fed and clean. Getting a shower was a challenge. Forget shaving. In pictures of us taken that first week I looked like somebody coming off a three-day drunk. I'd never say it to her face, but Kari didn't look much better. I found out babies were way harder than they looked.

I also found out they were way, way more fun than I would have ever believed. I'd always liked kids, but until we had Colton I'd never thought they were that interesting until they got big enough to talk to you and to where you could play with them. But Kari and I neither one could take our eyes off our son. Everything he did was the coolest thing we'd ever seen, and I do mean everything. Burps. Yawns. The way he sneezed. Kari laughed at me one time after I'd hung up the phone talking to Abe. Colton was five days old at the time.

"You realize you just spent ten minutes describing the color of Colton's poop to your best friend?"

"No, I didn't."

"You did. You told him it was green yesterday but it was yellow this morning."

I had to laugh. She was right. I'd given Abe the poop report. Having kids must do something weird to your brain.

Kari breastfed but sometimes she'd pump and I'd get to give him her milk in a bottle. Man. Those eyes of his. The way he could hold on to my finger with his little fist. After I'd get done feeding him I'd burp him. Then I'd stretch out on the couch and let him sleep on my chest. His head fit perfectly under my chin. Softest thing in the world. Sometimes I'd doze off too.

There's a picture of me and him asleep like that that Kari took. I've got it put in a frame.

I took off from work that first week after Colton was born, which was a good thing. Kari was exhausted from being up nursing him every two hours all night. I did the best I could to help out and some of her girlfriends came over and did stuff. They brought food. Mostly takeout. Darla did laundry one day. Somebody else cleaned up the kitchen and scrubbed our bathroom cleaner than I think it had ever been cleaned before.

Becoming a mother herself made Kari miss her parents, especially her mom, really bad. The day we brought him home I caught her crying. She was holding Colton, looking at a picture of her folks we had hung up in the hall outside his room.

"Your folks would have loved him," I said.

She wiped at her eyes. "I wish they could see him."

"Maybe they can," I said. I didn't know how all that worked, but I'd heard people say that when somebody passes they can look down and see what's going on.

"I don't know," she said. "If that was true I think I'd feel something. I don't. All I feel is I wish they were here and they're not." Kari wiped at her nose with a tissue she pulled out of the pocket of her pajama pants. I took Colton out of her arms, laid him down in his crib, sat down in the rocking chair we had in his room, and pulled her into my lap. I didn't say anything. What words would have done any good? I just held her and rubbed her back and let her cry it out.

Kari has always been one to keep things to herself. Back when we were married she wasn't a crier. It took a lot for her to lose it. It was no secret that in lots of ways she was way stronger than me. But being a new mom and not having your parents around to see their first grandchild was more than what anyone should have had to go through. I knew from hearing customers at the salon talk, when a woman has a baby, ninety percent of the time she wants her mother to come and help out.

What about my parents?

My mom left when I was five. At the time Colton was born, best I knew she was living in Arizona. I'd seen her a couple of times over the years but I didn't know her that well. I'm not even sure I had her number. What little I remember about my mom was that she slept a lot during the day and that she made me these really good chocolate oatmeal cookies.

It was tough growing up without a mom, but I try not to hold her leaving me against her. It could not have been easy being married to my dad. How can I put this except to say that it was way obvious to people who met my dad he was gay? That would have had to have been embarrassing for my mom. Growing up with him acting like he did was embarrassing to me. Maybe she thought leaving was the only thing she could do.

My dad lives in Texas, actually not that far from Eden Plain, which you'd think would mean we'd be close, but we weren't then and we aren't now. For ten years he's had a problem with prescription drugs. It started when he hurt his back. At first he held it together but over the years he's gone downhill. If you've ever been around somebody with a drug problem you know it will go one of two ways: It either gets better or it gets worse. My dad's not a bad person. If you ran into him and he happened not to be messed up at the time, and unless you've got something against gay people, you'd probably like him.

Things were not going so good with me and him around the time Colton was born. It sounds bad that I didn't call my own father about his first grandson. I knew he'd be thrilled to hear the news, but I thought it would be better for me and Kari if he wasn't too close around right then. When Colton got a little older and things settled down I'd give him a call. We'd go over to his house, which would be better than him coming to ours.

I hate it now that I waited. Colton was three months old when I got the word that he'd died. Overdose. We never knew how it happened, but to this day I believe it was an accident.

As crazy as those first months with Colton were, and as hard as it was losing my dad like that, things got better and better for the three of us. It doesn't make sense but by the time he was a few months old it was like Colton had been with us forever. Neither of us could remember what life was like before he was born. And what in the world did we do with our time?

Kari and I'd lined up full-time day care before Colton was born. After all, we both had to work. But after he came, taking him somewhere every day didn't sound like such a good idea. Just thinking about going back to the hospital and leaving him with strangers got Kari upset. He was so little. So after talking about it we decided that as long as we could afford it, she would work part-time. Two twelve-hour shifts a week. The rest of the time she would stay home. We'd just gone up ten percent on rates at the salon. That helped.

It is an amazing thing to see your wife turn into an awesome mother. Kari was incredible. I loved watching her take care of our son. She was so gentle with him, so calm. It was like she'd been a mother all her life. I got pretty good at changing diapers and dressing Colton and stuff but nowhere near as good as she was. Kari could do three things at once and all of them right. I used five times as many wipes as her to clean up a dirty diaper and only about one time out of three did I get the snaps on the crotch of his sleeper to come out right on my first go.

You wouldn't think it was possible, but Kari having Colton

made her more beautiful than she was before. Her hair grew out fast and was shiny and healthy looking—I figure because of the prenatal vitamins the doctor told her to keep taking even after he came.

She'd gained thirty-eight pounds while she was pregnant, but lost most of it all by the time Colton was six months old. Thing was, even though Kari weighed her normal 128, her body wasn't the same after being pregnant. She still wore the same size, but all over she was softer, more round, which looked good to me but not so much to her. I tried not to laugh at her for being embarrassed about the little tummy she had. No matter how many crunches she did, it did not go away. I thought it was cute. At night in bed when we lay on our sides, I'd put my arm around her middle and she'd move my hand to keep me from resting it on her belly. So of course, to tease her, I made sure I put it there every time.

We had so much fun that first year. Colton was what the women at work call a good baby. Like there's a such thing as a bad baby? He started sleeping through the night when he was four months old. He hardly ever cried. We switched him over from breast to bottle when he was seven months old. I was afraid he might have trouble with his stomach but he handled it fine. He went to sleep at night without fussing and in the mornings, he'd wake up happy—usually about six thirty, which was when we had to get up anyway.

Kari and I'd lay in our bed and listen to him talking to the stuffed animals in his crib. After a few minutes she'd hit the shower and I'd go in and get him. That was our time. Colton'd spot me in the doorway of his room. His head would pop up and he'd go to grinning. Like I was some rock star or something. After Kari quit nursing him, I'd change his diaper, carry him into the kitchen, and fix him a bottle and me a coffee. Then the two of us would watch a little ESPN together to start our day.

Can you tell being a dad was the best thing that ever happened to me? Nothing I'd accomplished in my life before he was born counted for anything. I couldn't believe how upset I'd been when Kari got pregnant. How stupid. It seemed like such a long time ago. I could hardly remember the person I was before I became a dad.

Except for that one thing.

I won't say I thought about it every day but I almost did. Memories of what happened would come over me. At the weirdest times. I'd be in rinsing a customer out, driving home from the store, or raking up leaves in the yard. Mental pictures would hit like flashes of lightning. Me and Leslie. Together. At my house. In her car. At the motel. For an instant I'd almost get sick. My hands would get wet and my heart would race. I never could figure out what triggered the memories but they were so real it would be like it had all happened only the hour before instead of months ago. The best way I figured out to handle it when things hit was to get really busy, to do something to occupy my mind. Which did not work very well.

I can't explain it but there was like this disconnect between myself now and myself then. Remembering back to Leslie and me was like remembering somebody else's life. Like it had happened a hundred years ago. If I didn't know better you could have convinced me all that was a bad dream, that it had never really happened.

What I would give if only that was true.

Kari and I bought one of those baby packs you wear, which I used to think looked stupid but I found out come in really handy. The three of us went everywhere together. People say married people should go out without the kids on a regular basis but Kari and I didn't see the need.

"You want me to ask Jill if she can watch Colton on Friday night?" I asked her. "We could go out to eat. Catch a movie."

"You want to?" she asked.

"If you do."

"I'm okay hanging out here."

"Are we getting to be one of those old boring married couples who never want to go anywhere?" I asked.

"Probably," said Kari.

We both laughed.

It's not like we didn't have time alone together. We did. Good times. Colton was in bed most nights before eight. After he went down we watched TV, listened to music, and cuddled on the couch 'til time to go to bed. Some nights we played backgammon. Kari beat me most of the time.

For us, that was enough.

Even though I liked working at the salon, I hated leaving in the mornings. "What do you two do all day?" I asked Kari one time. "What fun stuff do I miss being gone all day?"

She was standing at the sink in the kitchen at the time, holding Colton. "It's our secret, isn't it, Colton?" She shot me a grin. "We do all kinds of fun stuff while Daddy's gone. But we'll never tell."

"Hey, boy," I pretended to talk real serious to my son. "We men have got to stick together. None of this teaming up with Mom. You hear me?"

Colton giggled like I'd just told the funniest joke he'd ever heard.

I did miss the two of them. A couple days a week Kari'd pack some food and come up to the salon so I could play with Colton during my lunch hour. I never knew when she was coming. I'd be in the middle of a cut or a color and there the two of them would come walking in the door. Days she did that were the best. The customers loved it, too. While I'd finish whoever I was doing they'd fight over getting to hold him.

"He's perfect," Alice told me the first time she saw him. "A perfect little boy."

"Takes after his daddy," is what Brady said. That was the day Colton produced a stinky diaper almost the exact minute him and Kari walked in.

I can't explain how proud I was of my son. I mean except for getting his mother pregnant, what right did I have to take credit for how great he was? He was his own person. All I know is that I couldn't help it. Inside I swelled up like I was Superman or something whenever people admired him, especially strangers, which happened more often than you would think.

One time I was sitting on our couch holding Colton in my lap. I guess he was about six months old. I had my legs crossed. His head was in the crook of my knee, looking up at the ceiling fan watching it go around and around. Every so often he'd smile and kick his feet. Kari was sitting next to me. "Is he special?" I asked her.

She looked at me like I was nuts. "Of course he is."

"I mean when I see other babies his age they don't seem nearly as smart. They don't look nearly as cute to me. Is it me or is there really something different about him?"

"I know what you mean," she said. "Other babies don't seem as alert."

"Is he advanced for his age?" I asked her.

"I think he is. When I'm around other mothers and their

babies I don't want them to feel bad so I sort of downplay all the stuff Colton can do."

"There's no need to rub it in," I said, feeling amazingly lucky to have such a gifted child.

"Goo," Colton said.

Then he messed in his diaper.

chapter twelve

JULY 3, 2000, THE DAY COLTON was born, was the best day of my life.

May 18, 2001, was the worst.

My life imploded like one of those condemned old buildings they bring down with dynamite from the inside out. Once the fuse got lit there was no stopping the destruction, no going back in, no chance of saving any one last thing.

I got home from work a half hour early because things at the salon were slow. Kari's car wasn't in the driveway. Right off I caught a bad vibe. This being my late night, a nearly twelve-hour workday, it was past eight o'clock. I know. You're thinking, *No big deal.* She could have gone to the store or something last minute. But that didn't fit because it was too close to the time we always put Colton to bed. If we were out of something like milk or bread or toilet paper, normally Kari would have called me and asked me to pick it up on my way home.

I hadn't heard from her. Still sitting in the driveway, I checked my phone. No missed calls. No messages. Good signal.

When I got inside, my uneasy feelings got worse. The kitchen was a mess. Dirty breakfast dishes on the table. The pan where Kari'd cooked my oatmeal still on the stove. The milk was sitting out. Nearly a full gallon. The coffeepot was on but the dregs had evaporated in the bottom and it was stinking bad. There was an open can of Colton's formula on the counter, some of the powder spilled around it, and two nearly empty bottles next to it. Today was trash day. We couldn't put our trash out before noon because of a couple stray dogs that would get into it. Like always, I'd bagged it up and put it by the back door for Kari to take out later, except that she hadn't.

"Kari?"

It took me all of two minutes to walk through the house. Colton's toys were all over the living room. There was a load of wet clothes in the washer. A load of dry ones in the dryer. The little TV in our bedroom was on. Our bed wasn't made. Kari's nightgown was on the floor. There was two inches of cold, scummy water in the bathtub, Colton's floaty toys in there, too.

Kari wasn't a perfect housekeeper but she'd never leave the house like that. From the looks of it, she'd been gone all day. Where? Why? I dialed her cell but she didn't answer. There wasn't a note. No messages on the machine. The fact that we watched a lot of *CSI* and that I was so tired I wasn't thinking straight didn't help. You can imagine what was going through my mind. Had she been kidnapped? Was she hurt? Was Colton sick? Maybe they were in the hospital. But I'd been at work all day. Surely somebody would have called. Kari would have.

If she could.

I stood in our bedroom holding my phone without a clue who to call or what to do. Should I call 911? What would I say? My wife and baby aren't here and she's left the house in a mess? What would they do except blow me off? If they did then what was I supposed to do?

All of a sudden I heard somebody behind me. At the same time I felt a big hand come down on my shoulder. I guess adrenaline kicked in. I hadn't been in a fistfight since about the ninth grade, but like I knew what I was doing, my hands went up and I spun around swinging.

I didn't see it was Abe until after I landed the punch on his arm.

Which hurt my hand.

But didn't make him even flinch.

"What the?" I yelled at him. "How'd you get in?"

"Back door was open."

I paced back to the kitchen. Abe followed me. "Look at this place," I said.

Abe put the milk in the fridge, turned off the coffeepot, set the oatmeal pan in the sink and ran some hot water in it.

"I don't know where Kari and Colton are and I've got a bad feeling. She didn't call. There's no note. This isn't like her."

Abe pointed to the phone in my hand. "Who you calling?"

"I don't know. The police?"

"Give me that phone. This isn't nothing for the police."

"You know where they are?"

"Kari's over at Jill's apartment. Colton, too. Been there all day."

I let out a breath. "Why didn't you say? That's a relief. Why'd Kari go over there? She sure left in a hurry." I reached into the fridge for a bottle of water. "You want one, man?"

"Nah. I'm okay."

"Something wrong with Jill? Sh'dondra sick?" Being a nurse people were all the time calling Kari to come and check on their sick kids. I didn't want to hurt Abe's feelings so I didn't say anything, but I couldn't help wonder how smart it was for Kari to expose Colton to somebody sick. He'd just gotten over a cold himself.

"Jill's all right. Sh'dondra's fine."

I still had my phone in my hand. "Kari's cell must be dead. She's not answering. Give me Jill's number."

Abe looked off out the window over my sink for an instant, then at me straight. "Put your phone up. Don't call Jill's. Quit trying Kari's cell. Sit down. I got something to tell you."

There's times you know what's coming at you is going to be bad, and right then was one of them. I didn't feel relief anymore. None. The look Abe gave me was like a three a.m. phone call, the kind that wakes you up when you're sound asleep and is not somebody with a wrong number. It was like going to answer your back door and finding a cop standing on your step. It was like opening up your mailbox and pulling out a certified letter from the IRS.

Somewhere inside I must have already known what was coming because even though nothing made sense I didn't argue. Like me and Abe were going to play a game of poker or have us some lunch, I pulled out a chair and sat down at the kitchen table.

He sat down, too.

I waited. But Abe didn't say anything. He just sat there looking at me, swelled up like he gets when he's hacked off.

I fiddled with the salt and pepper shakers. They were red glass with silver metal tops. I picked them up. Set them down. Up. Down. Again and again. Until I couldn't stand it anymore. "All right. Tell me. What's up with Kari being over at Jill's? Why you acting so weird?"

"That chick Leslie. What happened with you two?"

I set the saltshaker down. "You met her. We used to be friends."

"You do her?"

There wasn't enough air in my house. "I haven't seen her. Haven't heard from her. Been over a year."

"You do her?"

I needed to get up, to move. To run. But I stayed put. Started to sweat. I couldn't get a deep breath. I kept on fiddling with the stuff on the table. First the salt. Then the pepper. Up. Down. Up. Down. It didn't take Abe long, even without my mouth moving, to know that the answer was yes.

"Joel."

The way he said my name it was like he didn't want to believe it but he knew it was true.

I didn't speak.

Didn't look up.

My hands got still.

Abe stood up. He walked over to the kitchen sink, turned on the cold water, and spit in the stream. What he said next pretty much summed it up.

"You're a real piece of work."

Except for the summer, when you can count on it being hot, you never know what the weather's going to be like in Texas. A November day we can have temperatures in the seventies. Then again, it could be in the twenties. Like it is on this Sunday afternoon. Way too cold to be outside but at least nothing's falling out of the sky.

Either way, everybody and their kids are inside my house and it is loud. Crazy. The bigger kids are back in my bedroom fighting over whose turn it is to play. Brandon and Chase brought their Xbox system over. Pete hooked it up on the little TV in my bedroom.

Even though Allyssa's getting to be a big girl Sh'dondra is

wagging her all over the house on her hip. Or that's where two-and-a-half-year-old Allyssa would be if Sh'dondra actually had hips. Since she started kindergarten Sh'dondra has decided she is one big bad mama. She's bossing all the little kids around. Acting like she's in charge, which Colton, who worships her, doesn't mind.

"You got an opinion on interracial marriage?" I ask Abe.

"What you talking about?"

"I'm thinking Colton and Sh'dondra might get married in about twenty years."

Abe snorts. "Sh'dondra ain't going out on any dates until she's at least twenty-five. Gonna lock her up. Keep her away from the likes of your boy."

Abe still comes over for our single-dad Sunday night get-togethers. He brings Sh'dondra even though he and Jill have been back together for going on ten months. It's all good but I got to give him a hard time about them going to church every Sunday while they're living in sin. He and Jill haven't gotten around to get-ting remarried yet, but he says they're going to do it pretty soon.

Tonight Casey's cooking chili on my stove. Two pots. A three-alarm batch for the dads. A false-alarm pot for the kids. We've got Fritos and cheese, cornbread, and of course some cut-up raw vegetables, courtesy of Abe.

Football game's on. Cowboys are playing. We're all in my living room, chilling, waiting for the chili to finish cooking. But then Sean, who's been pretty quiet since he got here, gets up and goes to the kitchen to get himself a soda. When he gets back, he sits down and drops a bomb.

"Brooke says she wants Allyssa to come live with her."

"No way," Casey says.

"When'd she decide this?" I ask.

"She called last night. Told me she's got things where she and him can take care of Allyssa. She wants me to pack up Allyssa's stuff and meet her halfway so they don't have to drive so far."

"That b—" Pete stops himself since there's kids in and out of the room. "Where the heck is she?"

"Oklahoma City."

"All this time you been taking care of Allyssa day and night not even knowing where her mama is and now she expects you to hand her over like she was some kind of a dog or cat?" Abe is mad.

We all are. What kind of a mother leaves her child like that? Brooke didn't give no thought to it. She hasn't even seen Allyssa in going on four months.

"You tell her that ain't happening?" Casey asks.

"I didn't tell her anything."

"Man," Casey says.

Sean takes a draw on his root beer. "After she told me she wants Allyssa to come live with her, she asked me for a divorce."

I haven't said it to his face, but why Sean hasn't already filed for one is way beyond me.

"She don't know what she wants," Abe says.

"Yeah, she does," Sean says. "She wants a divorce."

Nobody knows what to say. We all know Sean's been wanting Brooke back ever since she left. He blows his nose.

"What'd you tell her?" I finally ask.

"Like a fool, I told her I didn't see any need for us to rush into anything."

"That makes sense," Pete says.

"You two got time," Abe says.

"Actually, we don't." Sean gets this bitter grin on his face. "Seeing as how she's six months pregnant, it doesn't make much sense for us to wait on that divorce."

Brooke's been gone since July. It's November now. Everybody's doing the math.

"Six months. You sure——?" starts in Casey.

"It's not my baby," Sean says.

"But——"

Sean shoots Casey a look that shuts him up. He gets it.

We all do.

Kari found out about the affair from Leslie's husband. He found out about us from some guy at work who turned out to know Leslie's best friend who was the only person she ever told. Complicated, I know. But how she found out didn't matter. What mattered was that the lie I'd been living, the secret I'd thought I'd put behind me, wasn't a secret anymore. I suppose I should have been mad at Leslie for not being more careful, or at her husband for calling up my wife and giving her the news like that, but I wasn't.

I was only mad at myself.

At first.

But then I got mad at Kari. So mad. Because for a week after she found out about me and Leslie she wouldn't see me or talk to me or let me have any contact with Colton. That was what wasn't right. I deserved anything she threw out at me and I was ready to take it. But no matter what was between us, she did not have any right to keep me from my son.

It was terrible. Every day I'd try to get in touch with Kari. Every day she'd put me off. She didn't answer her cell. None of her friends would tell me anything. All Abe knew was that according to Jill, she and Colton were doing all right.

Whatever that meant.

How were we supposed to work this out? How was I supposed to tell her how sorry I was and how I'd do anything to make it up to her, if she wouldn't talk to me? I needed to see her. I needed her to let me see my son.

I was so desperate to talk to Kari that one night I went up to the hospital a few minutes before I knew she was supposed to get off. I got off the elevator in front of the nurses' station on the floor where she worked. Her coworkers, about half of them I knew, looked at me like I was some kind of an ax murderer or something. They told me she was busy in a patient's room. One of them headed down the hall. To head her off, probably. No one would say how long it might be before she got back to the desk.

Which was all right with me. I would wait as long as it took.

Finally one of the nurses got around to telling me Kari was scheduled to work a double shift. She wasn't getting off for eight more hours.

I figured at least she could take a break or something.

But no. I never did get to see her. Somebody told the supervisor who I was and without even saying anything to me, she called security. It was some guy who weighed at least four hundred pounds. Red face. Gut hanging over his belt. I guess he was supposed to throw me out or something. Sucker couldn't take five steps without starting to wheeze.

He was going to say something to me.

But I told him there wasn't any need.

I left on my own. Took the stairs down, got in my truck, and went on back home.

Finally, after a week of Kari blocking my calls, hiding out at different friends' houses, and not letting me know where Colton was at, I came home one day after work. Her car was in my driveway.

I opened the back door. My heart was beating like crazy. When

Kari wasn't in the kitchen like I expected I went down the hall towards the living room. As mad as I was at her for keeping me from seeing Colton, I've never in my life been so afraid to face something as I was to face her. Our hall was only about ten feet long but that day it felt like a mile. When I got to the end of it, I stood in the doorway behind this fake tree we had that I hated because it was ugly and always in the way.

From there I could see Kari sitting in the rocking chair I'd bought for her whcn Colton was born. Her back was to me. Her feet were flat on the floor. I couldn't see her hands. Our house has these creaky wood floors. There's no sneaking up on anybody with all the noise they make. Kari knew I was there but she didn't turn around.

I'm not suicidal. I wasn't then. But the pain in that room was so great that if dying would have made all it go away, at that moment I'd have gladly put a gun to my head.

"Kari," I said from where I stood at the end of the hall.

She didn't look up.

"Are you—are you all right?"

Only then did my wife turn to look at me. She didn't speak but I can tell you this: No, she was not all right. I wanted to grab her up. Confess everything. Tell her I was sorry. Beg her to forgive me. But I didn't. I stood where I was.

Until I saw him.

Colton.

Lying on a blanket she'd put on the floor to the other side of her chair.

"Joel," she said. "Don't. He just went to sleep."

I shot her a look. No way. This was my son.

And I already had him in my arms.

chapter thirteen

FIRST THING I DO WHEN I come in after a day off is put my lunch in the fridge. Then I look at my book.

Besides August, when everybody's getting ready for school, December is one of our busiest months at the shop. People want to look good for parties and for family gatherings and stuff. College kids are home on break. Most of the customers who come in are in a good mood and around the holidays the tips are excellent, which comes in handy for Christmas.

Me and Abe have talked about going out on our own, but I don't know. Start-up costs could eat you up. Neither of us got that kind money put back. Even though he and I both have good clienteles built up, it's not a risk either one of us is ready to take right now.

It's mostly Abe who thinks we should open a shop of our own. Most of the time I like it where I'm at. Mrs. Chan has her moods but she's basically a good person to work for. I get along okay with the other stylists. About the only thing that bugs me is I like my station to be real organized. Abe says I'm anal. Maybe. But it hacks me off when I come back after being off a day and somebody's borrowed something and not put it back or when I can tell they've dug in my supply drawer and it's not the same as when I left.

Still. Putting up with stuff like that's pretty minor when you compare it to all the headaches you have owning your own business. I've never been the overly ambitious type. I don't need a lot to be okay. A place to live. Something to drive. Food. Utilities. About my only thing is I buy too many CDs. Working for somebody else doesn't bother me. Money gets tight sometimes. Still. There's no reason why I can't keep getting by like I am. Except for my truck, which'll be paid off in ten months, I don't have any debt.

When Kari and I split up, she moved out. I thought about giving up our house and moving into an apartment. Rent would be cheaper and I wouldn't have to mow the grass. I still think about it sometimes, but it's nice having somewhere people can come over and hang out and make noise like the guys do on Sunday nights. It's good having a place to cook out on the grill. I like having room so if one my friends needs to crash, it's okay. If I lived in an apartment, there wouldn't be any place to put Colton's little plastic swimming pool he loves to get in when it's hot. If we moved I think he'd miss his room.

Last night I hung a Nirvana poster up over his bed. I know. Cobain's not exactly a role model for kids. It's about the music. Colton started recognizing them on the radio before he turned two. Every time he hears Nirvana in my truck, he goes nuts.

"Make it loud, Daddy," he tells me. "Make it loud."

When I found the poster I had to buy it for him.

It's not my place to say anything so I don't, but I worry sometimes about Kari and how she's managing her finances. In the past year she's bought a house and a new SUV. That's a lot of debt.

I know. RNs make good money. Kari probably pulls one-and-a-half times what I make. Plus I pay her $450 a month child support. Since I have Colton half the time, if we went back to court I probably wouldn't have to pay it, but I'm not doing it. Kari carries him on her insurance. She buys his clothes and most of the other stuff he needs. It comes out about right.

My book's nearly full. Only got one appointment slot open this morning, one this afternoon. Not much room for walk-ins. It never fails. Nine thirty, Sean comes in hoping I can cut his hair before he goes to work. I'm drying a girl's hair.

"Sure." I look up at the clock. "Take me about ten minutes to finish her up. You lucked out. My one open slot all morning." I motion towards my book. "Wouldn't hurt to call for an appointment next time."

"I know," he says.

"How's it going?" I ask him once he's in my chair.

"It's going."

I like that my station's in the corner. Against the wall. A little bit away from everybody else. I go and turn up the music so as to give us more privacy. Elevator, but it'll do. "You talk to Brooke?"

"No."

"Got an attorney?"

He nods.

"Stinks, man." I put a cape on him.

"She'll get Allyssa," Sean says. "My lawyer says it's almost a sure thing."

"You gonna fight her?" I'm thinking how glad I am Kari and I live close. Oklahoma is a long way to go for weekend visitation. Lots of Saturdays Sean has to work. How's he going to make an eight-hour round trip to see his little girl?

"Don't know. Haven't decided," he says. "Been talking to one of the pastors at church. He's telling me not to do anything stupid. Says I need to take some time. Think this out. Man's right. I got to remember, it's not about getting back at Brooke. All it's about is Allyssa."

"You're still going to church? The same one?"

Sean shrugs. "It's my church. I didn't do anything. Why should I leave? The guy got fired."

Makes sense. I suppose if you're a youth pastor, dinging one of the married lady members would tend to get you laid off from your job. "Hey, whatever works for you." Sean and me have never talked about religion but I know he and Brooke used to go together and take Allyssa. Every Sunday. To one of those big brick churches with the nice cars in the parking lot.

Sean tucks his chin to his chest while I clean up his neck. "You know what it's like. I need all the help I can get. There's good people in that church. They've helped me out. Praying for me. For Allyssa. I can use it."

"I guess we all can," I say.

We both get quiet.

Alice is all the time telling me she prays for me and Colton. I appreciate the thought. I tell her thank you. But honestly it makes me feel a little weird when she says it and I'm never for sure what I'm supposed to say back.

Sean pulls his hand out from under the cape to wipe at his eyes. He's embarrassed. "I got to believe what they say. God's with you when times get bad."

I get Sean a clean towel. Then I stand where nobody in the shop can see his face until he's okay. He's all right. It only takes him a second to get it together.

"Thanks," he says. He hands me back the towel.

"You need anything. Call me."

"Appreciate it."

I take off the cape and brush away the loose hairs on his neck.

"Can you keep Allyssa a couple hours for me tomorrow night?"

"Sure. What you got going?"

"Meeting with the real estate agent. Our—I mean my—finances are a mess. Putting the house up for sale."

"No prob. You want me to pick her up from day care on my way home? I'm off at five."

"That'd be great. I'll owe you."

"Don't worry about it. I'll have Colton. He'll be glad to see Allyssa."

When I'm finished Sean pulls out his wallet but I won't let him pay. It's the least I can do. "Next time," I tell him. "This one's on me."

Sean puts on his jacket.

Right as he's leaving I think of something else. "You and Allyssa need some place to stay, it'd be crowded, but me and Colton can make room."

"You're a good man," Sean says.

Then he heads over to Sears.

I never wanted a divorce.

I told Kari I'd do anything if she'd let me have another chance. We went to counseling. Out on dates. We read books, listened to tapes, and like they told us, wrote out lists of what it was we loved about each other. Kari and Colton even moved back into our house. Twice. The first time she stayed for four months. The second time lasted only three weeks. If both us had been trying, we might have stood a chance at patching things up. Key word, *both*. Thing was, both of us weren't trying.

Only me.

Which, let me tell you, got really, really old after a while.

Both times Kari moved home I believed we could put this thing behind us and move on with our lives. I was determined to make it work. Anything I thought would make Kari happy, I did it. She didn't have to ask me. I helped clean the house. I'm a terrible cook so we went out to eat a lot. I brought home flowers. Tamales. One time a crock pot and a new set of dishes.

And some days would feel okay. Normal, even. Kari and Colton would be sitting out on the back stoop when I'd come home from work. She'd smile at me and Colton would hold up his arms for me to pick him up and I'd think, *Yes, this can work. We're going to be all right.* I'd be hyper and happy, almost overcome with feeling optimistic and hopeful. Like a puppy who's so excited to see you he wets on himself.

But more days were strained. Tight. I'd come home and Kari's face would be closed off, blank. And I'd know right off she'd had a bad day and we were in for another bad night. There was no knowing what it was I'd done because she never would say. She'd be really quiet and really tired. More tired even than when she was pregnant and working and going to school. Those days were terrible. I never knew what to do. I'd try to be gentle with her, to comfort her. But her body would be hard and her eyes would look anywhere but at me. She wouldn't give me an inch no matter what I tried to do.

On one of those bad days, two weeks into the second time she came back, when I came in Kari was standing at the stove, stirring a skillet. She was making Stroganoff Hamburger Helper, which is one of the few things that I like but she hates to eat. Everything had been fine when I'd left that morning. We'd had breakfast, laughed at Colton, kissed each other good-bye.

It wasn't fine now.

The house was spotless. I could tell from the smell of Pine Sol in the kitchen, lemon oil in the living room, and bleach in the bathroom that she'd spent a lot of the day cleaning.

I stood beside her at the stove and watched her stir. Not talking, we stared at the stuff in the pan like we were checking out the most interesting thing in the world.

"House looks nice," I said.

"Thanks."

"Dinner smells good."

She nodded.

"Feeling okay?"

"I'm all right."

"How's your headache?" She'd had a bad one the night before.

"It's gone."

I stood there with my hands in my pockets, wanting to put my arms around her but knowing I better not.

Later, after I ate and she didn't, after I tried to make conversation and she didn't, after we'd cleaned the kitchen and put Colton to bed in his room, I sat down on the floor beside where Kari was on the couch. I leaned back against it. My shoulder touched her knee. She moved it away.

"Tell me," I said after we'd sat there for ten minutes not talking in our too quiet house. "Please. Tell me what to do. Tell me what to say. Anything. I'll do anything. You name it. I'll do it. I want us to be okay. I want things to be right between us. I'm not blaming you for feeling bad but you've got to talk to me. If you don't,

I don't know what's going on in your head and I can't know how to fix it."

"You can't fix this," she said real low.

Silence.

Nothing.

I was so tired of this. So ready to be done with it.

But obviously she wasn't. All I could figure was I hadn't suffered quite enough.

So we sat there. Her not saying anything. Both of us miserable. In our clean house with our beautiful boy asleep in his crib not ten feet away.

Finally Kari spoke. Her words came out hard as nails. "You want to know what to do so I'll get over this? I'll tell you. I want to know everything. Details. When. Where. How many times."

"No. Un-uh. We're not going there."

"I have to hear what happened from you. I'm stuck. If you tell me everything, I think then I can get past it. If you don't, I'm not staying in this house one more day."

"You don't know what you're asking," I said. "I'm telling you. You don't. Knowing is not going to help."

"I have to hear it."

I tried and tried but no matter what I said, she wouldn't have it any other way. I truly believed if I didn't say what she wanted me to say, she would have packed up and left that night. And so even though I knew in my heart it was the worst thing I could do, I gave in. I told Kari everything she thought she wanted to know. I described what it was like being intimate with somebody other than her. I gave her details. I answered her questions. I told her how Leslie made me feel.

It was bad.

Worse than bad.

My words cut. They made Kari bleed as surely as she would have bled if I'd come at her skin with a knife.

And hearing it once wasn't enough. At one point she even got up, went to the bathroom, and closed the door. I could hear her puking, which I thought meant we were done. But no. In only a couple minutes, she came out of the bathroom wiping her mouth, sat back down and made me tell her the same awful things again.

And again.

And again.

When Kari'd finally had enough, when she got to the point where she didn't ask me any more details, there was one thing I knew for sure.

My wife had been wrong.

I'd been wrong, too, for going along.

It would have been better if I'd let her leave.

Because some words are not meant to be spoken. Ever. They are too hurtful. Too damaging. The wounds they make can't ever heal.

I'd said those words.

Now all hope was gone.

Six months later Kari and I were divorced.

chapter fourteen

"HOW OLD'S THAT BOY OF YOURS?" Bradley's come in for a haircut. Like always, he tells me no, he does not want me to take a little more off the back.

"Colton's three," I say.

"He like dogs?"

"Loves them."

"My wife's got her a dog. Real smart one."

"You got married?" Last time I talked to Bradley he was single.

"Three weeks ago. New Year's Eve. Me and her been seeing each other off and on for four months. Decided real quick we'd tie the knot. When you're past fifty years old like me and her you can't be taking all the time in the world. Life's short."

"This your first marriage?" I ask.

Bradley shakes his head. Holds up four fingers.

"Oh. Well. Congratulations. I'm happy for you."

Bradley nods, moves his toothpick from one side of his mouth to the other. "Like I was saying, wife's got her a dog."

"What kind?"

"I don't know. Big dog. Maybe one of them Great Danes."

"Those are big dogs. Bet he eats a lot."

"That's not all he does a lot of. You should see the poop I have to scoop. Every day."

I laugh. "Thought you said this was your wife's dog?"

"I guess we share the dog," Bradley says.

"Sounds to me like you got the wrong end in that deal," Abe says.

Bradley ignores Abe's comment. "You boys ought to come out and see this dog. Bring your kids. You ain't never seen nothing like her."

"I've seen a Great Dane before," Abe says.

"Not one like her. This dog can talk."

"No way," I say.

"You're full of it, man," Abe says.

"I swear it. Didn't believe it at first, either. But she can. Me and my wife were sitting on the couch one night. Dog was over on the rug. I was in the mood for a little romance so I says to my wife, 'I love you.'"

I look over at Abe. I'm not sure we want to hear this.

"I give her a little kiss and she says back to me, 'I love you.' She's warming up to the idea."

I know I don't want to hear any more, but Bradley's not done.

"Then out of nowhere this third voice says 'I love you.' Shook me up but my wife wasn't surprised. She'd heard it before."

Abe stops what he's doing. "The dog said 'I love you'?"

"Plain as day. She can say other stuff too," Bradley says.

"Like what?" I ask.

"Let's see," he's thinking. "She can say 'Mama.' 'Cookie.' 'Water.' 'Outside.' 'Want a bone.'"

"And you can understand her?" Abe says.

"Same as I can understand you. Don't believe it, come see for yourself. You know where I live. Come on out. Anytime. Today. Tonight. After you get off work."

I'm thinking maybe me and Abe will. I've seen dogs on Letterman who whine and howl and make noises that sound sort of like real words. Pretty funny. Colton'd get a kick out of it.

"What does she call you?" I ask.

"Who?" says Bradley.

"The dog. Your wife's dog."

Bradley thinks for a minute. "She don't call me nothing."

"Not Daddy?" I ask. "Or Papa? Not even Brad?"

"Nope. She don't call me nothing."

"How come?" I ask. Egging Bradley on is not hard to do.

"Because, son," Bradley looks at me in the mirror like I'm a kid who's a little bit on the slow side, "she's a dog. There's just some words dogs can't say."

Abe cracks up. A couple of the other stylists who've been listening in laugh at me too. For some stupid reason I feel my face get red.

I finish up Bradley's hair, not saying any more about the dog. When I'm done he pays out.

"Later man," Bradley says.

I watch him leave. I don't give a rip about seeing the man's stupid dog.

After Bradley my book's open 'til after lunch so Abe and I go across the street to pick up some food at Church's Chicken. Strips for me. Two legs and a thigh for Abe. Mashed potatoes. Rolls for us both. Their's are the best. They dip them in honey. Abe makes an exception to his healthy eating rules when it comes to Church's.

When we get back, Kari's waiting on me, already sitting in my chair, talking to one of the stylists. She was down in my book. Except for the first few months after our split, Kari's never let anybody but me touch her hair. I hate to admit how glad I am about that.

She sees me and Abe coming in through the back door.

"Hi, Joel," Kari says to me. "Got here a little early."

"Hey, Abe." He goes over and she gives him a hug.

"Hey, girl," he says to her. "What you up to?"

She and I never hug.

"Needing a cut. How's Sh'dondra?"

"Good. Except she keeps getting in trouble in school. Talks too much. Tries to tell all the other kids what to do. Don't know what we're going to do with that girl if she doesn't settle herself down. Last week they made me come to kindergarten and sit with her the whole day."

"Did you learn anything?" Kari asks.

"Oh, yeah," Abe says. "I learned that the wheels on the bus go round and round and that ignorant spider makes it to the top every time."

Kari and I wish Colton had a little of Sh'dondra's spunk. He's shy and lets other kids run over him. At our last conference with his day-care teacher she told us he needs to learn to stand up for himself a little bit better.

I didn't say anything at the time but what I was thinking was *Lady, isn't that part of what we pay you to do?*

Kari bought him some books about a little bear cub who needs to learn how to growl. Maybe reading stories like that will help. It's too early to tell, I guess. We just got them.

Kari moves over to the shampoo chair. We're letting her hair grow out. It's past her shoulders. I put in some long layers. Looks good on her. She wears it up in a clip when she goes to work. I know that because on the mornings when she works and I don't she drops Colton off on her way to the hospital.

Since our divorce I've dated a few women. A few times. It's complicated knowing who to go out with. Girls my age and younger, the ones who don't have kids, like to party. Nothing wrong with having a good time but knowing I've got Colton, sometimes when I'm out at a club or something I feel more like a fifty-year-old man than somebody just going out. I've dated a few single moms, too. A couple were real sweet. But so many of them are wanting to get married. I don't have anything against that, but it's not something I can see me doing for a long, long time.

Our mutual friends try not to talk about it to me, but I know Kari's been seeing this same guy for going on three months. Abe I'm sure, because of Jill being one of Kari's best friends, keeps a lot what he knows to himself. What he has told me is that the guy's name is Nick. He's a respiratory therapist at the hospital. Thirty years old.

I don't know what respiratory therapists make, but I don't think it's that much.

Kari's never even told me she's dating anybody, but from what I can figure out, she only sees this guy when Colton's with me.

There's lots of things me and Kari don't discuss. We're probably the most polite-with-each-other divorced couple you've ever seen. We get along really good but only because we keep everything on the surface. We don't talk about the past. We don't talk about the future.

We mostly talk about Colton.

It's weird thinking about the woman you were married to, the woman you wish you were still married to, being with some other guy. It's not just weird. It stinks. Something in me would like to go to the hospital, find him, and punch him in the face.

But I don't.

Instead I lean Kari back over the bowl. I test the water to make sure the temperature is just right. Then I shampoo her hair. I put in conditioner. I rinse her out. And when I'm finished, I pat her dry with a towel and she goes back to my station. After I'm done with her cut I section her hair off and dry it with a big round brush. It takes me forever. Kari's hair is thick. I make sure every hair is right.

When I'm done she looks really good.

Today is Friday. The beginning of my weekend with Colton.

Which means tonight my ex-wife will probably be going out with that guy.

After my weekend with Colton, Kari comes a good hour early to pick him up on Sunday night. She knocks, then comes on in through the back kitchen door. The guys are all still over at the house. Me and Pete are cleaning up. We used paper so it's not so bad. Everybody else is in the living room.

"You had supper?" Pete asks Kari.

"No, but I'm okay," Kari says.

She doesn't look like she feels good. She's pale and she keeps rubbing her neck like she's got a crick in it. Her eyes look red.

Maybe something happened with her and respiratory guy.

Maybe they broke up.

Maybe he got hit by a truck.

"Abe cooked. Lasagna," Pete says. "Vegetable, but you can't tell."

"No, thanks," she says. "I'm pretty tired. Think I'll get my son and go home. Joel, is his stuff together?"

When Kari goes in to get Colton to take him home, Casey hits pause and everybody says hi. Sh'dondra comes over and gives her a hug. It's wall-to-wall people in the living room. The guys and the kids are watching *Iron Will* on the DVD player. It's kind of hard to find a movie kids can see that's not totally lame for adults. But this one's about some sled dogs and a race. If you're ever looking for a clean but good movie, this one would work. Been out a while. Maybe eight, ten years.

Colton sees Kari but he doesn't move from his spot on the floor in front of the TV. Brandon's on one side of him. Chase on the other. He's looking like he thinks he's hot stuff being down there with the bigger guys.

"Colton," Kari says. "Come here. Let's go home."

He's not answering.

"Colton. Mommy's here," I say. "Get up. Come put your coat on."

No way. He's not budging. At least not without a fight. He's having fun with the other kids. Doesn't want to leave.

Kari looks like she's trying to decide what she wants to do.

"Why don't you stay 'til the movie's over," I say. "Everybody'll be clearing out. He'll be ready to go then."

"How much longer?"

"Twenty minutes. Not much more."

Kari looks at her watch. I can tell she wants to go home now. I nearly offer to let her go on and tell her I'll bring Colton over to her house in an hour or so. But before I do, she decides to stay. She picks her way across all the bodies on the floor and squeezes into a spot on the couch between Abe and Sean. It's hot in here to me but Kari's shivering, so Sean hands her the afghan that's on his end of the couch.

Right at the end is where the movie gets good. Nobody talks. Even the kids are quiet. We've all got our eyes on the screen.

Since there's really no place to sit and the movie's about over anyway, I stand in the doorway and lean against the wall. I'm thinking I should go turn down the heat, but then I remember Kari being cold.

I look over at her. There's something different about the way she's sitting. She's sort of leaning. She looks kind of off. It takes me a minute to see something's bad wrong with her.

"Abe!" I yell.

I can't believe what I'm seeing. Kari's head, which one second ago was relaxed into the cushion of the couch, has gone stiff. She was just a minute ago joking with Sean. Now her eyes are rolled back in her head. Her hands are drawn up like those kids you see in wheelchairs who can't talk or walk or anything. She's twitching and jerking all over.

For what's probably two seconds but feels like two hours, nobody moves.

Then like someone yelled go, everybody jumps up. People are yelling. The kids are screaming. I'm trying to get to Kari but it's taking me forever because there's too many freakin' people between me and her. When I finally get to her, she's slumped over, still jerking and shaking. I can't tell if she's breathing but she's making some weird, weird sounds.

Abe takes charge. "Sean, get the kids out of here. Now. Pete, move this table. Lay her down. Casey, call 911. Tell them it's a seizure."

Abe checks Kari's pulse in her neck. He listens to see if she's breathing.

"What's the matter with her? What's happening? She was okay just a minute ago. What's going on?"

Abe shakes his head. He's had first-aid training but he doesn't know.

I'm kneeling beside Kari, holding her head to keep it from

bumping against the wood trim on the end of the couch. She's still jerking and it looks like she's peed on herself. "Hold on, baby, hold on," I tell her. "You're going to be all right. Everything's going to be all right." I don't know if she's going to be all right or not. It's too obvious she's not hearing anything I'm saying. The jerking's not letting up. She looks like an animal.

"They're coming," Casey says after he's made the call.

"How long?"

"Eight minutes is what they said."

"Eight minutes. You hear that, Kari? Hold on. The ambulance is coming."

She pukes. Yellow stuff. Smells terrible. Makes me gag.

"Turn her on her side," Abe says.

I wipe at her face with the afghan.

From the bedroom where Sean's got the kids I hear Colton screaming, "I want my daddy. I want my mommy." Any other time I'd have been right there but this time I let his screaming go.

chapter fifteen

KARI'S SEIZURE STOPS before the ambulance gets here. Which is a huge relief. But you can tell she's not all right. She's really sleepy. Weird acting. I can't get her to stay awake. It's like she's deep in this fog. She acts like she can hear what I'm saying but then she drifts off. Over and over she reaches up and rubs the back of her hand across her mouth.

When the paramedics get inside they take her blood pressure and shine a light in her eyes. They put in an IV. Takes them three tries. Kari doesn't even flinch.

"How long did the seizure last?" one of the guys asks. He and his partner are big guys. They talk loud. Them and their stuff fills up the living room.

"I don't know. Ten minutes?" I say.

"A minute and a half. I looked at my watch," Abe says.

It felt like an hour is all I can say.

After that they don't hang around long. They put Kari on a stretcher, fasten these big orange belts around her, and then they take off. Abe and I follow them in his car.

Soon as we pull up at the ER entrance, Abe lets me out. They unload the stretcher, the automatic doors open up, and they push her down the hall. I've been to the ER five or six times in my life. You know it's not good when they get you right in. I follow behind. This tall red-headed nurse stops me to fill out some forms. I try to watch where they're taking Kari, but they go around a corner and I can't see.

"Are you family?"

"Yes." I guess that's a lie. But except for Colton I'm as close as she's got.

"She have any allergies?"

"Un-uh."

"Current medical problems?"

"Headaches. Neck aches. When she's tired."

"Past surgeries?"

"Her appendix. When she was fifteen."

About halfway through the paperwork, which takes forever, the nurse lowers her clipboard. "Are you Joel?"

"Yes."

"Colton's dad."

I wonder how she knows.

"Kari and I are friends. I used to work up on the floor."

I'm relieved to know I'm talking to somebody who knows Kari. I'm thinking this gives me an in. "How bad is it? What's wrong with her?"

"She ever had a seizure before?"

"Never."

"She fall or bump her head recently?"

"Not that I know of.

"Seizures are usually caused by pressure on the brain. They'll take her to CT. Do a scan. Hopefully that'll show what caused it."

"But she's going to be all right." I want her to say yes.

"This is a good hospital. Kari's got lots of friends here. She'll get good care."

I look her straight in the eye. But she can't look back straight at me. I see her close down. They've got all these rules about confidentiality. I tell myself that's what it is. She raises her clipboard and we begin with the million questions again.

When we're done the nurse takes me to Kari's exam room, which isn't a room at all, rather a cubicle with curtains around it and one chair with a plastic seat. She's not there. They've already taken her down to CT. The nurse tells me I can sit down and wait but I don't. I stand up. I look around. There's not much to see. Blood pressure thing on the wall. Two trash cans. One of them red. Biohazard. I guess for blood. Abe comes in from parking the car.

"What'd they tell you?"

"Nothing. She's getting a brain scan done right now."

We wait for a good twenty minutes. People stick their heads around the curtain, but nobody tells us anything and Kari's still gone. I stand up. I sit down. I call the house.

Sean and Pete and their kids are still there. Sean's getting ready to take Colton home with him. Jill's come and got Sh'dondra so Abe can stay with me. Casey's gone home. He's got an early practice in the morning that he can't miss but Sean says he wants somebody to call him soon as we know anything.

"How's Colton?" I ask.

"He's upset, but he'll be all right," Sean says.

"Let me talk to him."

"Daddy?"

"Colton. It's me. You doing okay, buddy?"

"I want you."

"I know you do. But I need you to be a big boy and go spend the night with Allyssa tonight. I'll see you tomorrow. Okay?"

He's crying so hard he can't talk.

I hate this.

Sean gets back on the phone. "Don't worry about it, man. He'll be all right. You want me to take him to day care tomorrow?"

I haven't thought that far ahead. "Yeah. I guess so. I'll call if I need you to do something different. He's going to need some clothes. His backpack's in his room. I'm not sure where."

"Don't worry about it. I'll find his stuff. No problem. Let me know if you find out anything," Sean says. "Here's Pete."

"I'm locking your place. Then I'm coming up. Anything else you need me to do? Anything you want me to bring?"

"No. Nothing. Thanks."

Abe motions to me.

"They're bringing her back," I tell Pete, "gotta go."

Kari's awake. She's got an oxygen thing in her nose but she looks a lot better. Like a hundred percent. Some guy's walking beside the gurney. Another one's pushing it. I hear the one beside her crack a joke about how some people will do anything to get off work. She's actually smiling. Looking as much like herself as a person coming down the hall on a gurney can.

When they get her back into the cubicle the one guy doesn't leave.

"You feeling better?" I ask her.

"A little bit. I still don't know what happened," Kari says. "Where's Colton?"

"Sean's got him."

"You should go home. I'm all right."

"I'm not leaving you alone," I say.

Kari looks over at the guy who's stayed.

"Are you her doctor?" I ask.

Kari answers. "This is Nick Martinez. We work together. He's a good friend."

"Nice to meet you."

We shake. It takes me a second but I figure it out. Nick.

Respiratory therapy guy. He's about five ten. Stocky. Hair high and tight. Got on blue scrubs. And clogs. Which I have never seen any man wear.

"Kari's just been seen by the ER doc," the guy says. "He's the one who ordered the CT and some blood work. The neurologist on call's on his way. We probably won't know anything 'til they get the results of the scan." He and Kari make eye contact then he looks at me. "If you need to go, like to check on Colton, my shift just ended. I can stay."

I don't like the sound of this guy saying our son's name.

"That's okay," I say.

"Really," he says. "It's no problem."

"I'm not leaving." My voice is too loud.

"It's no problem," Abe moves in. "We got all the time in the world."

"Okay, then," the guy says.

Okay, then.

"How you feel?" I ask Kari.

"Little bit of a headache."

"You about scared me to death."

"They said I had a grand mal."

I don't know what that is.

"A big seizure," Abe says.

"Tell me what happened," Kari says. "You called the ambulance?"

"Yeah. You started shaking all over. Not talking. Like you couldn't hear anything. It came on all the sudden. Were you sick over the weekend?"

She looks over at Nick. "No. I was fine. Tired is all. I've been sort of run down lately."

"You haven't been eating right," Nick says.

Like he knows.

"I guess my electrolytes could be off."

She does look like maybe she's lost a little bit of weight. I don't know much medical stuff but I remember electrolytes are in your blood. "Can something like that cause a seizure?"

"Sometimes," Kari says. She looks up at the bag hanging over her head. "I'm getting sodium in my IV. Once they get the labs back they'll probably give me some potassium and let me go home."

"Tonight?" I ask.

"I bet they keep you overnight," Nick says. "Just to be sure."

It's another hour before we see the neurologist. Dr. Israel. The guy has a ponytail. Manicured nails. Eyebrows he ought to get somebody to trim. He talks to Kari, then to me about what happened. He tells us he'll be back, that he's going to go get the report of her scan. We wait and wait, thinking he's coming right back. Somebody comes in and takes more blood. Somebody else checks her blood pressure and puts this clothespin thing on her finger to check for oxygen.

Nick's been standing near the foot of Kari's bed. He moves to where he can get a look at the clothespin thing. "Your sat's ninety-seven," he says.

"I'm not surprised," Kari says. "My breathing's okay."

"You probably don't need the O2. Want to take it off?"

I think Nick's not the doctor and that he should leave things alone.

"Sure," she says.

He moves the tubing from where it's behind Kari's ears and up under her chin. He winds it up and hangs it over a hook that's on the wall.

I look at Abe. He looks at me. *She's not helpless* is what I want to say.

Pete comes in. Which makes it crowded, but I am sure glad he's here. He kisses Kari on the cheek. Tells her that Colton's okay.

"You take Brandon and Chase back to Erin's?" I ask.

Pete says that he did.

We take turns sitting in the chair.

Abe gets up and goes and gets everybody sodas. Except for Kari. They won't let her have anything. I feel bad drinking in front of her because I know she's thirsty but she says it's okay.

Finally two Asian guys come to get her to take her for an MRI. According to them the neurologist, who still hasn't been back, ordered it to be done. They say you can get information from an MRI that a CT scan doesn't show.

"What kind of information?" I ask.

They can't say.

So off Kari goes again. This time she's gone a good while. After half an hour, Abe calls to check on the kids. He says they're okay. I make a trip to the john.

"There a vending machine around here?" Abe asks when I get back.

"Across from admissions," Nick says.

"Think I'll check it out."

"I'll go with you," Pete says. Then he turns to me. "You want anything?"

"No, I'm fine," Nick says. He's got his head down, checking the messages on his cell.

I start to say something. Abe shoots me a look. So I don't.

"So," I say to Nick when it's just the two of us. "You got any kids?"

"No," Nick says.

"You divorced?" I ask.

"Separated." He closes his phone. Looks at his watch. Then he stands up. "I'm going to go upstairs for a second. Need to check on something. Kari gets back, you tell her I won't be gone long. Okay?"

I nod. *Okay nothing* is what I want to say.

He's only gone about ten minutes.

Not long enough.

The ER shift changes. They bring Kari back. A new nurse comes in. Somebody Kari knows. Nick, too. Other people come in to say hi to her on their breaks. This is a big hospital but Kari knows a lot of people who work here.

We wait. And wait some more.

A couple of times Abe stays with Kari and Pete goes outside with me while I have a cigarette. I smoke it fast, in case they come in and tell Kari she can go home.

But they don't.

It's five hours since we got here when the ER doctor comes back in. "We're going to admit you," he says. "Put you in a room upstairs. I haven't written orders yet so it'll be a couple minutes. Okay?"

"When do I get the results of the CT scan and the MRI?" Kari asks.

"Dr. Israel wants to review them a bit more before he talks to you."

"We want to hear what he's got now," I say.

"Sorry. No can do. Israel's gone home. Said he'd get with you tomorrow."

What a jerk.

Kari looks worn out. We're all tired. Pete can't quit yawning. It's after one by the time she gets up to a room and they finish asking her the same questions again and filling out the same bunch of forms they already did downstairs. Here's where I can't decide what to do. I want to stay. Kari wants me to go home. Respiratory guy really, really wants me to leave. He's already turned the chair in the room into a recliner and gone and got himself a pillow and a blanket off the laundry cart parked in the hall.

I'm waffling.

Abe puts his hand on my shoulder. "Come on, man. Let's go to the house. It's time."

He's right. It is.

And so Abe drives me home. Pete follows in his car.

"My book's full tomorrow but I don't think I'm going in," I say after we get inside my house.

"Don't worry about it. I'll take care of it," Abe says.

"You're off tomorrow."

"Doesn't matter. I'll go in. I'll do your customers that'll let me. Ones that want to wait on you, I'll reschedule. Won't be a problem."

"Thanks, man." I am so tired I can't hardly stand up, but I'm wired and I can't sit down. I'm out of cigarettes. I thought I had another pack but I don't. The guys halfway cleaned up before they left but there's stuff to put away in the kitchen and the afghan with Kari's puke on it is still on the floor at the end of the couch. I decide to go put it in the wash.

Pete stops me. "We'll get that."

"Leave it," Abe says. "Go to bed. Get some sleep."

"I will. Soon. Y'all go home. I'm okay."

"Yeah, you're okay. Now go on. Take a shower. Go to bed. We'll clean up."

They're right. There's no sense in staying up. Besides, they need to go home and I don't think they will 'til they know I'm headed to bed.

I get in the shower. I let the hot water run over my head, in my eyes, my ears, my nose. I turn it so hot I almost can't stand it. I shampoo my hair and get some in my eyes. It burns like fire, gives me an excuse for tears. Once I start, I can't stop rubbing at my eyes.

I wish I was at the hospital with Kari.

I wish Colton was with me.

I wish there was nobody in the world except for the three of us.

I get out of the shower when I can tell the water's about to go cold. My house is quiet. All the lights are off. I feel like I can sleep, but to be sure I decide to get some Tylenol PM, which I keep in the cabinet to the left of the fridge.

I grope my way down the hall. When I get to the living room on my way to the kitchen I see them.

Abe on my couch.

Pete on the floor.

Asleep.

But keeping a watch over me.

chapter sixteen

IT'S NINE O'CLOCK IN THE morning. I got back to the hospital at eight. Kari's taken a shower and eaten some eggs. We've seen old Nick twice in the past hour but only for a couple minutes at a time. He's on duty today. Pulling a twelve-hour shift.

Too bad for him.

"So how long have you been having headaches?" Dr. Israel has come in. He's at Kari's bedside making some notes in her chart.

I'm thinking a headache is not something you generally pay much attention to. At least I never have. I get them sometimes but I take couple Advil and they go away. But it turns out Kari's been having really bad ones for a couple of months. She tells Dr. Israel lately they've been getting worse. She says she's been seeing red and white flashes of light sometimes.

I didn't know.

He's not surprised about the headaches. Or about the seizure. Because according to the MRI they did last night and the two more they did this morning, Kari's got a brain tumor the size of a golf ball.

A brain tumor.

He says it no differently than if he was telling her she had a bladder infection or a broken arm. But that's not how it feels. Getting words like that is like getting hit in the chest during a flag football game and having the wind knocked out of you.

I've got a million questions but I can't think how to say even one.

Dr. Israel tells us tomorrow they're doing a biopsy. They're going to drill a little hole in her skull and suck some of the tumor out with a needle. A biopsy is the only way they can tell for sure what kind of tumor Kari's got. There's benign and malignant. You want benign.

"If it's malignant, can you cut it out?" I ask him.

Kari shoots me a look that tells me to let her ask the questions.

I shoot her one back. Okay. I get it.

"Unfortunately no. Because of the size and location of the tumor, we can't."

"What are my options?" she asks.

He says he'll give her those after the biopsy. Not before.

When he leaves we sit there not saying anything. For the first time today it's just me and her in her room. You wouldn't believe all the people who've been in and out all day. Kari's been here less than twenty-four hours and her room is covered up in flowers and balloons. A dozen red roses from respiratory guy. A stuffed bear from Jill and Abe.

When I was Kari's husband, I knew what I was supposed to do. What my role was. Now that we're divorced I'm all the time stepping across some line I can't see. I've been here all day even though Kari's tried to get me to leave.

"I'm sorry," I say after the doctor is gone. "About butting in. I don't think he's telling us everything he knows and I'm not sure I like him."

"I'm going to be fine," Kari says. "I am. The tumor's going to be benign." She fiddles with a corner of the blanket that's across her lap.

"What?"

Kari won't look at me.

"Come on. Say it."

"I don't want to hurt your feelings." She turns her head to me but then looks back down. "You mean well. I know you do. But I need you to back off. Just a little. You expect to be here. To know everything. And I appreciate how concerned you are. But we aren't married anymore. I'm okay. I've got people looking out for me."

She won't say it. So I will. "You've got Nick."

"Yes," she says. "I've got Nick."

"How long've you been seeing the guy? Couple of months?"

"That's not your business. I'm not going to discuss our relationship with you. All you need to know is he's a good person. He's good to me. To our son."

I open my mouth. Then I shut it. Then I stand up. I'm not listening to this. Not one more word. I look at my watch. "I got to pick Colton up. It's nearly three." I move for the door.

"Will you bring him up here so I can see him?"

"Yeah. Maybe. Okay. After while." I'm out of here.

"Joel." Kari looks at her hands in her lap. She reaches up and pushes her hair back behind her left ear. "You don't have any reason to be mad."

I look at her not looking at me.

"We're divorced," she says.

Yeah. Like I forgot.

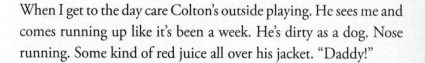

When I get to the day care Colton's outside playing. He sees me and comes running up like it's been a week. He's dirty as a dog. Nose running. Some kind of red juice all over his jacket. "Daddy!"

I scoop him up. He puts his arms around my neck. Even on a cool day he smells like a puppy. He seems okay. His teacher says he was all right today. Maybe he doesn't remember last night. Kids forget things pretty fast.

"Wanna see mama," he says after I've buckled him in.

"Okay. We will. After a while. First let's go home and change clothes." He's wearing jeans and his superman pajama top. When Sean was packing his things last night, I guess he thought it was a shirt. "First we'll go eat. Then we'll go see Mama."

He puts his thumb in his mouth. Three years old. Won't give it up. Mostly uses it when he's tired or upset. Today, I understand. His thumb is kind of like me and my smokes. He needs to quit. It's bad for his teeth. No way I'm starting in on him about it now.

"We're going to see Mama at the hospital."

He pops his thumb out. "Her go work?"

"Nope. She's sick. She's going to be in a bed when we see her. Okay?"

"Go see her now."

Casey's at the house when we get there. Sitting on my back stoop. "Whoa, buddy," he says to Colton. "Looks like you did some playing in the dirt today. You're a mess. How about we hose you off out here?" He picks up the water hose and acts like he's going to spray him. Colton giggles and runs, but Casey grabs him up and starts tickling him.

"Daddy! Daddy!" He's wriggling and laughing.

"Sorry, buddy. Can't help you. You're on your own." I'm unlocking the back door.

Casey puts him down. "You're getting too big. I think you broke my arm." He grabs hold his elbow, gets this awful look on his face. "What am I gonna do now?"

Colton backs away but he's still laughing. "You can't get me."

Casey grabs him up again.

Inside I put Colton in the tub. Casey sits on the john while I wash Colton's hair. I've got a thing about Colton being clean and dressed nice when he's about to see Kari. If just me and him are hanging out I don't care if he looks like a pig. Doesn't bother me if his clothes don't match. But whenever I've had him and he's going back to her, I want him to look good.

"What'd you find out," he says.

I tell him.

"And they're doing what tomorrow?"

"A biopsy."

"Which tells you what?"

"If it's malignant or benign."

"It'll be benign."

"I know. I'm not worried."

That's a lie. Casey knows it.

So do I.

After last night's butt-chewing from Kari about me being at the hospital all day yesterday, I came on in to work even though she's having that biopsy today.

Fine, I'm thinking. You don't want me there. I won't come.

Thing is, my body might be at the salon, but my mind's at the hospital. I keep looking at the clock. It's two o'clock. I worked through lunch. My stomach's empty but I don't feel like eating. Kari's biopsy was at eight. I've not heard a word. I'm cutting Alice's hair but it's hard to concentrate and it's taking me forever to section her off. I drop my comb on the floor.

"Sorry about that." I get a clean one.

Alice knows about Kari. I told her soon as she came in. "You sure you want to do this? I can reschedule. Come back some other time."

"No. Unless you do. I'm okay. Really. I am." I try to crack a joke. "I'm not going to mess you up."

Mrs. Chan looks over. She knows what's going on. So does every other stylist in the salon.

"I'm not worried about my hair," Alice says. "I'm concerned about you. While you're cutting, I'm sitting here praying those test results are going to be good."

"I appreciate that. You don't know how much," I tell Alice. And I mean it. I'll take every bit of help from anywhere I can get it. When it's time to blow her dry I can't find my bottle of styling lotion. I look in every drawer. Finally I snag some from Abe's station. It's a good thing Alice is not needing color today because even though I said I was all right, I'm not sure I'd be safe to mix it up.

Alice is paying when I get the news from Jill. She's at the hospital. Calls me on my cell. Everybody in the shop stops to listen when they hear it's Jill.

"How's Kari?"

"She's okay," Jill says. "They were late getting to her. She's been back from recovery a couple hours now."

"What the biopsy show?"

"They've only got a preliminary report but the doctor says it doesn't look good."

"Tell me."

"It's malignant, Joel. The biopsy showed Kari's got a malignancy."

"But she's all right," I say.

"You're not hearing me. Kari's not all right. She's got something they call a glioblastoma."

"Glio-what?" I've never heard of that. It sounds like some kind of an infection. Maybe she'll need an antibiotic. "But she's fine. You said she was fine."

"Joel. Shut up a minute. Listen to me. I'm telling you they're saying Kari's got cancer."

My hands go sweaty. I hold on to the phone and I try to think. Okay. Lots people get cancer. They do just fine. I've had some customers with cancer. Skin cancer. Prostate cancer. Even breast. They all beat it. I did a lady with colon cancer last Friday. Two years ago they cut it out. She's doing fine. Plays tennis. Does ceramics. All kinds of stuff.

"But it's something they can treat," I say to Jill. "Like with chemotherapy. Right?"

"I don't know what they're going to do," Jill says. "The doctor's back in there talking to her now."

"How's she feeling?"

"She's okay. Tired. I don't think she's slept since and she didn't sleep much last night. She's not saying much. She was eating some soup when the doctor came it. One of the nurses said she may get to go home tonight."

"Then it can't be too bad. If they're letting her go home."

Jill doesn't say anything. I hear her blow her nose.

"Come on, Jill. Please. It's going to be okay. It is."

"Joel. If Kari gets to go home, she wants you to bring Colton over. She wants him tonight."

If I've learned anything, it's that life can change faster than you think possible.

According to the doctor, Kari's got one of the worst kinds of cancer there is. Hardly anybody who gets it makes it a year. Pretty much nobody makes it five. It's worse for her because where the tumor is they can't take any of it out. If they did it would kill her. Best they can do is try to help her live a few months longer.

A few freakin' months.

There's times I wake up and I think they've made a big mistake. They must have gotten Kari's test results mixed up with somebody else's. I mean, she looks good. She's still having headaches some but who doesn't?

Kari says she's not giving in no matter what the doctors say. She's going to fight this thing. And win. There's a couple of people she's read about who lived way longer than they say you can when you have a glioblastoma. She's convinced there's no reason she can't do the same as them.

Most days I believe her.

Some days I don't want to get out of bed.

Alice has got Kari on the prayer list at her church.

Sean says she's on the one at his, too.

Abe and Jill put her on their church's list but Abe's not stopping there. He's been talking to this lady at the health food store about Kari seeing somebody who specializes in alternative medicine. Vitamins. Juice. I don't know what all. He's talked to Kari about it and she says she'll go.

Can't hurt is what I think.

Not that what I'm thinking is what Kari's going to do.

They've got her on a drug called Dilantin. Some other stuff, too. She can't drive because she might have a seizure while she's behind the wheel. I told her I'd take her anywhere she needs to go but she hasn't called on me yet. She's still working. Taking Colton the same days she normally does. She says she feels okay. But I don't know for how long.

Tomorrow she starts radiation. It doesn't take very long but she has to go twice a day. Eight in the morning. Two o'clock in the afternoon. Five days a week for four weeks. The doctors say it's the only thing they can do. Hopefully it'll shrink the tumor.

Abe keeps on her about seeing this alternative healer, but Kari's changed her mind. She doesn't want to go. She believes the radiation is going to work.

I hope she's right.

chapter seventeen

ONE WEEK OF RADIATION DOWN.

Kari's back in the hospital. Dehydration. They put her in this morning. She's been throwing up for two days. Not keeping anything down at all. She says not even Coke. I figured it was from the radiation, but they don't think so. Probably the cancer. But it could be a virus. Somebody said there's one going around.

I thought we'd know by now if the radiation is working but a couple days ago Kari told me no. They won't do another scan, which is the only way you can tell, until after her last treatment.

"Here's Mommy." I've brought Colton up to see her.

Kari's lying on her side with her back to the door when we walk in. When she hears us, she turns over and smiles. There's a button on the bed to make the head go up. She pushes it so she can sit up and still lean back. "Hey, big boy. Did you have a good day?"

Kari looks pretty good for somebody so sick. Except for the hospital gown, which is too big and which somebody snapped wrong. I want to fix it for her but I don't. Even here, in a bed with rails, I can hardly believe she has something so terrible inside her head.

I set Colton down on the bed beside her, on the side that doesn't have the IV. He's squirmy so I hand her a bag of peanut

M&M's, his favorite. She opens them up and starts giving them to him one at a time. I know you're not supposed to use food to get kids to behave but those M&M's work like a charm. He lays down next to her. Curls himself up in the crook of her arm. Instead of being rowdy, he's calm and good.

Kari strokes Colton's head from his crown to his nose. Every time she gets close to that place between his eyebrows he blinks. When he's ready for another candy he opens his mouth like a little bird and Kari drops one in.

"He needs a haircut," she says.

Colton's hair is fine and blond. His eyelashes too. He looks so much like Kari. Got those same blue, blue eyes and her fair skin.

"Yeah. I'll clean him up. Next week," I say.

Our conversation lags. I try to think up something to say.

"Census down?" I ask. Today's Saturday. I noticed when me and Colton came down the hall there's not too many patients on the floor.

"Yeah. They discharged seven today."

"Floor's quiet.

"Change of shift. Most of the nurses are in the report room."

"How you feeling?" I ask. "Still throwing up?"

"Not anymore. They gave me Phenergan. In the IV."

I've got Phenergan suppositories in the fridge at home. Left over from when Colton had the virus. You're not going to believe this but a couple months ago I came out of the bathroom and caught him with one in his mouth. Yes. A Phenergan suppository. He'd still been asleep when I'd gotten in the shower. But he hadn't stayed asleep. My son had gotten himself out of bed, gone into the kitchen, and opened up the fridge. Then he'd found the suppositories. He'd opened one up. I don't know how because they're wrapped up really tight in this foil. When I found him he was dipping the thing in a half can of leftover cake icing, then licking it off.

I don't know what will happen to you if you eat one of those things but I know they can't be good for you. When I took the suppository away from him he pitched such a big fit that, even though he hadn't had breakfast yet, I got him a spoon and let him dig right into the frosting. I was laughing too hard to do anything else.

Even though it was funny, I've never told Kari this story. If you're a divorced dad, you understand why.

"You think you could cut my hair when I get home?" Kari asks.

"Sure. You could use a trim."

"I'm thinking more than a trim."

"Okay. How short you want to go?"

"Short." She reaches up and touches her bangs. "They say with the radiation, since it's to my head, I'll probably lose it. There's already some coming out in my brush."

Oh.

For the first time since we found out about the tumor, I see Kari try not to cry.

What do I do? I want to get up in the bed with her and Colton. I want to put my arms around them both. I want to hold her and kiss her and tell her it's going to be okay, that I'll take care of her and that everything is going to be all right.

I reach out and touch her hand.

But when I do, she pulls away. Reaches for a Kleenex. Blows her nose.

"Mama?" Colton looks up and pats her face.

"I'm okay, baby."

"I got go potty."

There's a bathroom in Kari's room. I take him. After he's done, we go to the sink and wash his hands. He doesn't want to get back up on Kari's bed. It's okay for him to walk around in the room long as he doesn't sit down on the floor or put anything in his mouth. There are bad germs in hospitals. Ever heard of MRSA? It's one that even strong antibiotics can't hardly fight.

I go back to my chair. The one that makes a recliner. The one I guess Nick slept in last night. The chair's green vinyl. It makes a *whoosh* when I sit down. At least not a fart sound.

I'm here. Kari's here. Nobody else but me and her and Colton in this room. Before we got divorced, this would be the way it was supposed to be all the time. On normal days. We made vows to each other.

To love, honor, and cherish.

I promised her. She promised me.

In sickness and in health.

I feel like what I am. A visitor. Somebody who's on the outside looking in. Somebody who's not supposed to ask too many questions. Somebody who's not supposed to stay too long.

Forsaking all others and all else.

You break one of those vows and it pretty much erases the whole long list.

'Til death do us part.

I'm not going there.

Some people get divorced and it looks like they feel relief. Maybe that's what Kari feels. She looks and acts like she's gone on. Put the past behind her. But not me. Maybe it's worse for guys. Maybe it's worse for me because us splitting up was my fault. All I know is since the day of our divorce I've felt off-balance, crooked, like somebody trying to walk with one shoe on and one shoe off.

What God has joined together, let no man break apart.

How many meals did me and Kari eat together? How many times did we have sex? Night after night we went to sleep in the same bed. Morning after morning we got up, took our showers, and brushed our teeth in the same sink. We paid the bills together. We went out to eat. We bought groceries. When you're married and you do all those normal things, you don't even think about it. But those everyday things you do together change you. And it doesn't take all that long. The gaps between the two of you get filled in like grout between two pieces of ceramic tile. Even if you and your wife start out being as different as two people can be, you get connected.

Which is why divorce is so hard.

And why I feel as broken as a piece of cracked bathroom tile.

I'm not proud of being the kind of person who'll use a little kid to get what he wants. But that's exactly what I do. Kari wants to see our son? Fine. Since I'm the one who brings him, she gets to see me, too.

Kari takes a sip of the Sprite a nurse just brought in. "There's something you need to know," she says. "The radiation oncologist told me I have to stop working. She says I need to stay home until I finish the treatments and for maybe two weeks after. According to her, the fatigue is probably going to get worse."

"You shouldn't be working," I say. "I've thought all along you should take time off. Stay home until you get well."

"Hopefully I'll still be able to take Colton on my regular days. But I don't know how things will go. I don't know what to expect. I sure didn't expect to end up here after just a week."

"That's okay," I say. "I'll talk to the people at the day care. I'm sure with them knowing what's going on with you being sick and all, they'll let me bring him whenever I need to."

"But I'm still planning on keeping him."

"Sure. No problem. That'll be our backup plan."

"And it's only while I'm taking radiation. Soon as it's over, I should be getting my strength back. Things will get back to normal. I don't want Colton's routine messed up any more than it has to be."

"It won't be. Don't worry. He'll be fine. We'll do whatever we have to do."

"There's one more thing," Kari says. "You should hear this from me."

My heart skips. Not Nick. Tell me she's not getting married or something to Nick.

"I'm going to lose my house."

"No way." I feel relief it's not Nick but I try not to let it show.

"I shouldn't have bought it. I knew the payments were going to be a stretch but I thought I could swing it. I kept up at first. But they misfigured the escrow and my payments went up a hundred dollars."

"How can they do that?"

She shakes her head. "I don't know. They just can."

"How much is your payment?"

I can tell she doesn't want to say.

"Roughly."

"Seven-forty."

I've got nearly three grand put back. Enough to float her at least three months.

A nurse comes in. She checks Kari's IV. Listens to her heart and her lungs, asks her if she needs anything.

"You can't lose your house," I say when she's gone. "I can help you out."

"No. You can't. I'm not taking money from you. From anybody. Besides, it's worse than that. I'm behind already. Two months."

Two months? How'd she let that happen?

I have an idea. "You talked to the bank? I hear all the time about how you can refinance and get money to pay off your bills."

"It won't work. I haven't been in it long enough. I'm going to let it go back, which means I'll be moving. I thought you should know."

"That's going to screw up your credit."

"I know that. But I made a mistake. There's nothing else I can do."

"Don't be stubborn," I say. "I've got the money. Sitting in the bank. Not doing anything. It'd be a loan. You can pay me back."

Kari shakes her head.

She's not thinking. "Okay. Where you going to move? You get an apartment, you'll have to pay deposits. Even a small place is going to run you five hundred a month."

"I don't know what I'll do." She shrugs then puts her finger in her mouth and chews on her cuticle. "I'll figure something out. When I do, I'll let you know."

Right then Colton comes out of the bathroom. With me and Kari talking, I wasn't watching him close enough. I didn't even know he'd gone back in there. He's got something on his head. A hat. Like the pilgrims wore. Except it's white plastic.

Kari starts laughing.

"What is that?" I ask.

"Colton. Come here. Give it to me." Kari is laughing so hard it looks like she might wet her pants. I hope she doesn't throw up.

He's standing there in the doorway of the bathroom looking real proud of himself with whatever it is he's got on his head. It comes down so far you almost can't see his eyes.

"It's a hat," Kari says.

Well, yeah.

"It's to measure urine with." She can't hardly get the words out. "You put it on the toilet and you pee in it."

At least it's empty. "Colton. Come here. Give me that."

Colton's not budging. He thinks he's looking really fine. He's proud of his new hat.

I try to lift it off his head but he's got hold of it with both hands. I'm laughing so hard I can't hardly stand up. Finally, we talk Colton out of it, only because Kari's got more M&M's.

"You might want to wash his hair when you get home," Kari says. She's wiping her eyes from laughing so much.

"You think?"

Colton's back up on the bed with her. I'm in the chair. I can't remember the last time Kari and I laughed together like that. It feels good. We used to all the time.

Pretty soon me and Colton have to go. I put on his coat. He hugs her good-bye. Before we leave I have to say one thing.

"You could stay with me. And Colton. At the house."

"No, I can't."

I see her face get the look.

"Not like that," I say real fast. "Just as friends. And only 'til you're well enough to go back to work. Until you get back on your feet. You could have your old office. There's a bed in there now. I'd leave you alone. No questions asked. You could come and go as you please."

"I can't."

"Don't say anything else. Think about it. I wouldn't hassle you. No rent. No utilities. No strings. Give you a chance to get back on your feet."

She starts to say no again but I stop her. "Shh." I've got Colton by the hand and I'm at the door to leave. "We don't have to talk about it tonight. Me and Colton are gone. Get some rest. Take some more Phenergan. If you get to go home tomorrow, I'll bring him over to your house. If you don't, I'll bring him up here."

She shakes her head. But then she can't help it.

Kari smiles.

And I leave thinking *maybe.*

Maybe there's hope.

chapter eighteen

"I SHOULD START GOING TO CHURCH."

"And you decided this because . . ."

It's a workday. Me and Abe are at Taco Bell eating lunch.

I wipe hot sauce off my chin. Abe doesn't let anything be easy. "Why do you think?"

"Kari."

"Yep."

"You thinking you'd like to get to know the Man Upstairs. See if you can talk him out of a favor. Or a miracle."

"Something like that."

"Be a close thing to a miracle—the likes of your sorry behind on a pew."

"Ouch," I say. "I thought people like you were supposed to try to get people like me to come to their church."

"You need to come, all right. Just not for what you think."

I'm not going to ask.

"Sunday," he says. "Pick you up at ten."

What with Kari being sick, I figure church can't hurt. Lots of people go. Just not a lot of people like me.

If it wasn't for going with Abe, the biggest problem I'd have would be figuring out which church to go to. In Eden Plain it's easier to locate a church than it is to find a gas station. There's one place downtown where they've got four different kinds all on the same block. Church of Christ, Methodist, and two different Baptist, every one of them meeting at the same exact time.

Once I asked one of my religious customers, a guy that wears a cross around his neck and an American flag pin on his collar, what was the difference in the kinds of churches. Weren't they all pretty much the same? He said no. Not at all. Churches ascribe to certain doctrines. I didn't know what *ascribe* meant and I sure didn't know what *doctrine* was so I asked him to explain it to me. He said it means they have different views on things like predestination, the trinity, instrumental music, once-saved-always-saved, and women preachers.

"Those things are important?" I asked. I didn't want to show my ignorance but I didn't really know what he was talking about. "I mean are they important enough to make it worth having four big nice buildings on the same block?"

I wasn't trying to be smart. I just didn't know. It seems like a big waste of money. Like can't they see how much they could save if they pooled their money and built a place big enough to hold them all? They'd spend a lot less on utilities. Then maybe they could do some good. Right down the block from where all those churches sit, there's a low-rent apartment complex. Full of rats, drugs, and kids. With some of the money they save they could help those people. Clean the place up some.

But the guy got kind of hacked off at me asking him about doctrine. "You have to stand for the truth," is what he said.

"Like not telling a lie?" I said.

No.

He was talking about something different. This kind of truth meant believing certain things about certain issues.

Issues.

I guess like politics.

His church took the right stand on issues. I was welcome to go with him anytime.

Big surprise: I never did.

But I'm going with Abe this Sunday.

Yes, I'm going for Kari's sake. Not that she needs it. I'm sure the MRI they do after her radiation is going to show that tumor gone. But if there's a chance that me going to church will tip the odds in her favor, I'm willing to give it a shot.

There are a couple things about God that bother me. Okay, there are a lot of things.

They say God is in control.

Of everything.

That whatever happens is his will.

Hard for me to buy it.

Ever seen the movie *Hotel Rwanda*? Thousands of people. Slaughtered. Where was God during all that? Was that his will? Not to mention starving kids. You read about old people who get murdered, people whose houses burn down, people with cancer who don't get well. How come God lets things like that happen? What about September eleventh? Where was God then?

People say if we can put a man on the moon, surely we can find cures for diseases.

I say the same thing about God. If he created the world

like they say he did, surely he can put a stop to some of the bad things that go on.

People believe that he can.

It ticks me off that he doesn't.

At the salon there's always talk about religion going on. I mostly listen. What I hear is that people pray for all kinds of things. They pray that their team will win, that their grandma will get well, that they'll be able to pay their bills. They pray that their daughters won't get pregnant and that their sons will be able to stay off drugs. Old Bradley says he prays to win the lottery.

He would.

Kari's had two weeks of radiation. She hasn't had to go back to the hospital but man, has it ever knocked her on her butt.

"You want me to bring you something to eat?" I've called before heading out to her house. "Sonic? Chinese? Mexican? What sounds good?" She's not been eating. Nothing tastes good. She's really weak. Her hands shake when she tries to hold anything. Her hair has started to come out in certain places, I guess where they aim that radiation gun.

"Maybe some fried rice. Chicken," she says. "A half order. You sure you don't mind?"

Dumb question.

I call ahead to Golden China. Order Colton and me some shrimp egg rolls. Kari some rice. Hopefully she'll eat better tonight than last night. She took only a half cup of Jill's homemade potato soup before she said she couldn't handle any more and pushed it away.

Kari's plans of keeping Colton on her regular days haven't

worked out. She's too weak to take care of him. Which means I've got him-full time. It's been a change but we've got us a routine. He goes to day care. I pick him up when I get off. We go over to Kari's house so she can see him. Since it's dinnertime and Colton's always starving when I pick him up, unless she tells me somebody's brought something over, I pick up food for the three of us and we eat together. Sometimes it's just us, sometimes other people are there. Jill. Casey's wife, Darla. Friends of hers from the hospital. Nick.

I deal with it. I keep my distance and I keep my mouth shut around him because I don't exactly have any kind of choice. I hate it that he kisses her good-bye in front of me. I hate it that he's the one who knows where in her kitchen Kari keeps the salt. I don't like it when I get there and he's left the toilet seat up in the bathroom, something Kari hates and I never do.

Seeing him gives me grief but I never forget what I've got on him. Colton. That's not going to change no matter what happens between him and Kari. I'm Colton's dad. Forever and always I'm going to be in her life. Me and Kari made a child together. He's ours. Not just mine. Not just hers. Ours together.

You hear that, Nick?

Ours together.

You've got no part in that.

Kari says seeing Colton every day does her more good than all the radiation and medicine in the world. She says even though she feels rotten she can tell she's getting better. She says the worse the radiation makes her feel the better she figures it's working. I believe it.

Kari told me about a dream she had the other night. She was an old lady with gray hair, wearing a lime green dress and orange rain boots. She was playing the guitar, singing in a country band.

Pretty crazy if you ask me. Kari hates country. But she took it as a good sign. A sign that she was going to live to be really old.

Works for me.

I'll take any sign I can get that the mother of my child is going to be all right.

When we get to her house with the Chinese food, Colton gives Kari a hug like he always does. He shows her the coloring he did at school and the boo-boo he's got on his knee.

"Let me kiss it. Make it better," Kari says. She's on the couch.

Colton doesn't have time to spare. They must have given the kids cookies right before I picked him up because soon as she's kissed him he runs off. There's a basket of his toys over by the TV. He dumps it out and they scatter all over the place. As soon as he finds a truck he's on all fours, making truck sounds, driving it into the furniture.

"Colton, let's eat," Kari says. "Then you can play." She starts to get up. It looks like she doesn't feel like moving at all.

"Stay put," I tell her.

Kari looks worse today than yesterday. There's dark circles under her eyes.

"You care if we eat in here?" I ask. Kari's carpet is light tan. Her furniture is new.

"No. Go ahead." She leans back against back of the couch. Looks like she's glad I told her not to get up. But not like she's hungry.

I cut Colton's egg rolls into little bites and set him up on the coffee table with a sippy cup of milk. I get a towel from the bathroom and spread it out under him. Then I bring Kari a plate of her rice and a glass of iced tea.

I'm starving so I dig in.

She nods. Pushes some rice around on her plate. Takes one bite.

"Headache?" I'm on my second egg roll.

"No."

"Something happen today?" I know asking may shut her down but I can't help it. Something's wrong. Something other than me. "You hear from the bank?"

"Uh-huh."

I knew it.

"When do you have to be out?"

"Soon."

"Where you planning on going?"

"I don't exactly know."

"Not that I think it's a good idea or anything, but I thought you might move in with Nick." I try to sound neutral about this. I'm not. But it comes off pretty good.

"Not happening," she says. "He and I decided to take a break."

"Really." I chew on my egg roll. "I'm surprised. Thought you guys were tight. When this happen?" You have no idea how hard it is for me not to yell *Yes!* and punch the air with my fist.

"Today."

"I guess I should say I'm sorry," I say.

"Thanks. Try real hard not to get too upset." I can't tell if it's me or Nick she's hacked off at. Probably me.

I get up to get Colton more milk.

I think Kari should give me a little bit of credit.

I do smile.

But at least I don't skip.

Brooke and Sean's divorce is final. From what he hears from the people at his church, she and that other guy have already gotten married. He says at the divorce hearing, which was last week, Brooke was already big pregnant. His attorney was right. Because of Sean's history, she got Allyssa. The judge didn't take into account all the meetings he goes to, how he hasn't slipped up once in the past year and a half. All he saw was the drunk driving arrest and that time Sean got tagged for public intoxication.

After the hearing, Sean went to the house to tell Allyssa bye. Brooke told him it was okay. While he was there, right before he left, Sean went into the bathroom. When he came out, he heard Brooke talking to Allyssa about how she was getting a new baby brother.

"Hearing her say that, I felt like somebody kicked me in the teeth," Sean told me.

With his work schedule and Allyssa being four hours away he's only going to get to see her about one weekend a month.

If he's lucky and his schedule at work doesn't change.

Think about it. One day you're worrying about getting your daughter up, dressed, and to day care in the mornings, home, bathed, and to bed every night. You're wiping her nose. Picking up her toys. Trying to fix her hair. Every minute you're worrying about how you're going manage to work and take care of your daughter, too.

Then because some judge decides, it's all over.

Just like that.

And now Sean goes home to an empty house. He's got all this time on his hands. He doesn't know what to do with himself. It's no wonder most nights when Colton and I get back from Kari's he's pulling up in the driveway right behind us. Just wanting to hang out. Not wanting to be at his house by himself.

Seeing how bad Sean's hurting makes me think even more about how I screwed up my life. How I hurt Kari. What a stupid jerk I was. Not that our situations are the same. They're not. In my book what Brooke did is way worse than what I did. At least I was sorry. And ashamed. Brooke's acted all along like she was proud and glad about the whole thing.

You know what's weird? Brooke wanted to be free. I wanted to be forgiven.

What happened is things got switched around.

I got what Brooke wanted.

She got what I wanted.

Kari set me free.

Sean forgave Brooke.

After what she did to him. After all the hurt she's caused him. I do not see how. Or even why.

When Sean told me he'd forgiven Brooke I didn't believe him at first. Honestly, I'm still not sure I do. I've got a feeling Kari wanted to kill me when she found out about me and Leslie. Sometimes I wonder if it would have been better if she'd gone on and done it. Put me out of my misery like a dog that's gotten hit by a car and is too broken up to be fixed.

Me and Sean were sitting on my back stoop last night. "You ever want to kill Brooke for what she did to you?"

It took him a minute. "I did at first. I don't now."

"Just so you know," I said, "I want to kill both of them for you."

"Not necessary." Sean smiles. "But I appreciate the thought."

I flicked ashes from my cigarette into the dirt beside the step.

"I'm letting this thing go," said Sean. "Not holding on to it. It's too big. I made a decision. I decided to forgive them."

"You decided," I said. He was not making any sense.

"Yep. Don't get me wrong. It still hurts. Sometimes I can't believe what's happened. I wake up in the morning and for a second I forget I'm not married anymore and my little girl is gone. About twenty times a day I wonder how I'm going to make it. If it wasn't for Allyssa I'm not sure I could. It tears me up inside to think about her calling that sucker 'Daddy.' To realize he's the one's going to raise her instead of me. I hate it. But one thing I know. I'm not the judge of them. Only of me."

"You're crazy. They don't deserve your forgiveness. Either one of them said they were sorry?"

Sean shook his head.

"So what are you doing? You're letting them off the hook and they don't deserve it."

"That's right."

"Trying to do for them what God's done for me."

"Whatever, man." Then I leaned over and spit.

chapter nineteen

TODAY'S FRIDAY. KARI AND I are on our way home from her radiation appointment. Colton's over at Casey's house, playing with his boys.

We've got two more weeks of treatments to go. Kari's trying to hang on but the side effects are terrible. You'd think the doctors could do something about it. I guess they try but they say you pretty much have to go through it. She's got Vicodin for her headaches. Dilantin to keep her from having seizures. Not much you can do for her being so tired all the time. I guess the radiation takes a lot out of you. Which makes sense. Something strong enough to kill a tumor, I guess it would knock the rest of you back some, too.

You should see how much weight Kari's lost. Her clothes hang on her. They've got her taking vitamins and the nutritionist Kari saw says it's important she get plenty of protein. I bought her some Ensure. They say that's full of protein, but Kari took one sip and hated it. She said they make old people at the hospital drink it. I didn't buy any more.

Three days ago Kari fell on her way to the bathroom. When I got to her house after work her wrist was all swollen up. I was afraid she'd broken it but it turned out to be a sprain. I don't think she should be staying by herself but Kari says she's okay and that it is not my call to make. Her weight's down to a hundred and four because she's hardly eating anything. If she smells anything too strong, she throws up. She keeps a plastic trash can with her all the time. One of her medicines, Zofran, is supposed to help but I can't see that it does that much good. Loud noises bother her. A lot of her hair's gone.

I'm doing everything I can to help Kari out. Everything she'll let me do.

As long as I'm careful about what I say, things go fairly okay with me and her. Not because anything's changed. Well, Nick being out of the picture is a big deal. But mostly we're getting along so good because Kari's too tired to push me away. I've spent more time with her this last month than all of the past two years. I'm over at her house every day. Always careful to play things low key. To be a good friend. Somebody Kari can count on. Even though I've wanted to I haven't pushed her for anything more than a friendship. I'm afraid if I make one wrong move, if she starts feeling like I'm trying to get too close, she'll close down on me. Shut me out.

After everything that's happened, it could happen.

"You okay?"

Kari's looking pretty green.

I turn down her street then pull into her drive and turn off the truck. While Kari fumbles around in her purse for her house key, I go around and open the door for her. She slides out of the truck. I know from experience she's trying not to throw up until she gets inside. Puking in the front yard isn't something anybody wants to do.

When we get to her front door, she hands me her house key, holds on to the door frame, and takes some slow breaths. She's real pale and there's sweat on her upper lip. "Could you . . ."

"Sure." I take the keys, unlock her front door, and stand aside so she can go in.

I'm wondering, like I do so many days, do I get to stay for a while or does Kari expect me to leave her like this?

Because Kari is so moody, I feel like a yo-yo a lot of the time. Even though I'm being real careful, it's hard to tell what I'm walking into until I step where I shouldn't. There's days she acts like she's glad I'm around. Like she's happy to see me. But the other times I feel like she'd like to get rid of me but she can't because I'm the one who brings Colton to see her. Some days she tells me what she's feeling inside. She opens up. We talk about her being sick. How it's changed her life and made her think about what's really important. About what she wants to do differently when she gets well. But then another day I might say something like "How's it going?" She'll look at me like I asked her the most personal question in the world and clam up tight.

I guess today is my lucky day because Kari motions for me to come in. Soon as I do, she bolts for the bathroom. I can hear her heaving.

After a bit I go and talk to her through the door. "You okay?"

No answer.

"Kari?"

I hear a flush. Then the sound of her brushing her teeth. I move from the door, go and sit down in her living room.

Finally, Kari comes out. She's wiping her face with a wet washrag. "I'm okay. Nausea's a little better. But the couch is calling my name." She heads that way.

I don't understand how something as awful as throwing up can make you feel better, but somehow it does. A couple of Colton's toys and a magazine are on the couch. I move them so she can lay down. "Can I get you something? Maybe some crackers? You want some soup?"

"Sprite. Do you mind? There's a bottle in the door."

I bring her the Sprite.

She takes a few sips, then sits up and puts her feet on the floor.

She's starting to look a little bit better.

She sips some more. "I have to be out of this house by Monday."

This is not news to me. I've been counting down the days, wondering but not asking what she was going to do.

"Couple of friends told me I could move in with them, but no place actually worked out."

I'm not surprised. People mean well when they offer to help out but who actually has that kind of extra room? When you've got kids and a job, two or three dogs or a cat, and no telling what else, taking in somebody you're not related to is not an easy thing to do.

"I don't know how to ask you this," she looks out the window instead of at me, "I know you offered but maybe you've changed your mind."

She's stalling. Not wanting to say what I've hoped for all along.

"Would it still be okay if I came and stayed at the house until I get back on my feet?"

Would it? Well, yeah. *This couldn't be working out any better* is what I'm thinking, but nowhere near what I say.

"Sure. Whatever. That'd be okay." I've got to play it cool. This is hard for her, I know.

"It wouldn't be for long," Kari says.

"Of course not. Just 'til you get to feeling better."

"Until I can go back to work. Get my own place again. I figure a couple of months at the most."

"Sure," I say. "Whatever. Stay as long as you need to. There's that extra bedroom. The one you had as your office. I'll get you a key."

"Just so you know. This isn't something I planned on doing." She's got a wadded up Kleenex in her hand.

"I know."

"I never thought I'd be asking you, of all people, to give me a place to stay."

"Don't worry. It'll be okay. We'll make it work." Her words hurt but not any more than I deserve. I get up and go get her some more Sprite.

"Joel. You do understand—"

She's talking to me while I'm dropping ice in her glass.

"—me moving back in doesn't change anything. We have to make sure Colton doesn't get the wrong idea. I don't want him getting confused, thinking we're all together permanently."

"He won't," I say even though I'm pretty sure he will. "I'll tell him you're just staying for a little while. It'll be okay. We can make this work. Really. No big deal. You sure you don't want me to fix you some soup?"

When I get home, I call up Abe and tell him the news. He knows what this means to me.

"That's good, man," he says. "Real good. I'm happy for you."

I pace around my house thinking about what it'll be like having my wife here again. I'm trying not to hold out hope but it's hard. I never thought Kari and I would be living together again under the same roof. I hate it's because she's sick, but I'm so happy she's moving in with me I don't know what to do. I figure I've got this little window of opportunity to show her how much I've changed. To show her how good it could be. The three of us together again. I know it's a slim, slim chance anything will happen. I shouldn't have my hopes up but I can't help it even though Kari's made it plain as anything that her moving back doesn't mean anything's changed between her and me.

All I can say is we'll see.

The next day I'm over to Kari's house by ten. There's stuff she needs help with. Even though I'm off, I took Colton to day care. Thankfully they're open on Saturdays.

This is a hard day for Kari. Harder than I expected. She's cried off and on since I got here about having to move. Right now we're walking from room to room. Slowly. With her leaning against the walls. Holding on to the door frames. And me fighting myself not to grab hold of her and carry her in my arms so she doesn't get so worn out.

This may be hard to believe but after all the time I've spent over here since she got sick, this is the first time I've seen all of Kari's house. It's not too big, but a nice size. I'm guessing fifteen, sixteen hundred square feet. One of those open floor plans. Most everything's done in beige and brown, some light blue. Three bedrooms. Two baths. A little deck off the back. Nice place. A lot nicer than mine. No wonder she doesn't want to lose it.

"Leaving feels like I'm giving up. Giving in. And I hate it," Kari says. Her voice is small. It's almost like she's forgotten it's me in the room with her. Like she's mostly talking to herself. She wipes her nose on a tissue she's got in her hand. Her voice is almost a whisper. "This house was my fresh start."

I nod. A fresh start after our divorce. Some place to go to forget about me.

"It was supposed to be the beginning of the rest of my life."

I can't say anything. I shouldn't be hearing this. I wish I wasn't. It brings it all back.

"Leaving feels like I'm losing more than a house. It feels like I'm going backwards. Back to someplace I didn't ever want to go back to."

I can't tell you how bad Kari's words cut. I realize now how hard it is for her to decide to come live with me. Why she took so long. I'm the past she wants to forget. I'm the past that nearly did her in. I can't blame her but I want to tell her she's not coming back to the same thing. That I'm different now. Smarter. Less self-ish. That I'm now somebody she can trust one hundred percent. I want to say all those things but I don't. What if I'm wrong? What if I'm no different at all? What if I'm still the same jerk I was?

I'm glad when we get to her bedroom and Kari kind of snaps out of it. She starts in showing me what she wants me and Abe to put in storage, what she wants to bring with her to my house. Her clothes she wants moved. Her dresser. Her nightstand. We're moving her stuff tomorrow, right after Colton and me get back from going to Abe's church. We've gone the past three Sundays. It doesn't get out 'til nearly one, but that should still give us enough time.

"That's about all," she says. We're back in the living room. She's stretched back out on the couch. "It's not like I'm going to be there all that long. Six weeks, I figure. Two months tops," she says. "Once I'm back on my feet I'll be able to get a little apart-ment. Which will be fine. This house is too big for me and Colton anyway."

We haven't talked about what if the radiation doesn't work. Not one time. We don't discuss how bad the kind of cancer she's got is. How hardly anybody makes it. It's not that we don't know the facts. Kari's a nurse. She knows. I've read about glioblastomas on the Internet. Anything you ask me I could probably tell you. None of it good. But every day me and Kari only talk about what we'll do when she gets well. Because she is going to get well. We're not believing anything else. They say there's power in positive thinking. If that's true then between the two of us we ought to have enough power to run all the lights in my neighborhood for about the next ten years.

"Whatever you want," I say. I have to hide how glad I am she's moving in. All I want is to be with her. To spend time with her. To take care of her. "Colton's excited," I say. "When I was clearing out your room last night, he kept talking about how you were going to be sleeping at his house. You should check your bed before you crawl in. I think he put some toys under the blanket so you'd have something to play with. I saw two army men and a water gun. No telling what else."

"Was the water gun loaded?" Kari asks.

"Not if you're lucky."

"Be great seeing him all the time," she says. "But we have to be careful. This could confuse him. We'll have to make sure he understands that pretty soon I'll be moving somewhere else and things will go back to how they were before."

We've been over this before, but I can feel she needs to say it again. "Right," I say. "Sure. We don't want to confuse him."

Normally I don't cry. Most guys don't. Before Kari and I broke up, I honestly can't remember when I'd last shed a tear. But ever since all that, I'm a regular bawl baby. It doesn't take anything to get me started. All the women's magazines say crying is healthy. That you should do it. That people should not hold stuff back. All that is well and good if you're a woman, but if you're a guy, not controlling your emotions is embarrassing. People either look at you funny or they try not to look at you at all.

Every time I've gone to Abe's church, something has made me cry. I don't know why I keep on going but I do.

The first Sunday it was an old woman who told everybody what the Lord had done for her. She had to have been at least eighty years old. A little lady. I'm not sure even five feet tall. Shiny blue dress. Black skin. Gray hair pulled back into a bun. Holding on to a metal walker with green tennis balls stuck on the legs. Her ankles were swollen and you could see she had on knee-high stockings under her dress.

It took her forever but she came down to the front and told how God gave her comfort. How she knew he had a great reward waiting for her in heaven. All her life she'd had to work hard. Buried her husband and two of her kids already. She had one granddaughter in prison, one that was on dope. She had diabetes and congestive heart failure. The city had just condemned her little house and her kids were about to put her in a home. In spite of all that, life was good, but not nearly as good as what she said was coming after death. That was going to be even better.

Then she sat down.

And the pastor stood up. The guy's last name is Roberts. He wiped his eyes, cleared his throat a couple of times, and said the Bible says heaven is going to be wonderful for everybody who makes it there. More wonderful than we can imagine. But he said for the folks who've had the least and lost the most here on earth he personally believed for them it might be a little bit sweeter than for the rest of us.

At least that was how he saw it.

When church was over that day, I passed by the old woman

in the lobby of the church on my way out. Or I tried to pass her. Even though there were about ten people gathered in a circle around her, talking to her and hugging her neck, I didn't make it out the door. Somehow she saw me. I guess a six-foot-plus white guy in a mostly black church is hard to miss. She didn't call my name but I heard her tell one of the people standing beside her that she wanted to speak to me. When I came closer, she reached out, took hold of my hand, and pulled me to her. Her fingers were crooked and swollen, eaten up with arthritis.

Somebody must have told her. About Kari. About me. Because she motioned for me to bend down. When I did, her breath smelled like honey-lemon cough drops. She looked me straight in the face with eyes that were yellow where they're supposed to be white and said, "God is with you, young man. He's set His heart on you. You be on the lookout for Him. You hear what I'm saying?"

"Yes, ma'am," I said.

She squeezed my hand tighter than you would think an old woman could. "You look. You'll see Him. Sure as you're seeing me. But you got to look."

"I will," I said. She still didn't let me go so I just stood there, feeling like everybody was looking at me. Waiting for her to let go of my hand. Wanting to get in my truck and go home. She was freaking me out just a little but I couldn't move away.

So I coughed. Several times.

And she let go. With one hand at least. I thought now I was going to get to make my escape. But no. We weren't done yet. The woman reached into her pocket—I thought to get me a cough drop, but I was wrong. She pulled out two ragged dollar bills, folded them in half, and then put them in my hand.

I started to say no, but by then Abe was standing right by me.

I don't know where he came from because I'd sat at the back so I could get out quick. He and Jill had been up at the front. "Take it," he said in my ear. "Don't give it back to her. She wants you to have it. You have to take it."

So I did.

I told the woman thank you. Felt her dry lips on my cheek.

Then went and got in my truck.

And bawled all the way home.

chapter twenty

WE GET TEN DAYS OF VACATION every year. Even though it was short notice, Mrs. Chan's letting me take mine right now.

Kari's been living with me and Colton for nearly three weeks. I haven't been able to leave her alone at all for about the past week. She sleeps about fifteen hours a day but she has to get up real often to go to the bathroom and she can't get there without help. Part of the problem is she's gotten weak on her left side. Her arm and her leg. She drops stuff.

And for some reason she doesn't pick her feet up like she should. I remind her to but it's like there's this disconnect between her brain and her legs. She stumbles sometimes. I've taken up all the throw rugs in the house because they make her trip. The house feels drafty and loud without them but Colton thinks not having rugs is way cool. With hardwood floors everywhere except the kitchen and the bathroom, he can slide all over the place in his socks. He's got this pink towel he calls his cape. Every night I have to pin it on him so he can be Superman and fly around the house.

All the time I'm after him to pick up his stuff. To not leave his toys on the floor. He doesn't understand because I've never been all that good a housekeeper before. Thing is, I don't want Kari falling, maybe next time breaking something, because of some stupid plastic truck that I didn't see.

When I told Sean that Kari was having a hard time in the bathroom, that I was worried about her slipping, he brought over a plastic stool to put in the shower so she could sit down and some grab bars so she'd have something to hold onto when she got out. I never knew it but you can get that kind of stuff at Sears. I'm not very handy. I was afraid if I tried to put those bars up they'd fall down the first time Kari pulled on them. How are you supposed to find the studs in the wall just by banging and listening? I never have figured that one out. But Sean told me not to worry about it. He had his drill with him so he put them up.

Kari says they're a big help. Since no matter how weak she is, she still locks the bathroom door every time she goes in, I wouldn't know. I don't mention it, but while she's in the shower, I'm mostly standing and listening at the door hoping she doesn't fall and hurt herself.

If she does?

I've got a key.

Colton is loving being with Kari all the time. The two of them watch TV together in the mornings. *Rachael Ray. Dora the Explorer.* Sometimes Kari talks him into *The View.* She reads him books when she's awake. Every night she gets to kiss him good-night. And no matter how bad she's feeling or how tired she is Kari has to tuck Colton into bed and listen to his prayers before she'll go get in her own bed.

I never knew it, but when Colton was at Kari's house she taught him to pray. Guess it was their little routine, one that I get to be in on now. Kari sits on the bed. I stand in the door and listen. Colton's prayers are pretty cute.

Tonight he's wearing a Spider-Man pajama top. SpongeBob bottoms. Still got on his cape even though I've told him he can't be flying in his sleep. There's about forty-seven stuffed animals in bed with him. A couple of trucks, too.

"You ready?" Kari asks.

Not quite. Before he can go to sleep Colton has to fix his covers just right. He likes one foot under the blanket and one foot out. Just like me. Finally he's ready. He squeezes his eyes shut and folds his hands over his tummy. I never have understood why when you pray you're supposed to close your eyes but I guess you are because that's what Kari's taught him to do.

"Thank you, God, for the milk and the water and the nice baby rabbits," he says. Then he closes by whispering "Amen."

It's hard not to laugh. Where he came up with that one, I don't know. He had apple juice for dinner because we were out of milk. We have to make him drink water. He hates it. And there are no rabbits I know of anywhere around this time of year.

"When did he start saying prayers?" I ask Kari after he's settled in and she and I are back in the living room.

"I don't know. Awhile back."

"You teach him?" I get up and put an Alicia Keys CD on. One Kari likes.

"Yeah. My mom taught me to say bedtime prayers when I was little."

"You ever pray now?"

"Sometimes."

"You start when you got sick?" That would make logical sense.

"No. Before that. Actually off and on for as long as I can remember. Not every day or anything. Just sometimes. When I feel like I need to. Mostly when things aren't going so good. Honestly? Probably more in the past three years than the rest of my life combined."

I never knew.

I haven't taken Colton to day care at all. Since I've been on vacation, what was the point? It's been the three of us at home together. Which has been good, but with Kari feeling so bad, not like I expected it to be. Not normal, if you know what I mean. There's a lot to do when you're taking care of a child and a sick person, too.

People have asked what they can do to help out. So far, I've done pretty much everything by myself. But what with me having to go back to work, that's going to change. I'm not sure how I'll manage. Figure it out one day at a time is all I know to do.

Since she's feeling so bad, most all Kari wants to do is sleep. She sure does not feel like being up and getting out. But she has to because of the treatments twice a day. At first she tried to get dressed and put on her makeup. We got past that real quick. Now she just wears sweats or pajama pants, whichever she's slept in, house shoes, and a T-shirt. Not even a bra. Lots of times we're running late and Colton and me end up wearing about the same thing as her. We look pretty much like a family of homeless people. Not that it matters. Most everybody who uses the clinic has got some kind of cancer. They don't care what you look like.

Kari's got to where she has a hard time walking from the parking lot into the clinic, so I pull the truck up as close to the door as I can. Then I call inside on my cell and one of the nurses comes out with a wheelchair and helps her in while Colton and I go park. The treatments don't take all that long. It's the getting her and me and Colton ready and up there and then back home that takes up so much time.

I can't tell you how glad I'll be when these treatments are over. I'm counting the days until all the radiation gets out of her system.

Not just so Kari'll get to feeling better but because that's when they'll do another scan. We'll find out how much good it's all done. My bet is that tumor will be gone.

❧

"How's Kari?" Alice asks. She's in for a haircut.

"Not so good." While I'm shampooing her I tell Alice how it's been.

"I never knew radiation could make you that sick," Alice says. "When's her last treatment?"

"Friday," I say. Today is Monday. I've used up all my vacation time. One week from now is when they'll do the follow-up scan that will give us the news we've been waiting for.

"Maybe she'll get to feeling better when it's over," Alice says.

"She should. But not right at first. They say the effects usually last for about two weeks after the treatment's stopped." I put conditioner on her ends.

"Joel, you've got a lot on you," Alice says. "How are you managing to take care of Kari and Colton and work too?"

"Not easy. One day at time." I look at my watch, something I've started doing about a hundred times a day. "Soon as I'm done with you, I've got to go get her and take her in for her afternoon treatment. One of her friends, Darla, is staying with her this morning but she's got to leave right when I get there so she can go to work. Another one of her friends from the hospital is coming over to stay this afternoon but she can't be there until three. Which means Kari's going to be by herself for a couple of hours. That's not good but she's got her phone with her. Hopefully she'll sleep. She has to take some pills right at two so I've got to remember to call and remind her. Her memory is not so great right now, not to mention she'll probably fall asleep and not remember she's supposed to take meds."

I look at my watch again. "Since I'll miss an hour to carry her for her treatment, I have to work an extra hour this evening to make up my time off. Mrs. Chan's great letting me take off, but she only pays me when I work and I need to get in my hours."

"What about Colton?"

"He's back in day care. Abe's wife, Jill, is picking him up. She'll stay with both of them 'til I can get home."

"What a schedule," Alice says.

"Yep." It is what it is. I don't want Alice or anybody else feeling sorry for me.

"How are you keeping up with so many details?" Alice asks.

"Bought one of those big white calendars," I tell her. "The kind you can wipe off. Hung it up in the hall. I'm writing it down as I figure things out."

"You look like you've lost weight," Alice says.

I tug on my jeans. "Maybe."

"You're taking care of Kari and Colton. Cooking. Doing laundry. Working. Who's taking care of you?"

I shrug her off. "I'm a low-maintenance guy."

"Are you sleeping?"

"Some."

"How much are you smoking?"

"Too much. Have I got this rinse water too hot?" I don't like discussing my smoking with Alice. I know it's a bad habit but no, I'm not planning on quitting anytime soon.

Alice does not take the hint, but what she says surprises me. "Nicotine calms you down," she says. "I understand."

"You don't smoke."

"Not anymore. Quit a long time ago. But I remember what it's like to be doing more than what you can do. When my dad was sick and I took care of him for six months, I got up to over a pack a day. Cigarettes were my best friends. No way I was going to give them up. Only time I gave myself permission to sit down and not do anything was when I was with them."

"You got it."

"Someday you'll probably quit," Alice says.

"Maybe."

"Now's not the time, though. Take it from me. You don't need to be going through nicotine withdrawal when you're under so much stress."

This from Alice? I set her up. Pat her hair with a towel.

"Sounds like you haven't been leaving Kari alone at all."

"Not much. Not if I can help it. Wish I could take care of her twenty-four seven. Which is what I've been doing the past two weeks, but I can't afford to lose my job. I've got bills. And it's not just me. I've got to think about Colton. And Kari too, now she's at the house."

All of a sudden it hits me that I've been complaining since Alice sat down. I didn't mean to tell her so much. First rule a stylist should know: Focus on the customer. Not on yourself. People come to a salon to be pampered. Not to hear about somebody else's problems.

So I change the subject. "How's Pancho?"

"He's okay."

"How much you want me to take off your sides?"

"Whatever you think."

When I'm done blowing her out, Alice pays. Tips me five. I head home to pick up Kari so I can take her for her treatment. It's while I'm in the waiting room that Alice calls me on my cell. She must have got my number from somebody at the salon. I'm kind of funny who I give my cell number out to. People calling you can run up your bill. All I can figure is she forgot to sign her check or something. I don't remember if I looked.

"Alice? What's up?"

"Joel," she says, "can you talk? Good. Now hear me out. Don't say no right off. Here's the deal. I'm on winter break so I'm free all week. I'd like to help you out. I want to come over and take care of Kari and Colton these next few days."

Alice has never been to my house. We aren't even really friends. Not like that. We don't exactly have the same interests. The same lifestyle. The same anything. Our only real connection is me doing her hair. "Alice. That's real sweet of you but I couldn't let you do that."

"Why not?"

"You've got your own stuff to do."

"Not this week. I don't have one thing planned. Soon as I left the salon I came home and talked it over with Rich. It's fine with him. I could stay with Kari and Colton while you're at work. He won't need to go to day care. I can take her to her treatments. Do whatever you need me to do."

What should I say? Alice has caught me off guard. I've never seen her outside the salon. Never. I've never even run into her in the grocery store or Wal-Mart. Not one single time in five years.

"Think about it, Joel. I'd like to do this for you. Really. I would."

"Alice. I appreciate the offer, but—"

"Who've you got lined up for tomorrow?"

"I'm not sure."

"That's what I thought. You don't have anybody."

"Not yet."

"Then save yourself the trouble of finding someone. Let it be me."

Alice thinks she knows me.

But she doesn't.

Not like she thinks she does. Because if she did, she would not be offering to do something so nice.

"Okay?" she says.

Tell me. What am I supposed to say? I do need the help. I'm just not sure I want it to come from a customer who happens to be a forty-something-year-old church lady. Her coming to my house feels weird.

"I know I can work something out for tomorrow. It's just I haven't had time to call anybody yet."

"Forget finding somebody else. You live over on Meadow Lane. Right? What's the number?"

"Four Twelve."

"You go to work at ten. How about I come over about nine thirty? Give you time to show me where everything is. That sound like a plan?"

I guess.

Alice has got it all figured out.

chapter twenty-one

TUESDAY MORNING, I GET up a little early so I can pick up the house before Alice gets here. I'm putting last night's dishes into the dishwasher when Colton comes into the kitchen. He's not good awake, but he's crying.

"What's the matter, buddy?" I pick him up. From the feel of his soggy bottom against the sleeve of my clean shirt I figure out the problem. He's wet the bed. Great. "It's okay. It's all right." Colton tucks his face into my chest. I get him some juice. "Come on. Let's get you cleaned up."

I run a little water and put him in the tub. I know you shouldn't leave a kid in the bathtub alone but I do. For about two seconds. Only long enough to strip his bed and chuck the sheets, the mattress pad, and his bedspread into the washer.

By the time Colton gets out and I get him dressed, he's starving. We go to the kitchen. I lift him up so he can sit on the counter next to the sink. He loves it when I let him up there where he can see. I get out bowls for cereal. Then I realize we're out of milk. Again. "How about biscuits?" I ask him. He says okay but he's real hungry now. Me too. I'm not sure we can wait the eight to ten minutes it'll take for those things to get done. Good thing we've got Fig Newtons. Practically health food. I get one out for him. One for me. Then I whack the cold can on the counter, peel off the greasy wrapper, and put the biscuits on a cookie sheet. You're supposed to preheat the oven before you put them in, but I don't have time for that. Hopefully the bottoms won't burn before the tops get done. Do we have any jelly? I think so.

I've got my head in the fridge looking for the butter when I hear Kari calling me to come in her room. I get Colton down, set him in front of the TV with his cookie and his juice. Kari's trying not to cry, but she's woken up with one of her bad headaches, the kind where she gets nauseated, too. She hates throwing up. I get a wet cloth to put on her head and turn on the ceiling fan, which usually helps. When I go to get her a Vicodin, I see she's down to one left, which is not going to be enough to get her through the day.

Only a small problem. The pharmacy delivers. But when I try to call in a refill, the girl there says there's none left. She'll have to fax the doctor but it will be this afternoon before she does.

"No. That won't work. You have to call him now. My wife needs her pills now." Okay. She's not my wife. What am I supposed to say? My friend? My ex? I need action and who's going to pay attention to that?

"Sorry, sir. I'm not authorized to do that."

Great. Thanks for nothing.

I'll call the doctor myself.

I go back into Kari's room. I don't tell her about the problem with the pharmacy or about Colton wetting the bed or about us being out of milk. She does not need to know any of that. "You feeling any better?"

She's lying very still. "Maybe a little. Colton okay?"

"Yeah. He's watching cartoons. You remember Alice is coming over this morning. She'll be here pretty soon." I look at my watch.

"Yeah. I should get dressed," Kari says. She sits up, puts her feet on the floor. She's holding her head.

"No. Lay back down. I'll call her. Tell her not to come today. I'll stay home."

"I thought you couldn't miss any more work." Kari's talking with her eyes closed against the light coming in through the mini blinds because looking at it always makes her headaches worse.

I can't. But that's not what I say. I don't know what to do. All I know is that agreeing to let Alice come over was not a good idea. It's not right leaving Kari and Colton with somebody they've only met once or twice. Especially when Kari's started off with a not-so-good day.

"I'll work something out," I say. I don't know what.

Kari hands me my phone. "It was on the nightstand. You left it in here last night."

But before I can punch in Alice's number, the washing machine starts to buzz. Which it does nearly every time I do a load of sheets or towels. "You have to distribute the clothes all around the center so it doesn't get off-balance," Kari says. She's told me this about six dozen times. Okay. Maybe not six dozen. But enough times I don't need her telling me again.

"I know," I say. I head to the laundry closet. But I don't make it before Kari starts gagging, then throwing up, so I go back to her room. I'm getting used to the smell of vomit. I hold the trash can for her. Usually she hits it. This time she misses.

Which means I pretty much forget all about calling Alice.

Until I hear her knocking on the front door.

"What do you mean you've changed your mind?" Alice says she's not leaving. She's staying. And yes, I am to going to work.

She takes the biscuits out of the oven and feeds Colton his breakfast while I clean up the puke. After that I show her Kari's medicine and where everything is. She tells me not to worry about getting the Vicodin refilled. She knows one of the ladies who works at the doctor's office. Somebody who's got pull.

"Joel. I can handle this. If I have problems with anything, I'll give you a call. Now go to work. We'll be fine. Really. Now go."

By the time I get to the salon, I'm only an hour late.

"I like Alice," Kari says when I get home at the end of my work day. She's propped up on the couch, looking pretty good compared to how she was when I left her this morning. She has on lip gloss. Mascara. For the first time in forever.

"How long's she been gone?"

"Twenty minutes. She left right after you called to tell me you were on your way home."

"And it went okay? Was she pushy? She try to tell you what to do?" I'd been afraid she might.

"Not really. She pretty much took over, but not in a bad way. And she was really good with Colton. He loved her. Except he can't say her name."

"What did he call her?"

"Sally." She smiles.

I head to the bathroom. Sally. When I get out, I go into Colton's room. He's already asleep. I lean down to kiss him goodnight. From the smell of his hair, I can tell it's been washed.

"You put the sheets on his bed?" I ask Kari.

"Alice did. She changed our beds, too."

I hadn't intended for her to do all that.

"There's a pot of soup on the stove," Kari says. She's filing her nails. "And cornbread wrapped up in some foil. Soup's good. One of Alice's friends from her church made it and brought it over late this afternoon. Some kind of Italian. It's got spinach and meatballs and parmesan cheese."

I fix me a bowl and some iced tea and carry it into the living room so I can talk to Kari while I eat. She's right. The soup is good. So's the cornbread. "Alice got you to your treatments okay?"

"No problem."

"You get some rest in between?"

"I did. I guess it was while I was asleep on the couch she changed the sheets. I think she mopped the kitchen floor, too. She says she's coming back tomorrow."

"You're okay with that?" I ask. I'm glad it went so well. A little surprised. But mostly glad.

Today's Friday.

Kari's last day of radiation.

One of our busiest days at the salon.

I'm sweeping up. My next customer's already here. Abe and I have neither one stopped since we got to work this morning. We were booked before we started. Then there've been some walk-ins we've worked in even though we really didn't have the time. Lunch was in the break room. Scarfed down chicken burritos. Mrs. Chan's treat. They're good even cold. Tonight won't neither one of us get off until nine. But for once, I'm not worried about how Kari and Colton are doing. I've figured out they're in good hands. Alice is staying 'til I get home. Rich is out of town. She said it wasn't any problem at all.

"So," Abe says. He's doing a color job. "Alice been at your house all week. How's that going?" He's been off the past couple of days. Sick with bronchitis. We haven't had a chance to talk.

"Been good. It's not just Alice, though. Her and a bunch of her friends. A whole herd of church ladies has taken over my house. You would not believe all they've done. One of her friends is a massage therapist. She came over yesterday and gave Kari an hour-and-a-half massage. You know how much that would cost at a spa? She did it for free. One of her other friends is a manicurist. She gave Kari a pedicure. Colton, too."

Abe stops what he's doing to blow his nose. He cleans his hands with some of that alcohol stuff you don't have to wash off, then gets back to his client. "So's your son got pink toenails?"

"Blue." What the heck. He's only three. "That's not all. Man you should come over and see my house. It's spotless. They've cleaned it top to bottom. Brought over all kind of groceries. Filled up our freezer with homemade stuff to eat. Yesterday two women came over with boxes to organize all those hand-me-down clothes from Casey's boys I had in bags in the bottom of Colton's closet. Got stuff sorted out. Summer and winter. All by size. Everything he can't wear anymore they took to the Goodwill."

"That's good, man," Abe says. "I'm glad Alice could help you out."

"Guess I'm this week's good deed," I say.

When I get home that night, Alice is there. She's sitting in the recliner, reading Colton a book. She smiles at me. He's sucking his thumb, looking at the pictures, hardly letting on he knows I'm home.

"Hey, buddy." I go over and kiss the top of his head.

"Hi, Daddy," Colton says in his not-now-dad voice. He's a busy man. Into the story. Helping Alice turn the pages.

"Kari's not feeling good," she says over Colton's head.

"What's wrong?"

"I can't tell. She had a headache earlier. She may be asleep."

I go down the hall to her room. The door's open a crack so I stick my head in. Kari opens her eyes a little when she hears me. "You okay?"

She looks small. She's curled up in a ball. "Yeah. I'm okay. Just tired."

"Are you cold?"

She nods. Her hands are up under her chin.

I unfold the quilt that's on the foot of the bed and spread it over her. I put my hand on her forehead. It doesn't feel like she has a fever. "Want something to drink?"

She shakes her head. Closes her eyes. "No. Nothing. Tell Alice thanks," she whispers. "Can you turn out the lamp?"

I do. But first I make sure the trash can is where she can get to it. I leave her door open a crack. Then I jack the thermostat in the hall up a couple degrees.

Back in the living room I ask Alice. "She felt bad all day?" This being her fourth day over here, it's stopped feeling weird. It's like Alice is part of the family. Almost, anyway.

"She's slept a lot. More today than yesterday or the day before."

I go to the kitchen. A throw-away pan of enchiladas is sitting on top of the stove. Melted cheese on top. I open the fridge for some water. There's a banana pudding sitting next to the milk. These church ladies know how to cook. I'm hungry but I'll wait 'til Alice leaves to eat.

"Finally. We're done with all that radiation." I sit down on the couch. Doing hair is not exactly hard labor, but after being on my feet all day I'm always beat. I don't feel it 'til I sit down. Once I do, I'm like an old man when I try to get up. "It's taken a lot out of her. She should start feeling better. Back to herself in a couple of weeks. They say it takes that long to get it all out of your system. Monday's when she gets the follow-up brain scan."

"Are you taking her?"

"Yeah. I'm off Monday and Tuesday."

"What about Colton?" He climbs down off her lap, comes and crawls up next to me.

"I'll take him to day care."

"Would you rather him be at home?"

"Day care's okay." Alice's winter break is over today. She'll be going back to her school on Monday. Which means I've got the weekend to line up who'll stay with Kari next week while I'm at work.

"He like going?"

"Yeah. Most days. He likes to play with his friends. Don't you, Colt?"

He's scooting around on the floor, pushing a remote control police car he got for Christmas. The batteries have been dead in it since the first week he got it. I keep forgetting to buy new ones.

"That's good." Alice isn't making any move to leave. Every other night she's out the door within a few minutes of when I get home. I guess since this is her last day over here and all she's not in a hurry.

There's a long pause where neither one of us talks. I feel awkward. There's stuff I want to say. "Alice. I don't know how to thank you for everything you've done. You were so nice to take care of him and Kari this week. All the other ladies, too."

"We were glad to do it."

"Maybe I'll come visit your church some time." I've been thinking after all they've done I probably should.

"Aren't you going with Abe to his church?"

"Yeah. Some." Not for the past two Sundays but I don't throw that in.

"You like it there?"

"It's a nice place."

"If it feels comfortable, why change? You should keep going with him."

I guess Alice can see I'm surprised. For five years she's been trying to get me to come to her church. I finally say okay and she tells me not to bother. What's up with that?

"I didn't do this so you'd come to my church."

"Of course not. I didn't think that."

"You sure?"

I bend to pick up a piece of a cracker I see on the floor, raise up, then mash it into crumbles in my hand. "That wouldn't be such a bad thing. After all you and the other ladies have done. It wouldn't be out of line for you to expect me to come once or twice. I wouldn't mind."

Alice's eyes zero in on me. "Joel, if you want to come to my church you're welcome. I can tell you what time Sunday school starts. But that's got nothing to do with why I helped you out. Nothing to do with why the other women did what they did."

"I'd like to make a donation then. To your church." I pull out my wallet. I've got at least forty in cash from tips I made today.

"Joel. Stop it." Alice puts the foot of the recliner down and sits forward. "What are you doing? Put your money away. Don't you get it? Why I've been over here this week? Why strangers have done things for you, for Kari, for Colton? This isn't about getting you to come sit on a pew for a couple hours. It's not about you putting money in the collection plate."

"Why then? Why would you do this?" I've been trying to figure it out. "What you've done, how you've given up your vacation, doesn't make sense," I say. "It never has. You don't know me. I cut your hair. That's all. I'm nobody to you."

Alice hands me a Kleenex from the box on the table next to her chair.

"Daddy?" Colton's standing between my knees, patting my face.

"It's okay. Daddy's okay." I wipe my nose. My eyes. I cough a couple of times. Enough. I can't be losing it in front of him. I remember how it upset me when I was little and I'd see my mother cry. I'm not about to do that to him.

Alice doesn't answer me at first. I feel like she's trying to figure out the right words to say what she wants me to know. "Joel. You're wrong. About being nobody to me. Okay. Maybe we aren't really friends. Not the kind of friends who go eat lunch together. I'm not going to call you up just to chat and I doubt you're ever going to come over to the house to play cards with me and Rich. But it's not about that. I care about you. The first time I met you I saw something special. The way you talked about Colton. The way you grieved about your divorce. Even though you had it hard growing up, you try to be a good person, to be a good man. If I've ever seen a heart hungry for love, it would be the one inside your chest. Don't you know? Every bit of what's been done for you this week is about love. God's love. There aren't any strings. No expectations."

I blow my nose. But it doesn't do any good. I've got to get Colton out of the room because I'm gone. Bawling like a baby. He's been in my lap but I set him down so he can't see my face, and I nudge him towards my room. "Hey, bud. Go get in daddy's bed. You can watch TV in there. Okay?"

Alice means well. I know she does. But what she doesn't realize is that her words break my heart. I'm not anywhere near the person she thinks I am. She thinks I'm this great guy, deserving of love, but I'm not. Nowhere near.

For about five minutes I can't say a word. Alice just sits

there—quiet, too. I keep blowing my nose. Wiping my face. Finally when I do manage to say what's on my mind, my voice comes out so hoarse it sounds like a croak.

"This stuff about God loving me. What am I supposed to say? I don't understand it. I don't know what it means. I'm not like you. I'm not like your kids. I didn't grow up hearing people talk about God. Or about love. Nobody talked like that in my house. We didn't go to church. I never know what to say when people tell me things about God loving me. It's like somebody talking Spanish or something to me."

Alice moves from the recliner to sit on the couch next to me. She puts her arm around my shoulders. Her voice gets real soft. "Who said you have to say anything? God uses people. He used me this week. The other women, too. To take care of you. To give you His love. That's all this is about. "

I'm hunched over. My head down close to my knees. "And what am I supposed to do? I'm used to paying my way. No way I can pay you back."

"You aren't supposed to."

This is such news to me.

I expect Alice to say more, but instead, she stands up to leave. She puts on her coat, digs in her purse for her keys, then gives me a hug. "I need to get home. Take care, Joel. See you."

We stand at the door. I'm dog tired but I don't want her to leave.

"Thanks. Again. You don't know how much you helped me out."

Colton's come back into the room. He grabs Alice around the knees. She bends to kiss the top of his head. "Good night, you two. Hope Kari gets to feeling better. I'll be praying about next week."

I stand in the doorway and watch her Impala back out of my

driveway. I see her taillights get faint as she moves down my street. She stops at the corner, signals, and turns. I can't see her anymore, so I go in.

Colton's calling me from the bathroom. He's gone number two and he needs me to come finish the job. I'm starving. Soon as I get him cleaned up and in bed I'm digging into those enchiladas. I head down the hall. That's when I see the big calendar for the first time since I got home. There's names written on it. Some I know. Some I don't. I can't believe it. Every hour of every day of the next two weeks is filled in with the names of people who are coming to take care of Kari. Of Colton.

Of me.

My friend Alice has been at it again.

chapter twenty-two

KNOWING THE RADIATION IS behind us, that Kari won't have to go back for any more treatments, is a huge relief. It's like we've been carrying this big bag but now we get to set it down.

The three of us have a good weekend. Saturday's slow. I rent a couple movies. We order pizza for lunch. Since the weather's nice, I rake leaves and Colton plays outside while Kari sleeps. Later, she wakes up and he takes his nap. While he's down, she and I go sit out on the back stoop. We're side-by-side. Our shoulders almost touch, but not quite. Kari smells like honeysuckle. She's wearing a baby blue sock hat and a tan sweater I think she's had since middle school.

Since getting cancer, Kari stays curled up in a ball. Sitting beside me, she's hunched forward, hugging her knees to her chest.

"You cold?" I ask her. It's about seventy. Supposed to be down in the fifties tomorrow. February. Crazy Texas weather.

"I'm fine."

"Okay if I smoke?"

She shakes her head. "Your house."

I light up but I'm careful to hold my cigarette away from her and to exhale so my smoke doesn't go over her way.

Kari uncurls herself. She stretches her legs out in front of her and looks over at me. "I never told you this. Remember when we were married and you started back smoking?

"Yeah."

"I knew."

"Really?" I'm surprised. "I thought I hid it from you pretty good. How come you never said anything?"

"I don't know. Guess I didn't want to go there. So much was going on. Work. School. Being pregnant. Losing my parents. Don't get me wrong. I was hacked off about it. For sure. Mostly mad you were hiding it from me. Sneaking around like you were the kid and I was the mom. But I was too into my own stuff to take the time to go there with you. Everything else going on, it was just one more thing."

"We weren't exactly talking much then."

"No."

"Seems like a long time ago."

"Not that long," Kari says.

One of the neighbor's cats comes easing up our back walk. The little gray one.

"Hey, Smokey," I say.

He rubs against my ankles, then moves on to Kari. I don't know why we never got us a pet. Colton would probably like a cat. Maybe I'll start checking around. See if anybody's got a litter of kittens.

Kari pulls Smokey up into her lap. He's purring. She's scratching him behind the ears. "It wasn't all your fault, you know."

She catches me off-guard. I turn to look at her. She's only looking at the cat.

"What happened," she says. "It was my fault, too."

"No," I say. I've never heard her say anything like this before. "You didn't do anything. You were having a bad time. I'm the one that messed up."

"It wasn't just you, Joel. I was a witch. I know that now. I was a terrible wife. I blamed you for everything that was wrong in my life. If I'd treated you right maybe you wouldn't have . . . you know."

I've smoked only half my cigarette but I put it out. "It was a bad time for both of us."

"You're a good person," she says.

She thinks that? After everything that's happened? "Not nearly as good as I wish I was."

"I can't believe you let me move in."

"I can't believe you agreed to come back to this house."

"Not like I had much of a choice," Kari says. "Since I was pretty much homeless and broke."

"It's been nice. Don't you think? The three of us. Here together," I speak carefully.

Kari reaches up under her hat to scratch at her ear. "Nice? That's not how I'd describe these past few weeks. All I do is sleep and throw up. You've had to do everything. With all that, you can say it's been nice?"

"The best." I mean it.

"Joel." She punches me in the arm. "I may have a brain tumor but you're the one who's sick in the head."

We both laugh.

"Having you here is what's been nice. I hate being alone," I say. "Even when I've got Colton I feel like I'm by myself. I'm not very good at this single-dad stuff. Sometimes he gets to me. I'm not patient. It's been easier taking care of him just because you were in the house. He acts better. So do I."

"You and I did a lot of things wrong," Kari says, "but when I look at him I know we did at least one thing right."

"He's a great kid," I say. "I worry a lot I'm going to do

something that'll screw him up."

"You won't. You're a great dad. And you know—you were a good husband. Ninety-five percent of the time."

"It's that other five percent," I say.

Kari nods.

My hands are sweaty. I wipe them on my jeans. "You don't have to move out, you know. You could stay here. With us. This could work. The three of us together."

She shakes her head.

"Think about it. That's all I'm asking."

"What do you mean? Exactly. By the three of us together?"

"Whatever you want. As friends. Parents. Maybe something else."

"I can't stay."

"So you're saying there's no chance. No chance for us. For you and me. Ever."

Kari picks up a leaf, starts stripping it down to the vein. "Don't put words in my mouth. What I'm saying is that this is not normal. Two divorced people living together. As for us? I don't know."

I don't know sounds better to me than *never ever*. I'll take what I can get. "So there might be a chance? A little one. Someday."

"You should have been a lawyer instead of a stylist," Kari says. "Here's what I think. After I move out maybe you and I could spend some time together. See how it goes."

"You mean date."

"Maybe."

"Like boyfriend and girlfriend."

"Possibly."

"But until then, things have to stay like they are?"

"Yes. While I'm living here we're friends. Nothing else."

I look at my watch. "So," I tease her, "how much longer 'til you're out of my house?"

Kari shakes her head. Then she smiles. And you should see it. White teeth. Pink lips. Pretty, even chapped. My ex-wife has the best smile you've ever seen in your life.

It could light up a room where the bulb's burned out.

✦

The other day Alice gave me a Bible. First one I've had unless you count the one the Gideons came to our school and gave everybody in the third grade. I told her thank you, then said I didn't know if I'd ever get around to reading it.

Alice said that was okay. She wasn't part of the Bible police and she wasn't going to be asking me if I was reading it. She wanted me to have it. That was all. Whatever I did with it was up to me.

"Thing is," I told her, "me and the Bible—I'm not sure we're a good fit. All that stuff about homosexuals. I've told you about my dad." I held out the Bible for her to take back. "Maybe there's somebody else you could give this to."

Alice had to chew on this for a second. Finally she said, "Joel, there is stuff in the Bible about homosexuals. But you know? You could fit it all on about a quarter of one page. Which would leave," she looked at how many pages were in the Bible, "uh, a little over two thousand pages that don't even mention it."

"A quarter page? That's all?" I'd always thought bashing gay people was most of what there was.

"Yep," Alice said. "Lots of good stuff in here. Stuff that would surprise you."

I didn't know about that. But, "Okay," I told her, "I'll keep it. No promises about reading it, though."

"None required."

Sunday morning Darla comes over and stays so Colton and I can go to Abe's church. Being two of only a few white people there, Colton and I still stick out, but I'm beginning not to feel quite so weird about being there. I'm surprised but I actually like going. I don't know how to explain it but when me and Colton walk into the place something happens, even if we get there late, which we usually do. Soon as me and him sit down I start to feel this thing in my chest. Sort of a flutter. Not really a good feeling, but not a bad one, either. I don't know what it means but I figure it has something to do with God.

To be honest, I don't understand most of this stuff. And instead of getting answers when I go to church, mostly I come up with more questions. Abe and I talk about it. He says he doesn't understand most of it, either. Except for one thing. When I say it, it sounds cheesy but at the same time pretty much sums it up: God is all about love. Abe says wherever you see love, you're seeing God. He says forget that stuff about karma. Positive energy. Good vibes. It ain't about none of that.

It's about God.

I think about how much people have done for me since Kari got sick. Abe. Darla. Especially Alice and her church lady friends. Why do people help us? No way I can ever pay them back. There's that old lady who gave me the two dollars. People I don't even know have sent us checks in the mail. My customers are all the time telling me Kari is on prayer lists all over town. What is that about?

"What do you think it's about?" Abe asks me.

We're standing by my truck. I don't have an answer for him. Actually I need a cigarette but you can't light up in the parking lot of a church even if it is in a strip mall.

"It's what we been talking about," Abe says. "Love. God. All the same. Those people? The one's who've done stuff for you? If you'll just look, they're showing you what it's all about. It's not that hard, man."

I guess.

When we get back to the house, Kari and Darla've made plans for the rest of the day. Kari's dressed. Jeans and a pink sweater. Everything fits loose, but she looks good in real clothes. Darla's helping her put on her shoes. They're heading over to her apartment for a while. Kari says she'll probably stay all day.

"You up to it?" I ask. I'm surprised she's going. "You feel like getting out?" The past ten days Kari hasn't been anywhere except to the clinic for her treatments.

"I feel pretty good," Kari says. "Except for one thing. I need some girl time."

"She's having estrogen withdrawal," Darla says.

"I think I am."

"What this girl needs is gossip. A chick flick. Some dark chocolate. Doctor Darla's orders."

"I'm craving a mocha latte," Kari says.

"No prob," Darla says. "We'll stop at Starbucks on the way to my house."

I gather up Kari's medicine. Put it in a bag. She's glad to be getting out, I can tell. The two of them start out the door, Kari first. I hand Darla the trash can.

"What's this for?"

I give her a look.

"Oh."

"You probably won't need it."

"Right. We should maybe take it just in case." Darla's got it figured out.

"You got it," I say. I am the expert when it comes to this.

So now me and Colton have the afternoon off. Just us. It feels good. How long has it been? I think we might go to the playground. Or out to a movie. "What do you want to do?" I ask him.

He doesn't know.

I get on the phone. Call up the guys. It's been a month since they've been over. I'm afraid that on such short notice they might already have something to do. But no. I luck out. Within an hour Abe and Sh'dondra, Casey and his boys, Sean, and Pete and his kids are all over at my house.

Pete has gone to Chicken Express for us. We've got strips, fries, biscuits and gravy. Plenty. We fill the kids' plates. They sit at the table. Then we get food for ourselves and take it into the living room. Everybody's cool. Abe doesn't even make a fuss at there not being any vegetables. I guess today French fries count. Casey, who has not forgotten how I am about drinking around the kids, has brought over not just sodas, but a case of beer, too. I know he's waiting for me to say something. I don't.

Tonight? I don't care. I'll have a cold one. Two. Maybe three.

Everybody's talking. Laughing. The kids are acting crazy in the kitchen. They can tear the place up as far as I'm concerned. I stuff my face. Casey burps. While the kids are in the other room, Sean tells a raunchy story about one of the female managers at Sears. Somebody gets up and turns on the game. Arena football. Abe goes and gets a trash bag. We toss in our plates. Casey brings me another beer. I take it.

I claim the recliner. Put my feet up. And for a couple of hours I don't worry about anything but whether my team's going to make a first down. When everybody leaves, around six, my house is a wreck but I don't care. It's been a good day. A good weekend. I have that silly sense you get sometimes that everything is all right in your world.

And why not? Nothing's for sure. Nothing happens too fast. But I can't help but believe that starting now, things for me, for Kari, and for Colton are going to move in the right direction.

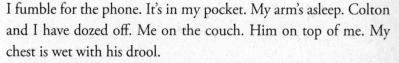

I fumble for the phone. It's in my pocket. My arm's asleep. Colton and I have dozed off. Me on the couch. Him on top of me. My chest is wet with his drool.

"Joel?" It's Darla on the phone.

What time is it? How long did I sleep? I'm all of a sudden awake.

"I'm at the hospital. With Kari. She had a seizure. You better come."

chapter twenty-three

"THE NEWS I HAVE ISN'T what we'd hoped for."

It's the neurologist, Dr. Israel, who I don't care for, with the ponytail, talking.

I'm sitting in a chair down by her feet on the other side of the bed from where he's standing. We've been here all night. Kari slept some but not me. I couldn't get comfortable. The chair I'm in reclines, sort of. Which last night would have been good except that every time I moved, it tried to close up on me. After about three I gave up trying to stretch out. Sean spent the night at our house. Since he's off today, he's keeping Colton there with him until I figure out what we're going to do.

They've got Kari hooked up to an IV. She's got a catheter. A heart monitor, too. I don't know why since there's nothing wrong with her heart. It looks like one of those old transistor radios but with five wires coming out attached with buttons to her chest. Last time they took her vital signs she had a hundred-degree fever, which sounds bad to me but must not be because I can't get any of the nurses to do anything about it.

"Even though I'm disappointed, you realize the findings don't come as a surprise," the doctor says. "As I told you when you were first diagnosed, a glioblastoma is almost never cured. It is a fast-growing, aggressive cancer. We were hoping radiation would slow down its growth. Decrease your symptoms. Give you more time. Unfortunately, from what we see on the scan, we did not get the results we were hoping for. The tumor appears slightly larger today than it was before you started radiation. I'm very sorry."

He's sorry? My ears start to ring. I look at Kari. This can't be right. I want this jerk out of her room. Now.

"I'm sure you have questions. I'm here to answer them as best I can." He sits down on the side of her bed.

Kari's cheeks are red from the fever. Her pupils are so big you can't hardly tell her eyes are blue. She licks her lips. She tries to say something but the way it comes out you can tell her mouth is too dry. I stand up and hand her some Sprite but when she reaches to take a sip her hand shakes so bad she can't hardly get the straw to her mouth.

Dr. Israel waits.

So do I. I want Kari to take charge. To tell him where he can get off. To fire this guy's butt so we can get somebody else in here who can tell us what's really going on.

"The tumor is bigger," she says.

"Slightly."

"Which means the radiation didn't work."

"It did not eliminate the tumor. Perhaps it slowed its growth."

"So what do I do now?" Kari asks. "What are my options? Is chemo the next step?"

He clears his throat. "That would be one course you could take. And if you want chemo we can certainly proceed with it. That's not my field of expertise but I can refer you to a specialist who can manage it for you. But speaking frankly, in your case chemo is not something I would recommend. Side effects would be severe. At most it would add a few weeks to your life."

Weeks?

"Maybe a month."

A month?

"You don't have to decide right this minute. I plan to keep you here for at least forty-eight hours. We need to adjust your Dilantin dose. Hopefully so you won't be having seizures, though with this kind of cancer we aren't always able to control them completely. We'll also work on getting your headaches and the nausea you've been having under better control. We want to do everything possible to make sure you're comfortable and that you have everything you need. Ensuring your comfort and optimizing the quality of your life is our goal."

The ringing in my ears has turned into the sound of a train. It's getting closer and closer. No whistle. Just the sound of the engine. I sit quietly, looking normal, I think. But I'm not. The train's bearing down on me. I want to run but it feels like my foot is caught in the track. Bright lights are shining in my face. I want to cover my eyes but I don't. This can't be happening. This isn't right. There's some mistake.

All that radiation. Back and forth two times a day. It was supposed to shrink the tumor. Supposed to make her well. Now we find out it didn't do any good?

I've got things I have to do. I should go to work. The oil needs to be changed in my truck. Bills have got to be mailed. Plus, we're out of cereal. What's Colton going to eat for breakfast if I don't go buy him some now? He likes Cocoa Puffs. Fruit Loops. Kari eats Wheaties. We're out of it all, which means I should make a grocery store run. I can't remember but my bet's we probably need milk, too.

For sure I should be doing something. Going somewhere. I should not be here in this room listening to somebody tell me the person I love most in the world is going to die and there's not one freakin' thing anybody can do about it.

"How long?" Kari says. "How long if I don't take chemo?"

"No one can say with certainty," Dr. Israel says. "But based on the size of your tumor and its location, I would say six months would be an optimistic guess."

Kari nods.

"You have a child?" he asks.

"A little boy." She licks her lips. Her eyes rest on a spot on the blanket somewhere near her feet. "Colton. He'll be four in July."

The hair is standing up on my arms. My feet itch. Kari has six months to live. Six months. Six months. I see a calendar in my head. The pages are flipping forward, like they're being blown by a fan. Faster and faster. How many months is six? March, April, May, June, July, August. That can't be right. I flip them back by hand, then forward by hand. Slowly. I count again. But it comes out the same. August. August. August is six months from now.

"Whatever course you take, chemo or no chemo, I recommend you get your affairs in order. We have an excellent medical social work department. They can help you. You may want to consider hospice care. With your permission, I'll have one of the case workers check in with you this afternoon."

And then the guy says he's sorry again. He wishes there was something more he could do. He stands up. Looks at his watch. Tells her he'll be back in the morning to talk to her again if she thinks of anything she needs to ask him.

Kari doesn't answer him. She's still looking at that same spot down by her feet.

So he leaves. Closes the door behind him. What a job. The guy must be some kind of a sadist. All day. Going from patient to patient. Delivering bad news. I don't care if he seems nice. I hate him. I wish he was the one going to die. Not Kari. Not my wife. Not the mother of my child. He's lying. I know it. He's a stupid jerk. This is some kind of sick joke. Kari and I should get out of here. Right now. This place stinks. I'm not putting up with this.

Kari's not either. She raises her eyes to meet mine. "I want to go home."

I nod okay but I don't move. It's weird. Like I'm in la-la land or something. But Kari snaps me out of it. "Joel. Get me my clothes. They're in the closet." I pop up and swing open the closet door. I hand Kari her jeans. Her T-shirt. They're all wadded up. Smells like there's pee on her jeans. I set her shoes down by the side of her bed but I can't find her socks.

By the time I raise up, Kari's already got her gown unsnapped at the shoulders and she's pulling off those sticky buttons that are attached to the wires. When she's got them loose, she winds the wires around the little box and puts it on the over bed table. "Hand me that alcohol pad, the one by the sink," she says. By the time I get it for her, she's already got the tape pulled off her IV. One of the nurses who I know is Kari's friend comes into her room right when she pulls the thing out.

"Kari! What are you doing?"

"I'm going home."

"But the doctor didn't release you."

"I'm going anyway. Take my catheter out." She covers where the IV came out with the alcohol prep but the thing bleeds through and blood gets on her hand.

The nurse has some gauze in her pocket. Real fast she puts on some gloves, covers the spot with it and stands there holding it. "I know. You got bad news. I'm sorry."

Kari won't look at the nurse.

"You should stay. Get your meds straightened out. See the

social worker. At least stay until tomorrow."

Kari shakes her head. She wipes at her eyes, then looks over the nurse's head at me.

"Dr. Israel is not going to release you."

"I'll go AMA."

I look at Kari. "What's that?"

"Against medical advice," the nurse says. "It means you have to sign papers saying you're leaving against doctor's orders and you won't hold the hospital responsible if anything happens to you."

This is beginning to sound like it might not be such a good idea. "Maybe you should stay," I say.

Kari cuts me off with a look.

"Okay. I'll bring the truck around."

"To the ER entrance," Kari says.

The nurse gives it up. "Give me time to let Dr. Israel know you're leaving. Then I'll get the papers and we'll get you out of here. Take me ten minutes. Tops."

Kari looks at me. "I'll be downstairs in five."

The nurse shakes her head.

Six minutes later Kari and I are in my truck, on our way home.

chapter twenty-four

IT'S BEEN TWO WEEKS since Kari's last radiation treatment. A week and a half since we got the news she's not supposed to get well. But you know what? Doctors don't know everything. We don't talk about the tumor. About her having six months or less to live. Because you know what? Kari's feeling better.

Every day she's stronger. You can see it. Most afternoons she still takes a nap but she's not sleeping eighteen or more hours a day like she was. She's eating better, too. Craving nachos. Pepperidge Farm Milanos. And chocolate milk, which I can't keep enough of in the house. Those patchy places where her hair came out are starting to grow back. Her skin isn't so pale like it was.

It's almost like the old Kari's back.

Thanks to Alice and her crew, along with Abe and Jill, Sean, Pete, Casey and Darla, and other people, too, I haven't missed much work. They've never stopped helping out, staying with Kari, taking care of Colton, bringing over food, doing lots of laundry, and cleaning up the house.

Even my customer Bradley's been helping out. When he heard about Kari being sick and her moving back in with me, he gathered up some the old drunks that go to his church. They came and cleaned up my yard, trimmed the trees, raked leaves, and hauled it all off. Did a good job. I tried to pay them. Some of them looked pretty hard up. One young guy had on Nikes about three sizes too big. No laces. No socks.

But they wouldn't take anything. Told me they were there to do God's work and that didn't include getting paid.

That's not all of what Bradley did. The other day I got home and found him and some woman in red stretch pants—I guess wife number four—up on two ladders. They were cussing each other loud enough I could hear it when I got out of my truck. Smoking, too.

"Hey, what y'all doing up there?" I asked them.

They were cleaning out my gutters.

Which was a real nice thing to do. Especially since they didn't set my roof on fire like I was afraid they might do.

It's Saturday. The first day of March. Me and Kari and Colton are parked at the Sonic. The weather's nice. We've got the windows down. They're playing Elvis on the loudspeakers. Kari and I are having Sonic's famous onion rings and chocolate shakes. Colton's got him a corny dog. Making a big old mess.

It feels good. The three of us together. Doing something ordinary. Except for the hat Kari's got on you wouldn't figure she was sick. You'd only see her as thin and a little bit pale. Except for neither one of us wearing a wedding ring, you'd think we were a real family. We look like any married couple and their kid. Just out together getting us all something to eat.

Kari sucks down the last of her shake. She reaches over and wipes Colton's face with a napkin then puts it in her empty cup. "I've been thinking. What about maybe next week I start staying by myself while you're at work?"

"You think you're ready?"

"I'm feeling good. Why wouldn't I be?"

I can think of a few reasons why not but I know better than to say them out loud. So I chew on my onion ring. Drink some of my shake. Smear some more mustard on Colton's dog. "What's the hurry?" I finally say. "Wait another week or two. Make sure you're all right."

"Okay. Whatever," Kari says. She stares out the window on her side of the truck. She gives me the silent treatment, which means I've gone and said the wrong thing.

But what if she's alone in the house and she has a seizure? What if she gets one of her headaches or starts throwing up and there's nobody there to help her? You never know.

Later that night, we put Colton to bed. There's nothing much on TV. I stretch out on the couch with *Car and Driver.* Kari's reading some book, but she's fidgety. She keeps shifting around in her chair, rearranging the afghan that's over her feet, and chewing on the ice that's left in her tea glass. After an hour or so, she puts down her book and goes to the bathroom. When she comes back, she doesn't get back in the recliner where she was. Instead she surprises me by coming and sitting down on the floor next to where I am. She leans back on the couch, close enough I can smell her shampoo.

"You okay?" I ask. I can't see her face.

She doesn't say anything.

I sit up. Put my feet down. Make room for her next to me. "Hey. Come here." I reach down to help her get up. "What's wrong? Does your head hurt?"

Kari moves up to sit on the couch but she won't look at me. She just stares at her hands in her lap. There is something wrong. What?

"Kari. Tell me. What's the matter? What do you need?"

Finally she looks at me, but when she does, her lips are together. She shakes her head like she does when she can't talk because she's afraid she might cry.

Quick.

Say something. Do something.

I've got to fix whatever it was I said or did wrong. "Is this about me not thinking you should stay by yourself? Because I could be wrong. Maybe you are ready. We could start with half days. I could ask Darla or Alice to check on you. It might could work. I didn't mean to get you upset."

Kari finally can speak. "Joel. It's not that. You're right. It was just a thought. And I'm probably not ready. Not yet."

Which gets me totally confused. If it's not that, then what? I thought we'd had a pretty good day.

"There are some things we need to talk about," Kari says.

Great. I may as well get ready. As long as Kari and I've been together the words *we need to talk* have not ever come before good news. She's either going to tell me all the ways I've been messing up or she's going to say she wants to move out.

"Okay. I'm listening."

"I was wrong." Kari is sitting Indian style in the middle of the couch, her hands holding onto a pillow she's got in her lap.

It would be easy, natural even, to reach out and rest my hand on her knee or foot, to show her it's okay, but I don't. Except for when I'm helping her in and out of the truck or holding her steady when she's throwing up or when she's got a headache and I'm wiping her forehead with a cold washrag, I don't touch her. Not because I don't want to. Man. Not that at all. But because I have no right to. No right to at all.

"Wrong about?" I ask.

"Us," she says. "I shouldn't have left you."

Whoa. I didn't see this coming. My heart starts thumping in my ears. Come on. Don't blow it. Don't say the wrong thing. Listen to what she has to say. I try to be cool but my voice comes out weird. "You had your reasons."

"Yeah. I did. At the time I thought they were pretty good ones."

"Most people would agree with you."

"I was so mad at you. So hurt."

"You had a right to be."

"It's still there. The pain. The hurt. But at least now that's not the only thing." She reaches up and touches her head. "We need to face facts. We don't know what's going to happen. To me. With this. That stuff the doctor said—we don't talk about it but I think about it every day."

So do I. Twenty-four seven.

"Being here with you. With Colton. The three of us in this house," she swallows.

"It feels right," I finish with what I hope she's going to say.

"It does. And no matter what happens I think it's what I want."

She thinks.

"You mean, staying here."

She nods.

"As friends? Like now? Or something else?"

"Something else. Like as your wife. Colton's mother. Us as a family. Like we were before."

I'm not all that cold but I start to shake. These are the words I never in my life expected to hear. The way I'm feeling must be like what it's like for a felon when somehow he lucks out and gets out on parole. Kari offering me a second chance is like getting a gift, one I no way deserve.

Kari's watching me. Waiting for my reaction.

I look her in the eye. "There's nothing I want more than for us to be together. I've always wanted it. But one thing. I have to know." This is hard to say but I have to be sure. "When you came back those other times, I wanted to believe it was going to work out for us, but it didn't. What's different now? Is it the tumor?"

Girl, don't be yanking my chain, is what I want to say. *Don't mess around with me.*

As much as I want to be with Kari, I am too tired. I am too worn out to go through that again. What do I want? I want us to be together. Really together. Not just housemates. But not if it means losing what we've got now. It's not the best, but at least it's working. For me anyway. And for Colton. He's got his mom and his dad together in his house. All's right with his world. Do we have any right to mess with that?

Kari blows her nose on a tissue. "Those times? They were bad, weren't they? For both of us. I know now there was no way it could have worked back then. You were trying but I was holding so tight to what you did we didn't stand a chance. Leslie was all I could think about. What the two of you did was the first thing I thought of when I woke up. It was the thing I went to sleep thinking about every night."

Why do we have to go over this again?

Her eyes are wet. "It was horrible. I couldn't get past what you and her did no matter how hard I tried. So you know what? After a while I quit trying to get past it. I decided you didn't deserve my forgiveness. You didn't deserve another chance. I was done. No more trying for me. When I moved out that last time, my plan was to hate you for the rest of my life. I didn't need you. I didn't want you. Except for us sharing Colton, I was putting you out of my life and moving on to something better."

"Nick?"

"For a while."

"But then you got sick."

"Yes. And you were there. You were still the jerk who cheated on me but that wasn't all anymore. You were the person who gave me a place to live. Drove me to the doctor. Cleaned up my puke. Do you know how much I hated needing you that way? But I didn't have anybody else. No other choices. Even days I was a witch you were still kind. Everything you did for me chipped away at my hurt. Not that it's gone. Maybe it won't ever be. But there's only a little bit of it left."

Kari reaches out. She puts her hand over mine. I'm wiping my eyes now.

"My plan to hate you forever pretty much got blown away by this tumor I've got in my head."

With my fingers I reach up and touch the place on her head where they say the tumor is. I'd give anything if it wasn't there. Even this. "So you mean you'll stay here? With me? With us?"

"Can I?"

"You think you have to ask?"

Kari nods. "I do." She looks at me with those blue eyes. Her hands are still in her lap.

"Come here," I say.

It's an awkward moment. But Kari turns herself around and stretches her legs out. Slowly, like she's not sure what I want her to do, she leans back against my chest. Yes. This is it. I slide my arm around her. She puts her hands on my arm and I settle my cheek against the top of her head. Fuzzy wild strands of her hair brush against my nose. They tickle a little but I don't mind. I love how Kari smells. How she feels.

It has been so long since I held her like this.

"I never stopped loving you," I say to the top of her head. "I never stopped wanting to be with you. I hate it that you got sick but I've loved every minute of you being in this house. It was like I was getting away with something. I've wanted you to get well more than anything. I asked Alice and Bradley and Abe and everybody I know to pray for the tumor to be gone. For you to be cured. At the same time, I knew when you got better, you'd be out of my life again."

Kari's fingers trace a path along one of the veins in my hand. "What a hard place to be."

"I want you to be okay."

"I want to stay." She licks her dry lips. "If you'll let me."

I answer her by pulling her into my lap and kissing her on the mouth. "Please," I whisper. "Don't leave. Ever. Don't leave our house again."

Kari and I lie side-by-side in our bed. It's too hot to spoon. We're covered up with a sheet. Because it's so warm, we have the windows open a little more than a crack, which lets some of the outside come in. I can smell our grass, which I cut today after we got back from Sonic. Some honeysuckle vines near the street are blooming early because it's been such a mild winter. They smell really sweet but not too strong. I can hear outside sounds, too. Somebody's dog is barking. The kid next door with the loud pipes on his car pulls into his drive. He leaves it running, goes inside his house, comes out, then leaves again. He's proud of those pipes.

Kari and I've talked so much I think we're done with words for now. So many nights when we were in separate beds in the same house I wished for just this. There is nothing better in the world than her lying here next to me, knowing our son is asleep across the hall.

I am happy, but so, so tired. Ready for sleep. And just about there.

I believe with all my heart Kari is going to be cured. I think maybe even she already is.

Please, God.

That's my prayer, if something so short counts as one.

Please. Please. Please.

When I hear Kari's breath slow down I prop up on one elbow and look down on her while she sleeps. Her mouth is open a little. She's lying like a baby, like Colton sleeps sometimes. On her back, her elbows bent, her hands on either side of her head. Open. Not afraid. Like she's not worried about anything in the world.

I lay back on my pillow, look up at the ceiling fan, which I remember coming home to find Alice dusting last week. Every once in a while it squeaks a little. I'll squirt some WD-40 on it tomorrow. Soon it'll be summer and we'll keep it on all day.

We're done with the cancer. I'm sure of it. I'm wrong about a lot of things but not about this. I can't be.

But I am.

chapter twenty-five

THE HOSPICE NURSE IS COMING today. Her name is Amy something. I don't know exactly what she can do but the social worker at the hospital set it up for her to come to our house. She says she thinks it's time we get help lined up.

Kari had some good weeks after she finished her radiation treatments. She got to where she could do things in the house. Cook a little. Do a little laundry. We did some fun things on my days off. Two different Saturdays we took Colton to the zoo. He loves the monkeys and the snakes but he's afraid of the cow. With all the walking Kari got tired, but when she did we sat down. She did okay.

Her birthday was two weeks ago. I surprised her by getting Abe and Jill to keep Colton while she and I went to the same hotel where we stayed on our honeymoon. It was really relaxing. They had a heated pool and a good breakfast buffet. We had a good time, except that on the way home she got one of her headaches, as bad a one as she's ever had. I had to stop twice so she could throw up. Dumb me. I thought maybe she had the virus or food poisoning from something she ate.

It was soon after that things started going downhill. Turns out those weeks Kari was feeling better were because of the radiation clearing out of her system. Which would have been something to be glad about, except for this: As soon as she finished with the radiation, the glioblastoma started growing again.

That's what the past two MRIs showed.

Now Kari's dizzy. Something's wrong with her eyes. She can't see well enough to read. Her headaches are back. I tell her she needs to eat but she says she can't because every time she does she feels like she's going to puke. The only good thing is that there haven't been any more seizures since that one when Darla took her to the hospital.

There's not any more talk of her staying by herself.

The calendar in the hall says June. There's a part of me that wants to take the thing down. I hate looking at it. After June comes July. Then August. On every date there are names and times written in. People coming to stay. Helping out. I don't know what I would do if it wasn't for that. I'm trying to work. To keep up on the bills. It's hard. I hate to leave in the morning. My mind is at home whether I'm there or not. Every minute I can spend with Kari and Colton, that's all I want to do.

There's a church I pass on my way to work. They have one of those big white signs you can put letters on in front. Yesterday it said *Keep the Faith*.

What exactly does that mean? *How do you do that* is what I want to know. This believing in God. Jesus. All that stuff. I want it to make sense. I'm not sure it does.

Kari says she believes. In Jesus. In God. That he is in control and that he's not going to leave her alone.

"Does that keep you from being scared?" I ask her. I'm sitting in the recliner in our living room. She's in my lap. She's lost so much weight, her hip bones are poky, but no way am I going to complain.

"Yes. No. Sometimes," she tells me. "Sometimes I feel good.

Positive. Peaceful. Like in the end it's all going to be all right. It feels like I'm holding onto a rope really tight and it's keeping me safe. But then I blink and it's like I lose my grip on that feeling. I start falling, falling. Really fast. I get so scared I think I can't bear it. Scared I won't make it. Scared of what it's going to be like if I don't."

My throat gets tight like I'm trying to swallow a towel. I want to tell Kari not to talk like that, because her not making it is not an option. She's not going to die. She can't. No way, no how. End of discussion. But I can't make any words come out because the truth is staring both of us in the face. She's getting weaker, not stronger. She's losing weight. She sleeps more all the time and she's forgetting things. Somebody has to help her walk to the bathroom. She can't get dressed by herself.

"What's going to happen to Colton if I don't make it?" she asks. "He needs a mother. He needs me to be around to see him grow up. This isn't fair to him. It's like I'm letting him down if I don't get well."

"You're going to get well." The words come out of my mouth even though my heart knows they aren't true.

Kari turns so she can look me straight in the face. "If I don't. You have to take care of him. You can't lose it. You have to be okay for him. Promise me."

If Kari doesn't make it—nothing will ever be okay. But I say what she wants to hear. "I'll be okay. I'll take care of him. He will always come first."

What am I supposed to believe? What exactly am I supposed to have faith in?

That God's going to fix this? That this is his will?

I don't know what to think. Sometimes I don't want to think about God. What good has it done? Believing, I mean. I think it would be easier to take this whole thing if I could see it all as random. But it's like it's too late. I can't shake the feeling that there's something out there holding it, us, *me* all together.

This God thing feels like when you have gum stuck on the bottom of your shoe. At first you don't realize you've got something extra attached to your foot. When you do, you reach down and pull some of it off, but there's still more. It's stretchy. A little wad can turn into a big glob real fast. It gets on your hands. Sometimes you get it on your other shoe. The more you pull, the bigger mess you get yourself in.

Which is exactly where I am. In some kind of a big mess. I did not intend to get in with God but it feels like I am and like I can't get him off of me. I go from begging him to cure Kari to being mad at him for letting her ever get sick. Sometimes I believe we're going to get a miracle. Most times I don't.

Me and Colton go to Abe's church every Sunday. Been going for three months. Over and over, on Saturday night I decide that tomorrow we won't go. We'll sleep in. But then Sunday morning rolls around and I'm wide awake at eight. Church starts at nine. So I get up. Get me and Colton ready and we get in the truck and head over there. Something pulls me.

Go figure. The guy who went to church maybe half a dozen times in his life is now the guy who can't miss. With all that going to church you'd think I'd have more faith than doubt. It's just the opposite. Every week I come up with more questions.

I ask Abe. "Why did this happen? Why doesn't God do anything?"

He doesn't have answers.

Neither does Alice. Me and her and Colton are sitting at the kitchen table having lunch. Somebody's brought over chicken spaghetti. Salad. Garlic bread. Chocolate pie. I don't know how I can eat but I can. I'm hungry all the time. Kari's losing weight. She's down to ninety-five. So far I've only gained four pounds, but if I keep on like this it'll be more. Colton eats real slow. He picks the mushrooms out. Puts them in his mouth first. Then the chicken. Guess he's saving the spaghetti for last.

Alice gets up and pours him more milk.

"If I could figure out a reason, maybe I could take it better," I say. "Doesn't there have to be a reason for everything? Isn't that how God works?"

"That would make sense wouldn't it?" Alice says. "Truth is, I don't know how God works. Nobody does. How does this fit into His plan? Kari having this tumor? I can't explain it. There's no way any of us can understand something like this. It's too big, too hard to wrap your brain around."

"So what do you do? How do you keep believing? I don't know if it's worth it. I think for me it makes it worse."

I feel like kicking something. The table. A chair. Good thing we don't have a dog because if we did I might kick him.

Alice wipes Colton's mouth and his hands with a wet paper towel. He's ready to get down. She comes back to the table. "Joel, I don't have the answers. What I know is I have hard places in my life. Things I wish weren't there and that I don't understand. Situations I couldn't face without feeling like God is in it all."

I never thought about Alice having problems in her life. I guess I've always been so busy telling her my troubles I never thought to ask.

"I need to believe in a God who's bigger than me," Alice says. "Even when I don't understand. Life is a puzzle. A mystery. I can't live my life without a belief that there's somebody behind all this mystery. For me it'd be like going rappelling without a harness."

"You've gone rappelling?"

"Couple summers ago. Went on this adventure trip with three of my girlfriends from college. Had a blast 'til I hurt my wrist," Alice says. She flexes her left hand. "Still gives me trouble sometimes. Joel, listen. I don't understand why this is happening. Anybody who thinks they can tell you why someone as beautiful and precious as Kari gets cancer is full of—you know."

I've never heard Alice cuss but I think she just nearly did.

"I don't understand why any of the bad things in the world exist. I wish they didn't and I wish God didn't allow them. I don't understand why He does. But there is one thing I do understand. One thing I know for sure."

Her voice comes out choked. She coughs. Then takes a sip of her tea. "None of this has anything to do with how much God loves us. When I start doubting, questioning—and believe me, I do, all the time," she says, "I think about the Cross. Does God love us? Does He care about us? Does He understand our pain? When I look at what happened on the Cross, at least for that moment my doubts fade. I know the answers to those questions. When Jesus died, He proved God's love."

I push a piece of spaghetti around on my plate. Talk like this makes me want to get up and move. But there's one thing I know. Without a doubt. Alice believes what she's saying. No way you could miss how sincere she is.

"No matter how down I get," Alice says, "no matter how upset I get with how things are going, I always know God loves me."

I'm not surprised Alice feels God's love. If I was God I think it would be easy for me to love somebody like Alice. "I can understand God loving somebody like you," I say.

Alice looks puzzled. "Somebody like me?"

"You're a good Christian," I say.

Alice actually laughs. "Joel. You tell me all the time that I don't really know you. Well, you don't really know me, either. I'm a bad Christian. I mess up all the time. So do the other women who've been helping you out. So do most of the people in my church. But you know what? I think us bad ones are God's favorite kind. He loves those of us who never seem to get it right. He loves churches who haven't got it all figured out but that keep trying to love people and do what's right anyway."

"I don't know," I say.

"No, you don't," Alice says. She gets up to carry both our plates to the sink. "But you will."

I look at my watch.

"What time's the nurse supposed to be here?" Alice asks.

"Ten minutes ago."

We're both nervous. We wish this day hadn't come.

I hear a car pull up in the drive. We both get up and look out the window that's over the sink. "Is it her?" Alice asks.

"I don't think so." Car's a green Volkswagen bug. Girl getting out of it's blonde. Cute. Young. Twenty-five maybe? She's got on a pink T-shirt and capri pants. "Probably one of Kari's friends from the hospital," I tell Alice. This friend must not have been here before because she goes to the front door instead of the back. I go around and open it for her. She's standing on the bottom step, which means that from the where I am three steps up, not even trying I can see straight down the front of her shirt.

Nice boobs. Fake tan. Purple bra. Little silver cross.

"Hi, there. Sorry to bother you." The girl looks at a piece of paper she's got on a clipboard. She's carrying a big flowery tote bag. Got a diamond stud in her nose. "I'm hoping I'm at the right place. Is this where Kari Carpenter lives?"

"Are you Amy? With hospice?" I don't know what I expect a hospice nurse to look like but this chick is not it. She looks more like a hair stylist than a nurse.

"Oh, shoot. Sorry. Yes." She sticks out her hand. "I'm Amy Lang. We're supposed to wear a lab jacket. But it's so hot. I left it in the car. My ID badge is clipped on the pocket. You want me to go get it?"

"No, no. That's okay. Come on in." This girl Amy's got a French manicure that looks pretty good but her roots are about two weeks past needing to be done. We go to the kitchen. I introduce her to Alice and Colton. They say hi. Alice's eyes meet mine. I know what she's thinking. *This girl is the nurse?*

"Give me a kiss bye." I tell Colton. "Be a good boy. Do what Alice tells you to do."

"Your little boy's a doll," Amy says when they're gone. "I've got two kids at home. Mattie and Marla. Twins. They'll be six next month. They keep me running. You mind if I use your bathroom before we get started?"

I show her where it is. She sets her bag down and heads down the hall. Kari's asleep behind our bedroom door, which is closed. "I'm not sure what we're supposed to do," I say when she comes back out. "I hate to waste your time. This was the social worker's idea. I don't know much about hospice. We probably don't even need it."

"Your wife," Amy says, "she has a glioblastoma? That's what they've got on my referral. Is that right?"

"She's not my wife. I mean she used to be. We're divorced. But we're, uh, together. She moved back in when we found out about the—"

"The glio. Gotcha," Amy says. "You're her primary caregiver?"

"Yeah." We're standing in the kitchen.

"How's that going?"

I shrug.

"It's tough," Amy says. "My husband's been gone three years. Leukemia. I tried to work and take care of him and the twins, too. Ten months. I nearly lost it. Maybe we could sit down somewhere and I could sort of explain how hospice works."

Two hours later I am just about positive Amy is an angel in really good disguise. First we filled out the papers. Then when Kari woke up Amy checked her over and asked a bunch of questions. I wasn't sure what Kari would think of Amy but the two of them hit it off good.

First off, she tells me to quit trying to make Kari eat. "Let her call the shots, Joel. Her body knows what it needs. And if it needs nothing but chocolate pudding three meals in a row, that's okay." She put her stethoscope to Kari's chest. "Your lungs sound okay but are you ever short of breath?"

"Sometimes at night. Not too bad."

"We'll get an oxygen concentrator delivered and a couple portable tanks. If you want, you can put the whole mess in a closet somewhere. Concentrator's about the size of a big ice chest. You may not need it but it's a good idea to have it on hand."

Amy looks at the medicine Kari is on and calls the doctor to get it all changed because it turns out what Kari is on for pain isn't strong enough. What she's been taking for nausea isn't working. Amy knows something better. And while she's still here, the pharmacy delivers exactly what we need, a pain patch I'm supposed to change every three days and morphine tablets to have on hand just in case. Amy says if the pain patch gets to where it doesn't work I'm supposed to put one of the morphine pills in Kari's mouth and let it dissolve. That's not all. We've got this gel stuff I rub on Kari's wrist if she throws up and some other gel stuff I'm supposed to put on her if she gets real nervous or can't settle down.

How's that for service?

"I'm leaving you a box of gloves. Make sure you wear them when you put the happy gel on her," says Amy to me. "Seriously. You're not used to it, stuff'll knock you on your butt. We can't have both of you mellowed out at the same time."

Before she leaves, Amy gives us her pager number. "Call me if you need anything. I'll be back day after tomorrow unless you page me before then." She gives us both a hug then heads out to her car.

She hasn't been gone a minute before Kari and I see she's forgotten her bag. I look at what's inside. It's got her stethoscope and her thermometer and her gloves and stuff. An opened bag of pretzels and some Dove chocolate miniatures, too. About the time I'm calling her to let her know we've got it, she's back at the front door. I hand her the bag.

"Thanks. I'd forget my head if it wasn't attached. See ya." She's gone again.

"That went good," I say.

"Yeah," Kari says. She's stretched out on the couch.

"Oprah's on. Want the remote?"

"Sure."

I go to the kitchen to get me and her something to drink. When I come back in the room, Kari's crying. She's got the hospice brochure in her hand.

"Hey, what's the matter?" I set the drinks down. Then I kneel down beside Kari's head. "I thought you were feeling okay."

"I was."

"What is it?"

Kari shakes her head.

"Was it Amy? Something she said? Something I said?"

Kari covers her eyes with her arm.

I hate it when she does this. I have to see her face. Still on the floor, I put my arms around her. "Tell me."

Finally. "It's the hospice thing. How can I — how can we — how can I keep believing I might get well when we need hospice?"

I never thought about it that way.

Kari shows me what she read. *One of the goals of hospice is to help patients and their families experience what we call a good death.*

I put in a page to Amy. She calls me right back. She must be at home because I can hear a TV on in the background. Sounds like when she answers she's got something in her mouth.

"Getting hospice," I say. "Does that mean there's not any hope? That we're supposed to give up hoping she's going to get better? Because if it does, you don't have to come back. We don't want it. We don't need it."

"Hold on a sec. Where'd you get that idea?" Amy says. "It doesn't mean that at all. You should have hope. You need it. Hospice is about hope. It's about having hope for a good end to a good life, however long or short that life is meant to be. Nobody is trying to take that away from you."

"Tell me. What's a *good death*?" I ask her. "This paper you gave Kari says that's one of the goals of hospice. I want the truth. What does that mean?"

There's a pause on Amy's end. I sense her trying to figure out what to say next. "A good death can mean a lot of things. Mainly it means one where there's no pain."

"Have you ever seen it happen like that?"

Amy hesitates again. "I'm supposed to say yes. And the truth is there's not usually physical pain. If somebody's on enough morphine they can slip out pretty easy. But if you're asking me if Kari dying is going to hurt. Yeah. It is. Whether it happens in two months or in twenty years. Death hurts. Always."

Kari's watching me.

"I see. Okay. Thanks."

"Anything else?"

"No. Sorry to bother you." I'm ready to hang up. "We're good now. You answered my questions. It's all good."

"No. It's not good," Amy says. "What you're going through stinks."

"Okay." I clear my throat. "So we'll see you day after tomorrow. Right?"

"Yep. I'll be there. Later, Joel."

chapter twenty-six

SINCE KARI MOVED BACK in with me and Colton, we've not had too many of our Sunday night single dad get-togethers. We usually had them at my house. With everything going on they just haven't happened.

But today we're all getting together at Casey's. Sean called me twice to make sure me and Colton were coming.

"Okay, okay. We'll be there," I finally told him so he'd quit bugging me. I wasn't sure about going. I hate leaving Kari any more than I have to. But since starting the new meds last week, she's feeling a little better. No more headaches. Hardly any throwing up.

It's Abe who finally talks me into going to Casey's. We're at work. He's doing foil highlights. I've got a cut going.

"You and Colton need to come," he says. "That boy needs to be around some men."

"Yeah. So he can learn to scratch and pass gas and miss the toilet when he pees," says the girl Abe's working on.

"All right now," Abe says.

"I don't know. Let me think about it," I say.

"You're in that house taking care of Kari. All those women helping you out over there all the time. 'Sides that, me and you, we work with chicks every day. No offense, girl," he says to his customer. "Just how it is. That has got to be getting to you. Come on, man. Jill says she'll stay with Kari. Sh'dondra's been talking all day about wanting to see Colton."

I don't answer him. "Where's my styling lotion?" Abe needs to quit borrowing my stuff.

"Casey's cooking outside. Three kinds of meat."

The food people have brought over has been really good, but mostly casseroles. Lots with chicken. A big slab of something that used to have four feet does sound good. "Okay. We'll come. May not stay long, but we'll be over. Around three."

When we get there, everybody's in the backyard. Soon as we get out of the truck, I can smell the food. Nobody does barbecue like Casey. His boys, Nathan and Andy, and Pete's twins, Brandon and Chase, have all got water guns. They're running around shooting not just each other, but everybody else, too.

"You boys squirt me one more time I'm gonna beat your butts," Casey yells. He's standing at the grill. Got a big meat fork in one hand, a beer in the other. You can tell the boys are really scared. They all run up and squirt him again.

"Wha's up, man?"

When Sh'dondra sees me she runs over for a hug. "Girl, who is that you've got on your shirt?" I ask her.

"Tinkerbell."

"It sure is pretty." She gives me a hug, then gets down to go play with Colton.

Sean's there. He's got Allyssa with him. He's sitting in a lawn chair. She's in his lap like a queen on a throne. "How's it going? Hey, sweetie. How's it been?" I say. I haven't seen Allyssa in maybe four months. She's gotten big. "You got her for the weekend?"

"Nah. I've got my girl for two months this time," Sean says. "Every other weekend. Eight weeks in the summer. That's how the judge worked it out. So me and Allyssa here are going to have us some fun, aren't we, baby? We're going swimming. To the zoo. Going to go play at the park."

Allyssa's sucking her thumb. She's nearly three. I sure hope her doing that doesn't mess up her teeth.

"How's it going with—you know?" I say. Sean's been tied up at work. It's been maybe a month since I've seen him.

"It's okay."

"She still with—?" I ask.

"Uh-huh. Baby's due any day," he says.

"You okay?"

"Got to be."

"Y'all ready to eat?" Casey yells.

Everybody is. We gather around the picnic table where he's got the food spread out. There's ribs, sausage, and steak. No telling how many pounds of meat Casey's cooked. To go with it we've got a bunch of loaves of white bread and a big bowl of coleslaw that Abe's brought. It all looks good. We dig in.

Around five, we're kicked back in lawn chairs, stuffed. It's just us dads. The kids have been inside a half hour or so. There's something they're watching on TV. Casey's got HBO. Hope what's on is something okay for kids.

"That was excellent," I say. "As always." I look at my watch. Doesn't matter if I'm at work or at the store or someplace else. Being away from Kari I get this uneasy feeling. "About time me and Colton head back to the house."

When I say that, Sean and Pete look at each other sort of funny.

"Hold on, man," Abe says. "Don't go just yet."

"We got something for you," Casey says.

"What you talking about?" I look around. Every one of them's got a weird look on their face. All of them except Abe is looking at the ground. He's the one who finally tells me what's going on.

"I talked to Mrs. Chan. She says it's okay you take off the next couple months."

What's he talking about?

"You can stay home. Be with Kari. Colton. Not have to worry about going to work."

He's lost his mind.

Then Sean gets up out of his chair. He hands me an envelope.

I look at the guys. None of my friends is staring at the ground anymore. They're all looking at me. Sean motions to the envelope, which I'm holding about as close to me as I would a snake. "Okay. I don't know what this is about. I've got to get home here pretty soon."

"Open the envelope already, you freak," Casey says. He's on probably his sixth beer.

"Okay." It's one of those long brown ones like you send documents in the mail in. It's sealed, then closed with one those metal clasp things. I tear it, then unfasten the clasp.

There's money inside.

"What the?"

I pull a wad out. Hundred-dollar bills. A bunch of them.

"You don't have to count it," Casey says. "I can tell you. You got fifty C notes there."

I drop my head. Chew on my jaw.

Five thousand dollars. No way.

"Ought to cover your rent. Your truck payment. Utilities. Groceries. A little extra. Keep you going a couple, three months," Abe says. "Take you through the first of September anyway."

"I can't take this."

"Yeah you can," Casey says.

"You guys."

I feel the weight of the envelope in my hand and I know what this means. None of my friends are rich. They don't have extra cash laying around. They've got rent, car payments, child support, groceries, and stuff they've got to buy for their kids. Like me, they all work hard but they live month-to-month.

"It ain't just from us," Pete says. "Bradley and his bunch put some in. Couple churches did, too. The one that lady Alice goes to and the one where you and Colton been going gave a little. Few more. Said they wanted to help."

Churches. People who've never met me. People who don't know me from Adam. They don't know whether I'm a good person deserving of their help or some dumb jerk, taking them for a ride.

"I don't know what to say. You don't know—"

"Yeah, we do. We know." Abe puts his big hand on my shoulder. The other guys come over and slap me on the back.

"She's going to be all right, man."

I wipe at my eyes.

"It'll be okay."

There's snot running from my nose.

"Hang in there."

I try to tell them thank you, to say to them how much this means, but every time I open my mouth I get choked up even worse.

It's Abe who tells me it's okay. That they get it. That I don't have to say anything. "Go home," he says. "Be with Kari. Colton. That's all we want. All this is about. We want the three of you to be together much as you can."

And so I do.

It's three in the morning. Kari wants me to go to Home Depot. She's got her days and nights mixed up. Been like this the past four days. I'm about worn out.

"Home Depot? What for?" I ask. She's sitting at the kitchen table in the wheelchair we got her. I'm making the pancakes she told me she was starving for. We just got finished ordering some knives she saw a guy demonstrate on TV. Supposed to never need sharpening. Lifetime guarantee.

"Let's get some paint. For Colton's room. I'd like to do it in blue. White trim. You think we could paint it this weekend?"

"Sure. I guess."

She's thumbing through a bunch of sale flyers from the newspaper. Not watching what I'm doing.

"Uh, can you make those pancakes chocolate chip? That would be so good."

I've already poured the batter onto the griddle. The pancakes are almost done. But I can make more. "Okay." I put the ones I've made onto a plate, go to the pantry and get the box of mix back out and the bag of chocolate chips. There's only a few left, but it looks like enough.

"While you're out, we need some things from Wal-Mart, too."

I hand her some paper and a pen so she can make a list. I know from experience she'll come up with more things than I can remember.

"We need a new mixer. One of those nice ones on a stand. They come in four colors and Wal-Mart's got them on sale this week. What do you think? Fire engine red or retro orange?"

Kari's on oxygen twenty-four seven now. We had to move our bed out of our bedroom because Kari's hospital bed took up so much room. I sleep on a camp cot next to her so I can hear when she needs something. Ten or more times a day I put her on the bedside commode because she can't make it to the bathroom anymore. Lifting her isn't hard. She doesn't weigh anything. Three weeks ago we started giving her morphine continuously from a little pump Amy brought over and showed me how to use.

She pushes her hair back behind her left ear. It's come in curly but she likes for me to blow it out straight. Her lips are dry. We try to keep stuff on them but they still get this way. Sometimes they crack and bleed. "I'm putting flower seeds on the list, too," she says. "Okay? Let's plant some zinnias. By the back fence."

This is July. I don't think you plant flower seeds when the temperature outside is nearly a hundred degrees. But I tell her okay. I'll get the seeds. How many packets?

"At least five. And be sure to read on the package and get the kind that gets really tall. We can plant them out by the street, too. In a long row. Don't you think that would look good?"

"I think it would look great." I set her pancakes on the table in front of her, pour me some coffee. "You want something to drink?"

"Milk, please." She takes two bites of the pancakes, then pushes the plate back. "These are good. Thanks for making them. I'm guess I'm not as hungry as I thought I was."

"That's okay," I tell her.

Because it is. Whatever Kari wants, these days, she gets. It's up and down with her but mostly down. Amy says all this is normal, that at this stage *anything* is normal. Kari'll go three or four days and do nothing but sleep. I'll have to wake her up to get her to take her pills, then she'll drift right back off. But then about the time I decide that's just the way it's going to be from now to the end, she'll wake up and be like this. Full of energy and ready to make all kinds of plans. Plans that her head thinks she can carry out but that her body can't.

The end.

It's coming.

Sooner?

Later?

How long can she go on like this? Hardly eating. Struggling sometimes to breathe. Getting weaker and weaker every day. Amy says there's no way to predict how long Kari will live. She says the end of life is like a birth. That sometimes a baby is born quick and easy, before you expect it. Other times the baby takes a long time to get here. She says when a person dies it's the same way. Not only that. We do the same thing when someone gets to the end of their life we do when a life is getting started. We wait and we watch.

People ask me how I'm able to hold up. How I'm getting through all this. I don't know. If you'd told me a year ago that this would be my life I wouldn't have believed it. Most times I still don't. One thing I do know: Looking at the big picture is too hard. You can't do it. For very long. What you do instead is you take care of the little things minute by minute. Day by day.

You empty the bedside commode.

You put in the new morphine cartridge.

And you make pancakes.

Abe comes by around eight. It's his day off. He lets himself in the back door. Me and Colton are in the kitchen. Colton's days and nights are not mixed up. He's up ripping and roaring by seven, most days. I'm barely awake but I've got last night's pancakes, the plain ones Kari didn't want, heating up in the microwave for him to eat.

"Man," Abe says to me. "No offense but you look like run-over dog poop."

I butter Colton's pancakes. Pour syrup on them. "Thanks. I feel much better now."

"Up all night?"

"Most of it."

"Kari asleep?"

"Yeah." I can't stop yawning.

"Then go to bed," he says. "Not on that stupid cot thing. Go lay down on the bed you've got in the extra bedroom. Close the door. Turn on the ceiling fan and get you some sleep. I'll take care of Colton."

I am tempted, but no. I tell Abe I'm really all right.

"Un-uh. You're not all right. You aren't no good to anybody, tired as you are."

"If Kari—"

"She needs something, I'll call you. Go. Get some sleep."

I'm so tired, he doesn't have to say it again. I go, take off my clothes, and fall into bed. It's a good six hours before I wake up. When I do, it takes me awhile to figure out where I am. I'm not sure if it's morning or night. Then I look at my watch and can't believe I've slept so long. Abe should have come and got me. I shoot up, put on my pants, and come out to see if Kari's okay.

Darla's in the kitchen. Colton's watching TV. I find Kari in our bedroom. She's sitting in front of the window, looking out through the lace curtains, still and quiet like a photo. A really pretty one like you see in those women's magazines. I could stand in the door-way and look at her like that forever, but when she hears me come in she looks up and smiles. "Hi, sleepyhead. Did you dream sweet dreams?"

"I did. Dreams about you."

"Were they sexy?"

"Of course."

I go over. She lifts her chin for a kiss, puts her arms around my neck, and pulls me down to where I'm on my knees in front of her wheelchair. She smells like lavender. Ivory soap. And Blistex.

Her eyes are close to mine. "I love you," she says.

"I love you, too."

"How much?" she asks.

"Enough," I say.

"Enough to do something for me?"

"Of course. Anything."

Here we go again is what I'm thinking. This time she may want a new blender. Or a parakeet. She may ask me to build her a gazebo. Or add a deck onto the back of our house. Which, by the way, we are only renting.

"You'll do anything I ask you to do?"

"Name it," I say. I give her a peck in the cheek. "Try me." There's no way I could ever tell those blue eyes no.

"Okay," Kari says. "Here's what it is. Let's get married. Again. Could we do that? Please?"

Can we get married again? Of course.

I can't think of anything I want to do more than get married again to my wife.

chapter twenty-seven

THE FIRST TIME KARI AND I got hitched we did it at her mom and dad's church. A bunch of people we didn't know came. Her parents' friends, I guess. Probably some distant relatives. Two days from now, Kari and I are getting married again. This time in our living room. About twenty people are coming. All them our good friends.

She's in her hospital bed. I just finished sponging her off and now I'm rubbing lotion on her feet. "Anybody special you want to do the ceremony?" I ask her. For a couple who a year ago didn't go to church, Kari and I know a lot of pastors. When word got out about her being sick, they came out of the woodwork. I don't mean any disrespect. I guess that's what pastors are supposed to do when they hear about somebody being bad off. For the most part they've been nice. There's two different guys from Alice's church that come regularly. One man from Sean's. Some others I can't remember where from. Bradley calls himself a pastor but I'm not sure he counts.

"I'd like Pastor Roberts to do it," Kari says. Abe and Jill's pastor. I guess mine too if you get right down to it. By default, you could say. Since I haven't joined his church or anything. He comes by at least once a week to see how we're doing. Colton likes him because he's always got grape gum in his shirt pocket. Kari likes him, too. She says his glasses and his gray hair make him look wise. Sometimes the two of them want to talk with me out of the room.

Which, even though I wonder what it is they're saying, is all right by me.

"Okay. I'll go ask him if he's free."

It's hard to reach Pastor Roberts on the phone. He doesn't have a cell. The guy can't make a living just off the church. The people who go there are too poor to pay him what he needs. Besides pastoring the church, he and his twin brother are partners in a little home cooking restaurant a couple of blocks from downtown. A place they've had going on thirty years. That's where I go to find out if he'll do me and Kari's wedding for us.

"Of course, Joel. I'm humbled you asked," he tells me. We're sitting down in a booth. He's got one of those red aprons on over his clothes. Velcro shoes on his feet. It's three o'clock. Too late for lunch, which I missed today. Too early for dinner. The place is empty. From the smell I'm guessing fried fish was one of today's lunch special choices. Not bad. Just a little strong. Pastor Roberts motions to his brother. The guy nods, goes to the back where the kitchen is, then comes and sets a bowl of peach cobbler topped off with vanilla ice cream down on the table in front of me.

"What's this?"

Like I don't know.

"On the house," the brother says. "Enjoy." Then he brings me a tall glass of sweet tea. The cobbler's hot. The ice cream's cold. I shovel it in and man, is it good.

"About the ceremony. Anything special you want me to say or include?" Pastor Roberts asks. His brother goes to the back.

Special? I can't think of anything. "Just the usual, I guess." I wipe my mouth with a napkin out of the holder that's on the table.

"It's going to be real small. Just us and a few friends."

"So you and Kari want the traditional vows."

"I guess so." I don't know any other ones.

Pastor Roberts takes off his glasses. Wipes them on the end of his apron. Puts them back on. "You want the vows that start off with, 'for better, for worse'?"

I nod okay. Sounds good to me.

"For richer. For poorer."

"Uh-huh." I wish I had some more tea.

"In sickness."

It hits me where we're going with this.

"And in health."

I set down my spoon. I push back my bowl. I tell myself this it not the time or the place to let go. "Yeah. That's what we want." I can barely get the words out. "Like I said. The usual."

Pastor Roberts is quiet for a long minute. He's got a napkin in his hand, which he opens all the way up, then folds back into exact thirds. The AC kicks on, which is good, because it's hot in here. "Son," he finally says, "there's nothing *usual* about you or about what you've done. Taking care of Kari. Of that little boy. Yes. Saturday I'll come to your house and perform the ceremony. I'll join you and her even though you're already joined together in my eyes and I'm fairly certain in the eyes of God, too."

I blow my nose. Stand up. Shake his hand. "Thanks. I appreciate it. Three o'clock?"

"See you then, son."

Everybody's here and, let me tell you, it is loud in my house. People are hugging and laughing and talking at once. Pastor Roberts and his wife made it. All the guys. Their kids. Alice. Sh'dondra and Jill. Bradley and his wife. A couple of Kari's good friends from the hospital. Amy, who came over to help Kari get ready. And Darla, who's made us a cake.

I've been up since six, dressed in my wedding clothes, jeans and a white button-down shirt. Abe and Pete came over early. They helped me move the big furniture out of the living room so there'd be room for everybody. We took everything out but Kari's piano. Too heavy. It's staying right where it is. Wasn't no place to put the furniture except out the back door. We laid down tarps so nothing would get messed up. Hopefully stuff will be okay long as it doesn't rain before we're done. From the street, looks like we're having a yard sale. I keep expecting somebody to ring the bell and make me an offer on my couch.

Sean brought over some folding chairs he's borrowed from his church. They're set up in rows of five, two on each side with a space in the middle for Kari to come through. The house is clean, thanks to Darla and Jill. They've been running around busy all day. There's chicken salad sandwiches and punch to go with the cake once the ceremony is done. It's all set up in the kitchen.

And it's nearly three.

Pastor Roberts and I go and stand together in front. Abe turns on the CD player. Percy Sledge. *When a Man Loves a Woman.* Everybody gets still. Even the kids.

At my first wedding I was nervous. Scared I was going to do or say something wrong. This time I'm not nervous.

Just glad.

We can hear Kari's wheelchair coming down the hall. Amy's pushing it. Before we can see them we hear Amy ask Kari if she's ready. She says that she is.

When they get to the living room everybody turns around to

see. Kari looks beautiful. She's wearing a white skirt with lace on it and a long sleeve pink T-shirt because these days she's always cold. We were hoping she'd be strong enough to stand during the ceremony but since today she's not, Casey and Sean have decorated her wheelchair with white ribbons and silver balloons. Colton likes those balloons. He's sitting in Kari's lap, batting at them and helping Kari hold her bouquet. She's got pink daisies. Tied with white ribbon. I've got one pinned on the collar of my shirt, which is tucked into my jeans. Neither one of us wanted to be all that formal this time around. Pastor Roberts is the only man here who's wearing a tie. He looks nice, but I think what me and Kari have picked out to wear is just right.

Amy pushes Kari up to the front, straightens out her oxygen tubing, then goes and sits down on the end, next to Sean, who's got Allyssa in his lap.

Percy finishes his song. The room is really, really quiet.

So Kari doesn't have to strain her neck looking up at me, I squat down in front of her and Colton.

"Daddy," he grins like he hasn't seen me in a week, like he's surprised I'm here even though he watched me make him a peanut-butter-and-banana sandwich two hours ago. He pats my arm, then squirms out of Kari's lap and climbs up on my knee. Then he waves at everybody in the chairs. Some people laugh. Sh'dondra waves back.

Pastor Roberts smiles. "Thank you all for coming," he says. "I know it means a great deal to Joel and Kari to have you with them today to witness the rejoining of their family in the presence of God. Let's begin by going to Him in prayer."

Kari and I bow our heads.

God.

You may not get what I'm about to say, but here it is. It hit me.

One day not so long ago. Out of the blue. All of a sudden I realized I wasn't mad at him anymore. Not like I was. I can't explain it except to say I think what happened is I got tired. Being mad at God wore me out so bad I couldn't keep it up. It got to where it wasn't worth even trying. Better to let it go.

Alice says the way she sees it, that's a step in the right direction.

They say you're supposed to love God. More than anything. But I'm not there. Not anywhere close.

Alice says it's okay to feel like that. For now. She says God has lots of patience. Maybe soon I'll be ready to take another step.

I tell her I'm not making any promises.

She says that's all right. God's not going anywhere. He'll wait.

I tell her we'll have to see.

Pastor Roberts finishes his prayer. We raise our heads. He puts one of his hands on my shoulder, the other one on Kari's. He smells like Irish Spring soap. I can feel how warm his palm is through my shirt and I think about what a good man he is. Then I look into his eyes and all I see is love.

Pure love.

I look out at the people who've come to be with us. To share this with me and Kari. I see the same love in all their eyes. Alice. Abe. Sean. Even Amy. Everybody in this room is looking at us the same way and it makes my throat want to close up. If there's anything I've learned through all of this it's that people can show you more love than you ever knew existed.

My wife. My son. My friends.

Everything I want.

More than I deserve.

All in this room.

Colton gets down from my lap. Abe comes and scoops him

up, sets him in a chair next to Sh'dondra. Kari and I stare into each other's eyes. She gives me that look. The one like me and her are sharing some secret or an inside joke. Her face is so thin I can see the blue veins in her forehead. When she speaks her vows to me, I don't think anybody but me can hear because her voice is so low. Her hands shake when she tries to put my ring on me. She can't do it. So I help.

Not many people get a second chance. As grateful as I am, as glad as I am about getting to be with Kari, there is one thing I hope you know. No question. I would turn around and leave this house, close the door behind me, and never come back if it meant she could live even one more day than what she's going to get.

When it's my turn to say my vows I can't stop my tears. It's like somebody turned on a faucet. They run out of my eyes, down my cheeks, and drop off my chin onto my shirt. Pastor Roberts pulls out his hanky. The way it's folded you can tell it's clean. He hands it to me to use but Kari takes it out of my hand and starts wiping me up.

Pastor Roberts gives us some time. Then he tries again with my vows. But when I open my mouth I can't get anything to come out. I'm bawling like a baby. The harder I try to stop the worse it gets. I hear people sniffling. I see a couple dab at their eyes. Everybody in the room is sympathetic to what me and Kari are going through, to what I'm feeling, to my tears.

But my bawling goes on too long.

Way too long.

After about five minutes of me trying to quit crying I hear Casey snicker. I hear Sean cough. And Abe clear his throat. I even catch Alice letting out a little snort. Alice, of all people. Which gets Kari tickled. "I'm sorry," she whispers. "Maybe if you'd blow your nose."

"Okay." I blow. It doesn't stop my tears, but I can see the corners of Kari's mouth twitching like crazy.

Amy gets up, goes to the kitchen, and brings me back a glass of water. I try to take a sip. All I do is get choked. No way I can say those vows.

Finally Pastor Roberts comes to my rescue. He bends down, puts his mouth close to my ear. "Joel, do you love this woman?"

I nod my head.

"Do you want to be married to her?"

I still can't talk so I nod again. Kari's trying not to laugh at me. I'd like to go hide.

"Well, then. I do believe that's good enough for me," says Pastor Roberts. Then he looks out at the crowd. "These two should be married. Do you all agree?"

"We do," our friends say.

Put me out of my misery is what I want somebody to do.

"All right, then. Joel. Kari. Your friends have spoken. By the power granted me by the state of Texas, I pronounce you husband and wife."

Everybody claps. I wipe at my eyes some more.

"Joel," Pastor Roberts says, "whenever you're ready, you may kiss your bride."

Finally. I get hold of myself. My tears stop like somebody turned them off. My back is killing me from squatting for so long so I stand up. But then I bend down and lay a big wet kiss on my wife's lips.

"Woo-hoo!" Casey says.

"Congratulations," Jill says.

"Daddy," Colton says.

"Ladies and gentlemen," Pastor Roberts says, "Mr. and Mrs. Joel Carpenter."

I look at Kari. She looks at me. We smile. *Mr. and Mrs.*
Are those great words or what?
I'm as happy today as I've ever been in my life.

chapter twenty-eight

AMY WAS RIGHT. NO MATTER what the doctors tell you, no one can predict how long a terminal cancer patient will live. The doctors gave Kari six months. I don't know how, but she made it a year. Some of that year she felt good and was up and around. Some of it she wasn't able to get out of bed.

We got those flower seeds planted and we painted Colton's room. Blue, with white trim, just like she wanted. I bought her that mixer. The red one. A new microwave, too.

In September we had a garage sale because Kari wanted all the closets cleaned out. With the money we made, me and her took a little road trip. We didn't go all that far. Just to Dallas for two nights, but we had a nice time. The three of us had Thanksgiving together. Christmas was good. On New Year's Eve we had a party. Everybody came. At midnight, Kari and I shared a kiss.

February sixteenth was the day she died.

Two days before, Amy told me she thought it wouldn't be long. There were signs. Cold legs and knees with purple spots. Kari's breathing would get shallow and fast, then deep and slow. Sometimes she struggled like a fish on the bank. She got to where she didn't talk. I don't think she was scared. Thanks to the morphine I don't believe she was in pain.

The last day, she kept looking up at the ceiling, staring at a certain spot. Amy told me she'd seen hospice patients do that same thing lots of times before. Kari might be seeing angels.

It was a comfort, thinking maybe she was.

People thought it would be harder for me if Kari passed away at home. Even Abe tried to convince me to take her to the hospital. But Kari and I'd talked about it. She wanted to die in the same place she'd lived.

Those last few days I lost track of when it was day and when it was night. There were lots of people at our house, lots of people in and out of Kari's room. Lots of people coming to check on me and to tell her good-bye.

When Amy let me know it was getting really close, I asked everybody to leave the room where Kari was. I wanted to be alone with her when she drew her last breath.

Yes. There were tears.

If you've never been through something like this you might think Kari getting those extra months would make the end easier. That a person would feel some sort of relief when the end finally comes. It doesn't work like that. You're never ready to tell somebody you love good-bye, even if you believe they're going on to something better than what it is they've got. I held Kari's hand. I kissed her lips. I stroked her hair. One second she had breath. The next she had none.

When I came out of her room, I closed the door behind me. I didn't have to say anything. Everyone knew. Colton was sitting in Alice's lap in the living room reading a book. I picked him up and headed out the back door. Abe, Sean, Casey, and Pete followed us outside. None of them knew what to say, but that was okay. If it hadn't been for my friends just being with me, I don't know what I would have done.

While we were out back, the women took over. It was Amy

who told me later what they did. They went in to Kari's room and surrounded her bed. Jill and Darla on one side. Alice and Amy on the other. They got a pan of warm water and a bunch of towels. They bathed Kari, put lotion on her, brushed her hair, and dressed her in a pretty nightgown. They took the pink Valentine roses I'd sent and scattered the petals on her pillow and her sheets.

When I brought Colton back inside, he got to see his mother looking and smelling like a sweet sleeping angel.

I'll always be grateful for them doing that.

Colton is eight years old now. He's in the third grade. Good at reading; not so hot at math. It was hard on him when Kari died. He kept getting hold of my cell phone, trying to call her up, and he started pooping in his pants. People ask me if we prepared him for her death. The answer is no. We didn't even try. There's no way you can prepare a four-year-old for his mother to be gone.

But he's doing better these days. Playing soccer. Taking piano lessons. He's got a big yellow Lab named Jake and a couple of older stepsisters who love to boss him around.

The way hospice works, they keep in touch with the family for a year after their patient passes away. You get phone calls checking to see how you're doing. They mail you stuff and they've got grief support meetings you can go to. Sometimes they stop by, which is what Amy did every few weeks. She was a big help with Colton. When I didn't know how to answer his questions, she could usually come up with something for me to try.

Right after the funeral, people pressured me to give all Kari's stuff to Goodwill. They said I should get it out of my house so I wouldn't have to see it every day. But Amy disagreed. She told me

I should hold on to it as long as I needed to. She said her husband liked clothes. He had a lot of shirts. After he died she slept in a different one every night for two months.

A year and a half after Kari's death, Amy and I started seeing each other. One year after that, we got married at the courthouse. Just me and her and the justice of the peace. The past eighteen months have been good. So good. Both of us understanding what it's like to lose somebody, there's a lot we don't have to explain, a lot of things we just know.

Like how precious life is.

How you can't take it for granted.

How you don't want to do anything to mess up the good thing you've found.

A few weeks after Kari died I was back at work, doing Alice's hair. We were talking. About how Colton was doing. How things were for me. About how I'd had so much loss in my life.

"Joel," she said, "I don't begin to understand why some people suffer so much and others live their lives unscathed. It's an awful mystery. But I believe this with all my heart. In spite of everything that's happened, you and Colton's story is going to have a happier ending than you can dream. God has more good ahead for you and him than you can imagine."

I didn't answer Alice right then. I couldn't. Because at the time it was all too fresh and what she'd said was too much to take. So I changed the subject. I started in about the new Thai restaurant opening up down the block, and about how Mrs. Chan was talking about putting in a couple more stations, which was going to make the salon too crowded, I thought. Then, because me and her both love Norah Jones, I asked Alice which one of her CDs she thought was better, the first one or the second.

No big surprise. Alice went along. She says what she thinks, but she doesn't push.

"The first one. Of course. When's she releasing her third?"

When I finished her hair, Alice put her earrings back in and dug through her purse for her checkbook. I'd warmed up her color a little bit this time. "I love the change," she said. "Darker than I was expecting, but I think it looks good."

"I like it, too. Brightens up your face," I told her.

"Guess we'll have to keep it like this then." She paid me with a check, insisted on a tip, and got up to go. "See you in a few weeks, Joel." She buttoned her jacket and put her purse up on her shoulder.

"Later, Alice. Thanks," I said. Then I gave her a hug and I kissed her on the cheek and I whispered in her ear that I hoped what she'd told me would turn out to be true.

I don't smoke anymore but I still like sitting out on my back stoop. Especially after a long day at the salon. It's nice out here. Peaceful. Quiet. A good place to think. To pray. To wind down. Colton's dog Jake likes to sit with me. He slobbers a lot and he'll chew up anything that's not nailed down, but he's good company. When I scratch him behind the ears, his big old tail thumps against my leg.

It's springtime and Amy likes the fresh air. She's got every window in our house opened up wide, which means even out here it's not hard to tell what's going on inside.

She's cooking dinner. Pork chops. Something with onions.

The girls are in the kitchen with her. Probably doing their homework at the table. Their voices are quick, high-pitched, like cartoon voices on TV. Colton's at the piano. He's supposed to practice a half hour every day. I think he's got some of his mother's talent. He just thinks playing's fun.

After twenty minutes of sitting on the concrete, my rear is numb. The sun's going down and it's getting chilly outside. "Let's go in, Jake. What do you say?"

He gives me a big dog grin. I'm not the only one who's smelled pork.

It's time to join everybody else and I'm ready.

After a few minutes alone, I always am.

Because Alice was right.

There are happy endings.

And mine is inside.

etc.

bonus content includes:

Reader's Guide

1. What is your first impression of Joel? Of his friends? What motivates him? What motivates Abe? Casey?

2. Is Joel a good dad? What mistakes does he make as a father? Describe how his methods of parenting Colton differ from the ways a married dad would parent his child. How does Joel's relationship with his own dad affect the way he relates to Colton?

3. Why is Joel so distrusting of organized religion? What keeps him from believing there's anything there for him? Why does he feel comfortable at Abe's church? What can today's church do to make people like Joel feel welcome and accepted?

4. Is Joel completely to blame for his affair with Leslie? Did Kari contribute in any way?

5. In what ways did the affair change Joel?

6. Did you want Joel and Kari to get back together? Would they have remarried if she hadn't gotten cancer?

7. Joel believed Alice was trying to push religion on him by inviting him to church. Was she? What changed Joel's mind about Alice's motivation? How did their relationship change over the course of the book?

8. Joel struggles with believing he is worthy of love and of forgiveness. Which people in Joel's life model unconditional love and acceptance? How does that change his views of himself and of God?

9. When Kari gets sick, Joel turns to God. Yet Kari does not get well. How does a Christian reconcile the power of God with the realities of tragedy and death?

10. How do you think Colton handled his mother's death? How will it affect him in the years to come?

11. Does Joel's life have a happy ending? He told Leslie that he wanted what her parents had. Do you think he got it?

A Conversation with Annette Smith

Q. Where did you find the idea for this book?

A. Two years ago, at my daughter's urging that I *do something about my hair*, I visited a new salon. It was there I met Paul C., the stylist who gave me a new look. Not only did Paul give me a great color and style that day, he also gifted me by sharing snippets of his personal, bittersweet history. Leaving the salon after our first meeting, I could not get his story out of my mind. As soon as I arrived home, I sat down and began writing. While not in any way a factual account of his life, much of the voice, tone, and feel of *A Bigger Life* came from Paul, who has since become my friend.

Q. What made you decide to tell the story from Joel's viewpoint instead of from Kari's?

A. Writing from a male's point of view was a challenge. My other novels have all been in a woman's voice. However, I wanted to explore the way a man thinks, the way he views marriage, and how male friendships are maintained. Because Joel worked in a female-dominated setting, I had an understandable setting from where to begin.

Q. There are lots of medical descriptions and situations in *A Bigger Life.* How did you research these details?

A. Since I'm terribly lazy when it comes to doing research, this book didn't require much. I've been a registered nurse since age twenty, which explains my knowledge of medicine and hospital routines. I love my work and continue to serve part-time as a hospice nurse.

Q. So is hospice nurse Amy based on you?

A. No. Alice would be the character that most resembles myself.

Q. Joel has little use for organized religion. How do you believe the mainstream church is viewed by people like Joel?

A. Unfortunately, oftentimes not very well. I hear young non-believers express their feelings that the church is concerned with mainly two issues: abortion and gay marriage. They are not consistently getting the gospel message of grace and reconciliation. My belief is that lives are changed and Jesus is made known most often through personal, sacrificial relationships. Joel's life is changed not by a sermon, rather by the love of an assortment of imperfect believers who provide tangible help when he needs it most.

Q. What do you hope readers gain from reading *A Bigger Life*?

A. My first goal, in writing fiction, is always to provide readers with excellent entertainment. My desire is not to instruct or even necessarily to inspire, though if that happens — great.

If I provide a few hours of escape, if I transport readers to another time and place, then I've done what I set out to do.

Q. Can you explain the significance of the Scripture you quoted at the beginning of the book?

A. Sure. Psalm 51:17 beautifully expresses the theme of *A Bigger Life*. No matter how broken or messed up we are, God never loses sight of us. It is through the actions and words of people placed in Joel's path—Alice, Abe, Pastor Roberts, and even Bradley—that God's love and care is poured out on Joel.

Q. What type of books do you enjoy reading? What books are currently in your to-be-read pile?

A. Like most writers, I am a voracious reader. Give me a spare second, I've got my nose in a book. I read everything from the Bible to the back of the package my bath soap comes in. Currently, I'm reading *The Soul Tells a Story: Engaging Creativity with Spirituality in the Writing Life*, by Vinita Hampton Wright. On my waiting list are *Watching the Tree Limbs*, by Mary E. DeMuth; *Gilead*, by Marilynne Robinson; and *The Inner Voice of Love*, by Henri Nouwen. I've also recently purchased a volume of collected works by Flannery O'Connor, which I plan to read in small bits.

Q. May readers contact you?

A. Yes. I love to hear from readers. My website, www.annettesmithbooks.com, has a contact page. My postal address is P.O. Box 835, Quitman, TX 75783.

About Hospice

Hospice is compassionate care for patients and families facing life-limiting illnesses. Provided by a team of physicians, nurses, social workers, chaplains, and volunteers, hospice care focuses on comfort rather than on cure. The ultimate goal of hospice caregivers is to see that the terminally ill patient experiences a pain-free, dignified death, and to support his or her family.

Care is provided most often in the home. However, services are also provided in inpatient hospice facilities, hospitals, and nursing homes. Medicare, Medicaid, and most private insurance companies cover hospice care. Many hospice organizations also serve those with no means to pay.

If you or a loved one has need of end-of-life care or if you would like to become a hospice volunteer, contact your local hospice organization.

The following websites offer helpful information and education about hospice:

www.caringinfo.org

www.nationalhospicefoundation.org

About the Author

ANNETTE SMITH is a lifelong Texan, a hospice nurse, and an accomplished storyteller whose book of short stories *The Whispers of Angels* has sold more than 100,000 copies. She is also the author of the *Coming Home to Ruby Prairie* novels. Annette lives in Quitman, Texas (population 3,000), with her husband, Randy, and an affectionate, shaggy mutt named Wally.

MORE GREAT READS FROM THE NAVPRESS FICTION LINE.

Balancing Act
Kimberly Stuart   1-60006-076-5

As maternity leave comes to an end for Heidi Elliott, so does virtually everything she thought she knew. Pushed into accepting an invitation to the Wednesday night Moms Group, she finds herself in a sea of polyester, polka dots, big hair, and strong women who just might hold the lifeline she didn't think she needed.

A Mile from Sunday
Jo Kadlecek   1-60006-028-5

Can this reporter find a good story among the church bulletins for barbecues and bingo? One tip can change—or end—a career, as Jonna Lightfoot McLaughlin, the *Denver Dispatch*'s religion reporter, soon learns.

Stealing Adda
Tamara Leigh   1-57683-925-7

It'd been a long time since *New York Times* best-selling author Adda Sinclaire had experienced more than a fictional dose of romance. But when publisher Nick Farnsworth walks into her life, everything changes.

Visit your local Christian bookstore, call NavPress
at 1-800-366-7788, or log on to www.navpress.com.
To locate a Christian bookstore near you, call 1-800-991-7747.

NAVPRESS
BRINGING TRUTH TO LIFE
www.navpress.com